Because of Them

BECAUSE OF LOVE SERIES 2

DEVON MAY

ISBN: 978-0-6486356-5-9

Edited by: Ashleigh Van Arkkels at AVA Book Editing

Cover Design: Books and Moods

Formatted by: Stacey at Champagne Book Design

Books by
DEVON MAY

BECAUSE OF LOVE SERIES

Because of Us (Prequel Novella)
Because of Her
Because of Them
Because of Me

Author's Note

The Because of Love series is a steamy contemporary romance set in Melbourne, Australia. To stay true to the characters and the author, it is written in Australian English. There may be times you spot a *u* where you weren't expecting one, or an *s* instead of a *z*. It is my hope that you are so invested in Michael and Audrey's story that you don't notice them.

Trigger Warning: *Because of Them* is a story of accepting change and love, even when you aren't expecting it. It involves sexual content between two consenting adults who are learning to accept their flaws. If any of the below is potentially triggering for you, please read on with care.

- Pregnancy, birth trauma, emergency caesarean, Newborn Intensive Care Unit (NICU)
- Body dysmorphia related to pregnancy
- Infertility (brief mention, not explored)

For anyone who feels a little lost in the mess that is life.
I hope you find a little *fun*.

Because of Them

Chapter One

AUDREY

The smile on my face grows tighter than the knot forming in my stomach. I've been standing here, looking brighter than I feel, for over an hour. I stand even taller, pushing my shoulders back and loosening my grip on my clipboard. My wide smile never wavers, but my cheeks are beginning to strain. My feet hurt inside my professional kitten heels, my stomach is all twisted, and all I want to do is pull in the damn flags. But I still have a horde of potential buyers waiting their turn to traipse through the upmarket four-bedroom townhome with the biggest backyard in the suburb. Standing in a line across the manicured front yard, that is just a fraction of the huge outdoor space, each small group looks ready to throw down an offer and call it theirs.

The afternoon sun blasts down on us all, suspiciously bitey for late winter. I use the back of my sleeve to wipe the beads of sweat from my forehead. The black cotton fabric comes away wet, and for once I'm thankful for the dark tone that forms the unofficial 'uniform' my boss insists on.

In the line, women stand in front of their partners, hiding away from the blinding glare and finding whatever small sliver of shade they can. A gentleman takes off his suit jacket, draping it over his shoulder to roll up the sleeves of his white business shirt. Too bad for all of them I already have the perfect buyer in mind. Securing such a prestige sale will be a huge boost to my career, and just what I need to finally convince my boss that I don't need his head over my shoulder all the time. I wasn't willing to risk it on the gamble of the open market.

There is no doubt in my mind that my ex-husband will want to snap this property up for himself.

I don't blame him. The back garden is the perfect blank canvas for growing flowers, and there is plenty of space for our daughter Maisie to play and grow. The modern facade and clean lines remind me of the renovations he used to plan for our house.

Callum and I officially divorced almost six months ago, but emotionally, we've been separated for much longer than that. It took me a while to get used to the idea of him moving on, and a fling of my own before I was ready to accept it. But as our relationship as co-parents continues to improve, I'm finally ready to help him move on with his life. In a professional capacity, at least.

My bitterness stopped me from helping him search for a new house early on. It was fun, watching him move into a tiny two-bedroom unit. How petty I was … and it turns out that two-bedroom unit was exactly what he needed to find his true love.

If only the same could be said for me. But no. My brief adventure into the world of dating apps was cut ceremoniously short. Turns out everyone blushes over a single dad, but single mums are much harder to love.

My fling with Michael was … everything and nothing all at once. He was young and immature, but I sat across the picnic table from him, and I was transfixed. His body builder physique was overpowering in all the right ways, and no sexy man bun could steal my attention from the way his henley clung to his rock-hard abs. I craved to feel what it would be like to be under him, if only for a night. It was incredible. More intensely electric than anything I'd felt before, as though our bodies were hardwired with the same cables.

I wanted more, and I got it … a few times. Until he ghosted me. For weeks. And I was left with nothing more than the memory of his weight settling over my core and butter-flies that slowly started to die with his lack of contact. It still haunts me, pulling at my gut and beating against my heart.

His nonstop messages now won't make up for the utter drop off I experienced then. Sure, he was fun and had all these little ways to show me that he cared, but I was only in it for the mind-blowing sex anyway. At least that's what I've been telling myself these past few weeks.

"When will the owner stop accepting offers?"

A cheery couple bursts into my line of sight as they skip through the wide-open front door. They stand too close, fin-gers looped together as they bounce on their toes, no idea of the bubble around them. The one that's sure to burst.

I don't believe in everlasting love, not anymore.

I swallow down the lump that's been sitting in my throat all day. "A few weeks, I think. But my understanding is that they are ready to sell as soon as possible. It's safe to assume they will sign as soon as they get the right offer."

As soon as they get Callum's offer, that is.

A fresh wave of nausea rushes over me. My immaculate posture softens, and I throw my hand onto the doorframe to steady myself. I haven't eaten since breakfast, that's all. And I haven't had anything to drink the whole time I've been stand-ing here. This opening was supposed to end an hour ago, but if I don't get food soon, I might pass out. Or vomit, oddly.

The couple takes a card, promising to email through their offer. Ignoring the twisting in my stomach, I bid them fare-well before turning my attention to the final group wanting to check out the property. I check my watch after they pass me. If they can be in and out within twenty minutes, I won't be late to pick up Maisie from kindergarten.

My phone buzzes with a string of messages in my pocket.

"Maisie?" My boss asks from the other side of the front

porch. His head gestures towards my hip, where the lit phone screen shines through my dark linen pants.

"Probably not. They would call, not send a barrage of texts."

I don't need to pull my phone out to know it's Michael. As if his almost daily attempts to win me back weren't annoying enough, the man doesn't know how to compile his thoughts into a single message before hitting send. It's infuriating. Especially while I'm trying to remain professional.

My career in real estate is finally taking off. It stalled, as so many mother's careers do, when Maisie was younger. Stalled again when my marriage fell apart and I took some extended leave. Now that Maisie is in kindergarten, and the custody agreement is properly underway, I'm back. I can focus more of my time and energy into selling the kind of homes I wish to buy for myself one day.

In a few short months I've climbed the top seller ranks, even if my boss is struggling to give me the credit I deserve. When I chose this career, I never imagined making the top ten realtors in the area, let alone being number two. But that's where I am. If I can sell this house with a big enough return, I might even hit the number one spot. I just have to get through this open first.

Regardless of how much I believe I've found the perfect buyer, ethically I need to do the right thing here. Other buyers have the right to look through the property, and however slim it might be, there is always the chance that some other rich hot shot will swoop in and make a better offer than Callum does.

I know it's wrong to judge books by their covers, or in this case, a buyer's bank account by their appearance, but my instinct on these things is rarely wrong. I doubt any of the families or so-called investors that walked through today have the same bargaining power as my ex-husband.

My stomach lurches again as my boss bids farewell to the final couple.

"Are you okay?"

I swallow down a lump of bile. "I'll be fine."

"I'll lock up here, you get some food before you get Maisie. You look pale." He huffs, a smug look on his face as he dismisses me.

I nod, unsure if I can get any words out without heaving. I hate the thought of leaving my boss to do my work and giving him ammunition for his crusade against working mothers. More than that, though, I hate myself for not being about to handle the constant juggle. I was starving earlier, but the hunger pains have been replaced by an utter emptiness that has left me feeling ill.

More ill than I've felt since I was pregnant with Maisie. It was more than five years ago but I can still remember the tightness that would start like hunger but rapidly shift into a pain that made me heave. I haven't felt anything like it since. Until this.

Shit.

The thought slams into me as I step into my stuffy, sun warmed car. I turn the car on with the door still open, waiting for the air conditioning to blow cool air before closing myself into the hot box. That can't be why my stomach is in knots. But I'm left scrambling through my thoughts, counting backwards, sifting through my memory. I can't remember the last time I had my period, but I always skip the little yellow sugar pills, so it's impossible to figure out if I'm late.

Besides, Michael used a condom. Every time. Except, *shit*, that one time it broke.

Broke.

Like something out of a movie or a teenage nightmare. I hadn't thought it would matter, I kept taking the pill long after my ex and I stopped needing it, so when I did need it again there was no doubting its effectiveness.

But there was that day when Maisie was sick. And then

I was sick. Was that before or after the broken condom incident? Does that make a difference? Surely I can't be that unlucky. Can I?

As I continue to spiral, the twisting and nausea in my stomach falls lower. Despite the heavy heat that still lingers in the car, I wrap my cardigan around my middle, curling in on myself. Cramps erupt over my lower abdomen. I just *know*. Like I just knew with Maisie.

Only then, it was planned, even if the timing threw us by surprise. And I had Callum to calm me down, to reassure me, to promise me everything was going to be okay.

I don't have anyone now.

Fifty-one … fifty-two … fifty-three …

The chill from the bathroom tiles numbs my toes and I bounce side to side with each count. I track the seconds against the faint tick from my watch, too scared to leave the bathroom for my phone so I can time the test properly. It sits beside the sink, blinding me. Pressing my palms to my eyes, I will myself not to look early until I count out the instructed three minutes. But it calls to me like a siren, singing a song I know all too well.

I reach for it, pulling the plastic stick into view. A glance is all it takes to confirm what I've known since this afternoon.

Two pink lines.

Maisie is going to be a big sister. I'm having a baby.

The test shakes in my hands. I drop it onto the counter at the same time my knees buckle and I fall to the floor. The plastic tube rattles around the sink, as sporadic and uneven as my now hasty breaths.

Unprepared for the iciness of the ceramic to permeate

through my leggings, I tense at the chilling sensation when my butt hits the floor. Wriggling on the spot, I heave in oxygen. Every muscle cramps inside me, tears clump at my lashes. I taste the salty liquid as it trickles over my cheek and into the corner of my mouth.

I can't do this.

A thud sounds from down the hall, echoing through the house. Maisie, most likely rolling in her bed and kicking into the wall. I hold my shaky breath, listening for any signs the collision may have woken her. Instead, only silence follows, broken only by my hushed sobs and Maisie's loud, sniffly inhale.

The air I was holding in escapes my lungs.

One by one, I stretch out my aching limbs, scrambling to stand like a baby giraffe. My body lurches out of the ensuite and I collapse onto my bed. Sobs muffle against the pillow until it's wet from my tears and sticking to my cheeks.

Somewhere below me, my phone vibrates. I let my arm flail around me, finding the cool brick of my years old phone near my thigh.

The screen is lit with messages from Michael. All the ones I haven't answered over the past week and the string of new ones from today. The latest one is short, but it tugs at the muscles in my heart.

Michael: Please Audrey. I miss you. I miss us.

I close my eyes, dropping the phone onto my chest. I can't remember the last time someone other than my daughter missed me. If it wasn't for the thirty-seven messages that came before this one, it might have been nice.

Besides, Michael and I had nothing in common. I have a career, a daughter, and a house. I have, by all considerations, a successful adult life. Minus the long-standing relationship. Michael, on the other hand, has none of those things. Instead, he has a job he refuses to progress in, a dog that follows him everywhere, and an apartment that screams 'bachelor pad'.

At first, the only thing that worked about us was the way our bodies moved so well together. And it was fun, God was it fun, but I wanted more. Little by little he showed me pieces of himself, and I started to think that with Michael I could have more. I wanted to fall, I was ready to fall, head over heels for him. I wanted a man who was sure of himself, and his place in life, and I wanted him to fall head over heels for me too. Michael might have still been working on the first part, but I thought he might be ready to fall for me. For a while it seemed like he was. We were good. No, more than good. We were golden.

Then he got a glimpse into what a lifetime with me would be like and ran for the metaphorical hills.

First he ghosted me, now he haunts me.

So, after a failed marriage and a fling that turned into nothing, I no longer believe in the love I somehow still crave.

Especially not with Michael. Not with the way he had no idea what he was doing with his life, still riding on the coattails of his father's business. Not with the way he shrunk at the thought of being a parent or how he shied away from Maisie. Not with the way he ran as soon as he realised that waking up next to me also meant waking up in the same house as my child.

Oh God, I have to call him. Despite how I feel about him, I have to tell him that I'm pregnant. With his baby. That we have decisions to make that will change our lives. I'm not ready for those decisions, how on earth can he be?

This man, who spends more time at the gym than at his house, who told me he loved kids but wasn't sure about babies. I might not be ready to be a mother again, but he sure as shit isn't ready to be a father.

Chapter Two

MICHAEL

The morning sun is hot on my back, waking me up with its burning glaze through the window. I carry my pillow with me as I roll over, covering my face. I must have slept in, with the way the sun streaks lines across my sheets through the vertical blinds I never bother to close. I live on the top floor of the tallest building in the suburb; no one can see me anyway. Not that I care if they do.

Stretching my arms above my head, the pillow falls onto my lap as I push myself to sit and swing my legs off the side of the bed. Baxter's head pops up from his spot on the floor, plodding over for his morning pat. He lets out a bark when he sees the pillow in his favourite resting place, giving me his best puppy dog sad face until I move it away. Crouching on the floor beside my Golden Retriever companion, I soak in his unconditional love. The only kind I'll ever get.

Rostered Day Off Fridays. My favourite day of the month, the best part of working for my dad's construction company. A mandatory day off. A whole day to do whatever the fuck I want.

Baxter lets himself out onto the balcony and I flick on the coffee machine in the kitchen. After adding a splash of cool water, I down the shot of espresso in one go. Tastes like fucking shit, but I need the boost first thing in the morning. Without it, I'll never get through my session.

Weights line the walls of the spare room; an all-in-one lifting machine sits in the middle. My one Friday off every month might be my favourite day, but Friday workouts are the ones I hate the most. Leg day.

I tried to be one of those gym guys who neglected his legs. I hate the exercises and frankly, I didn't see the point. But the competitions demanded I build form in my thighs and calves, so I did. It became a habit. And although I haven't done a comp in over a year and I loathe the exercises and the way I struggle to walk down the stairs after them, it's kind of nice having some form where a lot of guys don't. Gives me an edge, and something to stir shit over.

After my rounds of calf raises and lunges and squats, I emerge from my makeshift gym on shaky legs to the buzzing of my phone.

Weird. No one calls me, especially not in the morning.

My dad's face lights up the screen when I pick it up from the charging pad on the bench.

Not today.

It's my RDO and the very last thing I want to do is spend it talking to my father about his business. About how he wants me to run the thing one day. I can't think of anything worse.

Rejecting the call, a stabbing in my heart reminds me of the one person I wish *would* call me. I fucked things up with Audrey. Bad. But no matter how many times I try to call her, how many texts I send. She never answers, never replies.

My mates all say to forget about her. The guys at work tell me to get over the wild few weeks we had. I can't. I tried.

It doesn't matter how big—or little, technically—the red flag was. I can't forget about Audrey. I can't forget about how her body moulded under mine, the way her breasts pushed against my chest when I sunk myself between her legs. We were perfect together, physically at least. And I doubt I will ever find another woman who fits so perfectly against me.

We had something most couples spend their relationships wishing for. An unmatchable sexual chemistry. But it started to evolve into something more and I began to freak out. Audrey's older than me, not by a lot, but by enough. She's thirty-two, which is so far from being old, but the differences in our lives were glaring. At twenty-six, I have a lot of my life still to sort out. But I shoved down my worries, hoping they would ease with time. Thinking that maybe I was destined to be with someone after all. Until I was rudely shocked out of the daydream.

I knew she had a daughter. She never tried to hide it. I figured I would get used to it. A kid is different to a baby, and for some reason it felt easier to grow into the idea of a kid being in my life than the thought of one day having a baby. I never knew how to act around Audrey's daughter, but I was getting used to her being around. And that was something.

Until all my wishful thinking was destroyed in one tiny moment, by one tiny voice.

I woke up, erection pressed against the small of Audrey's back. Moaning into her, I imagined all the things we might get up to before ever leaving the bed. My hand snaked down her front, toying with the band of her panties.

"Mummy!" Her daughter's shrill voice had called down the hall. "Can I put Bluey on?"

Audrey had groaned at the rude awakening, calling out "yes" and pressing her behind into me. But the moment was gone.

Maisie's tiny little voice had awoken a panic in me, and I rushed to get dressed, leaving before breakfast had even been served. I didn't feel ready to be such a big part of the little girl's life. I still don't know if I am, I'd still bet on me making a fool of myself, but I'm willing to try. Properly.

As soon as I left, I regretted my hasty decision and I knew the impression it gave. Audrey is perfect, in every way. Her daughter doesn't subtract from that, and I hate that I made her think it did.

If only Audrey would let me show her how I feel. It took more than a week for me to build up the courage to message her again, and my radio silence must have been so loud after how I ran out, so I don't blame her for not wanting to give me a second chance. Only now I'm trying to get back what we had, and she is the one ignoring me.

I fucked up. But I'll never stop trying to make things right.

A message pings from my father.

Dad: I know it's your RDO but call me. As a son, not an employee.

Well fuck, his message hits a chord, but it's the chain under it that catches my attention.

A little blue dot next to Audrey's name. She messaged me. In my haste to open the thread, I fumble with my phone, dropping it to the counter. Picking it up, I have to read the message four times before the words sink in.

Audrey: Hey Michael, can we chat?

My body screams to type *Yes* and hit send, but my brain holds me back. *Chat?* In what way?

There's chatting like how I used to chat with multiple women at a time, trying to find the one that felt right. I haven't done that since I met Audrey though. Or chatting like catching up on each other's lives. Or—and God I hope it's not this—chatting like a final talk. I have no idea where she wants this chat to go.

The message log says she sent the text this morning, while I was doing my stupid leg workout. My stomach cramps, part hunger, part a ball of anxiety at the thought of calling her back. I have to call my dad back too, even though it probably will be work related despite his message. I reach for a banana, needing fuel before I attempt anything else.

When I've shoved the final bite in my mouth, my stomach feels a little better. Audrey first, then I'll tackle the call with my dad.

The phone rings twice, but when Audrey answers, the sound of cartoons blasts into my ear.

"Maisie, turn it down!" Audrey yells. I hear her shuffling away down the hall, muffling the obnoxious music.

"Sorry Michael, how are you?"

She sounds out of breath. Dread mixes with the anxiety in my stomach, swirling against my pre-breakfast snack.

"Audrey, I'm … good. How are you?"

"Oh, you know, work, motherhood, life."

I don't know. The conversation is all forced small talk, doing nothing for the storm inside me.

"Audrey what's—"

"Can we see—"

We cut each other off. "Sorry, you first," I prompt.

Audrey blows out a long puff of air. "Can we see each other? Like, go for coffee or something?"

My cheeks burn. She wants to see me, finally. I can't help but wonder what prompted her swift change of heart. But then, I suppose it must have felt the same for her when I started calling her again too.

"I'd like that. Today?"

"Not today, I have to get Maisie to school and get to work."

Right, I forgot the whole world doesn't get these blissful days off like the trade industry.

"On the weekend. I'll see if Maisie can go to her dad's. Can I text you?" Audrey gulps down her words.

"Okay," I strip the concern and confusion from my voice. "I'm looking forward to it."

I try to convince myself it's true as I end the call. I try not to think about the way each word caught in her throat, or how she sounded on the verge of tears. I try to imagine all the ways it could go right, instead of focusing on the way my hairs stand on end like they know something I don't.

I wait until what's left of the morning has passed before calling my dad, delaying the inevitable berating as long as possible. I eat a proper breakfast, binge some more of my favourite true crime podcast and take Baxter for a walk before the clouds give up. I wipe down all my weights, order a delivery of groceries, trim the fraying ends of my shoulder length hair and contemplate cutting it off altogether. I fill time with mostly meaningless crap, until enough has passed that whatever work crisis my dad thought needed immediate attention will be long past, or at least he would have dealt with it himself.

"Son." His voice echoes down the line as he drives. I despise when he calls me son, it's too formal, like we belong on some prissy upper regency drama show.

"Father," I respond in jest, adding an unnecessary inflection just to spite his choice of language.

He scoffs. "Quit the shit. It's been hours. What if your mother was sick?"

"She's not though."

"Fine. She's not. But we are getting older."

Collapsing on the couch, I let my head fall back against the cushions. "Dad, I don't want the whole 'I want to retire and I want you to take over the business' spiel. We've been through this."

I don't add the 'over and over and over again' that cycles in my head. Dad has wanted me to take the reins from him for years, but despite his constant and incessant conversations about it, I still don't want to. Once upon a time, maybe I did.

But I was even younger and dumber then than I am now. And who knows, maybe in a few more years I'll want to again. But not now, and the more he keeps bringing it up, the further away that hypothetical moment becomes.

According to Dad, at twenty-six I should be ready to take over the company he started as a teenager. The reality is I'm far from ready. I don't have control of anything in my life, I can't add a national company to the mix of things I always manage to fuck up.

"And before you can come up with your usual arguments, I know you were younger than I am when you started this business. I know you want to step back and watch it grow instead of working on it day in and day out now. And I know you want to pass your legacy onto your son. I know all of those things Dad, but I don't know the first thing about running a business. I still make a mess of every job you leave me in charge of."

Baxter pads his way across the room, sensing my rising mood and the way my pulse is spiking. He'd make a great service dog if I ever needed one. Clambering onto the couch, he drops his front paws on my lap, resting his head between my knees. He's big, even for a Golden Retriever, far too big to be a lapdog, but he insists. I'm happy to oblige, happy for the comfort from someone who doesn't seem to always expect *more* from me.

"Michael, stop. I don't expect you to know how to run the bloody business. I just expect you to try."

His disappointment leaks through the phone. The way it always does.

I want to live up to the expectations he has of me, but the truth is I'm not sure I can. I was barely a day over fifteen when I left school to start my apprenticeship under his instruction. For a while, it was great. Working with my dad and not having to go to school like the rest of my mates. But over time the appeal waned. Now, I'm only in this job because everything about it comes so easily. Because I have no idea what else I would do with my life.

After finishing my apprenticeship, I stopped pushing myself to learn. I'm far from the most skilled carpenter on any job site, but I know the basics and that's all I need to get a house built. The other blokes can fine tune the cabinetry and do all the precision work, I'm more than happy just focusing on the basics. The foundations and having a good frame are more important than the insides looking pretty. And I'm pretty good at assembling a frame.

Aside from that, I like having no one depend on me on the job site. And I like being able to depend on my father when things turn to shit. If the wood delivery is wrong or the owner wants us to work faster, I can palm off the responsibility of dealing with the shit to my father—or whichever lackey he assigned as project manager.

"I have tried, Dad. Remember?"

It was a disaster. The job was delivered five months late when everything imaginable went wrong. It baffles me that even after that atrocity cost the business thousands of dollars in late penalties, he still wants me to try again.

"Michael, that was three years ago. I was stupid to think you'd be able to handle project management only a few years out of your apprenticeship. But you're not that young kid anymore. Stop pretending you are."

"I still feel like that young kid though."

It's the first time I've admitted it out loud to my father, the first time I've come even close to opening up to him. But it feels good.

"Well, maybe the way to change that is to try again?"

I hate that he is right.

"Fine," I choke on the word as it comes out, regretting it instantly. "What's the job?"

My father's booming laugh echoes through the phone line. "There is no job yet. I honestly didn't think you'd finally agree to it. I called you to see if you could look after the dog in a few weeks. Your mother is sick of the cold, she wants to go to Port Douglas."

I reach down to scratch Baxter's neck. He shifts his head in my hand and wags his tail against the armrest of the couch. He'd probably enjoy the company for a few days, even in the form of mum and dad's tiny Cavoodle Miffy. I won't be able to leave her alone in the apartment while she is here though, her eyesight is pretty poor and she won't know how to use Baxter's doggy door.

"You know I will. But, you actually didn't want to talk about work?"

"Nope. Unless you wanted to talk about work"

"No but …"

I fade out, and the conversation stalls in the uneasy way it often does between us. Neither of us knowing the expectations we place on each other, neither of us willing to test the boundary between our father-son relationship.

"Enjoy your day off."

"Thanks Dad, bye."

Hanging up the phone, I'm still caught on the fact he wasn't calling for work. He hadn't wanted to berate me about my work ethic or pressure me into stepping up. He just, I don't even know, wanted to chat, I guess. Which is unusual. It's always been easier talking to my mother, I find comfort in telling her everything and feel safe letting her know my woes.

Dad on the other hand, not so much. He is a typical, hardworking, Aussie tradie. Work tough, live tough. If he had a motto that would be it. Growing up, he never cried, barely hugged me, struggled to show any emotion. Good or bad. I knew he loved me. I know he loves me. He just isn't the kind of man to make a big deal about showing it. So, I've never been the kind of son to open up to him. About anything.

I can't figure out why he is starting now. Or *if* he is starting now. That phone call felt like a big moment, but really, we didn't talk about much. He asked if I could dog sit. I told him I would have a go at project managing a job again.

In the grand scheme of family discussion, it was nothing. But for us, it was something. I think.

Chapter Three

MICHAEL

The bell rings above the cafe door. The sound of cars out on the street mingles with the steady chatter and the whirring coffee machine from inside. My coffee begins to churn in my stomach, and I push the half-drunk glass towards the centre of the table. Dark pink rose petals bunch around it, and I gag at how … *lovey* the whole place looks.

I look up from the table and see Audrey, frozen just inside the door. She casts her eyes over the cafe, her gaze lingering on the floral wall at the back. Even from across the room I notice the way her eyebrows pinch together.

I should not have recommended this cafe.

It was my go-to, once upon a time. With its overly done floral theme and pink everything, it was just what I needed when I was looking for cutesy and romantic brunch dates. The kind I hoped would become more but never did. Maybe it was fate that I never brought Audrey here. The coffee is overrated anyway, and the dates never panned out.

I try not to let my mind wander to the last date I had here. The girl ceremoniously walked out when I accidentally let slip that I had dinner plans with another woman. And lunch plans. That was probably a mistake too, but the lunch date that followed it? That was when I met Audrey.

I'd slipped onto the bench beside her in the park across town, and every other woman on the planet disappeared. She reached out an arm to shake my hand, and my fingers tingled from her touch. In that moment it felt as though all my fuck ups were worth it to be right there, in the park, meeting her for the first time. I'd cancelled the dinner date within minutes.

I kept fucking up after that though, just like I fucked up choosing this cafe. I thought the romantic vibe was just what we needed to reconnect, but something is off. Audrey isn't glowing like she used to. Beauty still shines off her, but her face is a little pale, and her eyes seem sunken. Her short blonde hair has grown out of the chin length style she sported when we first met, now dusting across her shoulders in gentle, messy waves. The highlights have grown out too, leaving a mousey section at the top of her head. The unkempt style suits her, but it doesn't feel like *her*.

Audrey holds the back of her hand against her mouth as she searches the room. When she sees me waving, her body shrinks into itself.

I shiver, but not from the way my long hair is still damp from my post gym shower. *Fuck,* I should have given myself more time to make sure it was dry. Should have packed more appropriate clothes than the grey sweats and tight tee I keep in my gym bag.

Squeezing between the tables, Audrey makes her way towards me, pulling her maroon cardigan around her before bringing one hand back up to her mouth.

She pulls out her own chair and sits down opposite me before I realise I should have got up to greet her.

"Sorry this place is a little …" I wave my arm towards the giant floral backdrop, tilting my head towards the rose petals spread across the table.

"Tacky?"

I shift my gaze between Audrey, the petals on the table, the flowers on the wall, and the hot pink coffee machine.

"I was going to say nauseating," I say, reaching my hand across the table. I nudge a pile of petals out of my way and rest my fingertips on her elbow. They tingle, just like they did that first day. The sensation crawls up my skin, under my shirt until it settles on my chest. Audrey scoots back in her chair, out of reach.

"Don't say that." Her voice is a whisper, barely audible through the fist she still holds over her mouth.

"Are you okay? You look … tired? Sick?"

Audrey pushes out of the chair, standing in a rush. It clambers behind her, knocking into the woman seated at the next table, but Audrey pays her no attention.

"I'll be back." She chokes out the words before darting through the tables and rushing to the back of the cafe. She slips into the hallway, following the sign to the restrooms.

My knee bounces under the table while I wait for her to return. I shouldn't have said she looked tired. *Fucking idiot.* If she is tired, she probably knows it. And if she wasn't I just turned around and told her she looks bad. That's not what I *meant.* I only wanted to know if she is okay. *Why?* Why is it only with Audrey that all my charm melts away and I'm left with nothing but my awkward self?

I stand up, shaking out my arms as though I can brush off the nerves and anxious energy.

The guy behind the coffee machine freezes to check what I'm doing. Giving him what I hope is a reassuring smile, I turn around the room.

"Were you leaving?"

Audrey looks even more pale than she did five minutes ago. Her glassy eyes flick between the table and me, and a loose strand falls from the haphazard bun she tied in her hair. I reach out, desperate to tuck it away from her face, to comfort her, to hold her through whatever it is that's making her feel this bad.

She flinches away from me, one hand on the back of her chair.

Shit, this is going terribly. I plonk back onto the seat.

"No, Audrey. I was just stretching my back." My eyes shift side to side at the half truth, even as I try to hold them steady.

Audrey presses her palms against her eyes.

"Michael, I can't—"

"Wait. I wasn't 'stretching my back'. But I wasn't leaving either." I cut her off, spitting the words out as fast as I can. "I'm sorry, okay. I didn't mean to say you looked like shit, and I didn't mean to pick out some super loved up cafe. I couldn't sit still so I stood up while I waited for you to come back. I keep fucking up and—"

"Stop."

I snap my mouth shut, the harshness of her voice mixes with a hint of despair. She sits in her chair, resting her elbows against the table. My fingers twitch against the table, aching to reach out to her. To pull her close and show her that I care and that I'm more than some idiotic young man who has no clue.

"Can we just order some food? Please?"

Nodding, I turn my attention to the waitress wandering between tables. Her slick long hair flicks against her back when she pivots towards us. We make quick work ordering food, I don't need the menu to know I want the biggest breakfast meal available. Bacon, eggs, hash browns, and all the toppings to go with it. But Audrey keeps her order light—raisin toast with a fruit juice—and I'm left wondering if I overestimated our date. If she wants to leave sooner rather than later.

"I am sorry, you know," I reiterate while we wait for our food. "For choosing this place. I've been here a couple of times and the coffee is okay but the food is good. I just forgot how cutesy it is."

"It's okay, Michael."

"No, it's not. None of it is okay. I've spent weeks trying to get you to see me again, and now you are, I keep messing it up."

"Michael, it's not the cafe."

It's not? I reach up to scratch underneath my bun, where

the hair tie pulls against my scalp. If the cafe isn't the problem, I'm really at a loss. Because as much as Audrey is stunning, she's looked miserable from the second she arrived. I hadn't said a word to her and she was already clutching at her stomach.

"Okay, well let's start again then," I try.

I push out of my chair, hovering in a semi crouched position before changing my mind when I see the thin line that forms on Audrey's mouth. She drops her head into her hand.

Pulling my chair back under me, I sit on my fingers. My knee bounces under the table and I fight the urge to pick apart my nails.

"How are you, Audrey?"

From behind her hand, a puff of air blows from Audrey's mouth.

"No? Um, how about … I've missed you?"

Her eyebrows reach her hair.

Shaking my head, I try again. "I'm sorry?"

"*That's* a good place to start."

I close my eyes, processing her abruptness. Something unexpected crackles through me. Disappointment. In myself. My skin crawls as I piece together the words to form a decent apology.

"I never expected to find what we had Audrey, and when I did, I didn't know how to react."

Audrey leans back in her chair, her hand falling from where it rested against her mouth. "Mike that's not what I—"

"Don't call me that, not you. And please, let me finish. I'm not an adult, not in the way you are. You're a mother, you have your career on track, you own a house. I have none of those things, and I'm not ready for them either. But I still think we could work. What we had was too incredible to walk away from, just because we are at different stages of our lives."

In my peripheral, I spot the waitress coming over to our

table, coffees propped on her tray. Audrey slams her hands down on the table. The waitress's long ponytail flicks over her shoulder as she pivots to deliver drinks to a calmer table first. I don't blame her.

"That's just it, Michael. You're not ready to be a parent, you're too scared to even *try* to take a step forward in your career, and I don't give a shit about whether you have a house or rent an apartment but you have to learn to own your decisions."

Her head drops, resting back on her hands for a moment. When she looks back up at me, her crystal blue eyes glisten with new tears. "Life is not all about good sex, Michael." She whispers the words, glancing around us as though she is making sure no one heard.

"No," I admit. "And a relationship shouldn't be built on that either. But you have to admit it was pretty good."

I wink, and Audrey's cheeks glow with a blush. Colour returns to her face and I see a hint of the playful woman I fell for. As quickly as the glimmer of a smile came, she drags it off her face.

"Good sex is not all it's hyped up to be. It has consequences."

My thoughts scramble. We always used a condom, and I hadn't been with anyone since I was tested for any sexually transmitted infections or diseases. Audrey stands before I can work out what she means, before I find the words to ask for clarification.

"I'm sorry, Michael. This was a mistake."

Reaching down to grab her bag from beside her chair, Audrey sucks in a long breath. She doesn't look at me when tucks it over her shoulder, croaking out a swift goodbye and turning on her heel.

I sit and watch her exit, coming to my senses as the bell above the door chimes and she steps onto the footpath. The waitress steps up to the table with our drinks, preventing me from rushing out to Audrey.

"Sorry, please cancel the order." I throw my wallet on the table, already scooting around the chairs.

"Wait, you can't—" the waitress calls out, but she doesn't move. Either she knows she can't stop me, or she can't be bothered.

I call over my shoulder as I head to the door, "I'll be back."

Stepping onto the footpath, I spot Audrey a block down the street. I scurry between the crowd, wrapping my fingers around her wrist when I catch up to her. Last time I touched her, electricity sparked through me. But this time, something softer tickles its way up my arm, settling back into my chest.

"Audrey, what do you mean?"

"I shouldn't have said anything," she sobs.

Pulling her towards me, I spin her around and wrap my arms around her back. Her soft curves fall into place against my chest as she nuzzles into my shoulder.

"It doesn't matter," she adds. "Really, don't worry about it. But please, stop calling me. Okay?"

I nod against her hair, even though I don't mean it. I don't want to stop calling Audrey, I don't want to stop trying to make her see that we are right together. But with everything I keep doing and saying? All the mistakes I keep making? Maybe we're wrong after all.

Chapter Four

AUDREY

Thump, thump, thump.

The steady, echoing sound drills into my ears with each rhythmic beat. I close my eyes, trying to block out the sound of my neighbour's latest DIY project. Surely there are noise restriction rules about using power tools at midday on a Saturday.

My head pounds along with the pulsing thuds, my stomach churning with each distant bang of a hammer. Too late, I realise I should have stayed to eat the food I ordered at the cafe, or stopped to pick something up on the way home, or at the very least grabbed something from the kitchen before hiding out back here. Bile rises and I rush out of my art studio towards the bathroom.

Nothing comes up, it never does. It never did with Maisie, and I doubt it will this time. Mostly because I can never stomach enough food in the first place. All I can manage are little nibbles of pre-approved 'safe' foods. But they do nothing to stop the twisting in my gut and the unbearable heaves that leave me panting.

When my body has finally had its disgusting moment, I splash water on my face and wipe the sweaty tears from my cheeks. I hobble to the kitchen, crouched over like an old witch, and pull an apple from the fridge before making my way back to my art studio.

I've always found calm here. Through the darkest days of my marriage breaking down, through the exhausting moments of Maisie's first few years, the spare bedroom I converted into an art studio has been something of a safe place for me. With its large north facing window, there is plenty of light, even through winter, to paint, and plenty of natural warmth to dry my artwork. We pulled up the carpet when we redid the flooring through the house, using the same ashy floorboards from the hall. The cupboard doors were removed, replaced with open shelving to store all my supplies. Various types of paints, canvases of all sizes, and more brushes than I can count fill the shelves.

Career ambition has always taken a strong first place when it comes to my interests outside of my family, but painting is a strong second. In high school, I hated the pressure that studying the visual arts put on the creative process. The planning, the explaining, the analysing. I just wanted to paint, to create. And that's all I still want to do.

Sometimes my pieces are beautifully abstract. Swirls of colour to match my mood, like the deep stormy blue stage I went through when my ex-husband first moved out. Other times, I recreate landscapes and plants and flowers in my own unique, colourful way. And occasionally, I find myself attempting portraits. Like the one I'm working on now. Tiny baby Maisie, snuggled and sleeping, wrapped in a tiny sage green blanket.

Stepping back into the room, the gentle energy washes over me. I crunch into the apple, chewing slowly through the nausea still swirling in my stomach, right alongside the baby currently growing in there.

By instinct, my free hand finds its place resting on my belly. There's no bump yet, but I'm bloated already, soft around the middle far sooner than my body changed with my last pregnancy. Maybe it's a second baby thing, like my body already knows all the right places to grow, or maybe it's just because I was so obsessed with crunches before I had Maisie, so my muscles were all tighter.

Either way, I'll have to start living in leggings until I buy some maternity pants.

I unbutton my jeans and let my stomach relax at the reduced pressure. All the weight I never managed to lose after having Maisie, the weight I finally came to accept and even love, feels almost excessive now. I wonder what will happen to my body with this pregnancy. Putting on weight is a given, it comes with the parcel, but will my belly grow out like it did last time, or will every part of me swell up? How long will it take me to love my body again?

Sitting on my stool, I spin the seat a few times, trying to get comfortable. Naturally, my legs cross underneath me and I lean forward over the back support. I've never been one for sitting 'normally', always berated at school for hooking my legs under the seat or fidgeting too much while we all sat on the mat. Here in my art room, I decided early on to ignore all the 'sit straight' memories and just make myself comfortable.

While I finish my apple, I admire the painting in front of me, comparing it to the reference photo I have pegged to the top of the easel. Portraits are always harder to get perfect. There's less freedom and I always want them to look exactly like the picture in my head. So far, Maisie's eyes aren't quite right, and the swirls of dark hair atop her head need some attention. I force my focus to the blanket wrapped around her. I used a little creative licence on the colour, turning the minty green into a deeper sage to give the whole piece an earthy feel. I'll pull out the contrast between the shadow and highlights in my final layer of paint, but for now I love it. The colour is perfect, the woven strokes and gentle bunches look soft to touch.

I'll have to find where I stashed the blanket, for the little baby growing inside me now. We donated almost everything as Maisie got older and we settled into the idea that she was it for us: the cot, the pram, the car seat, the toys. But I *know*

I kept the blanket somewhere, in a box with a few other precious memories.

From the day Maisie came out, announcing her presence with the most beautiful wail, Callum and I knew we were done having kids. It wasn't what I originally wanted, and we'd fought over it time and time again. But pregnancy was hard, and deep in the midst of my twelve-hour labour I said never again. I backflipped a few times, but Callum stood his ground.

As the days, then months and years went on, I became happier, more content with our decision to be a 'one and done' family. Maisie was our world. But I also enjoyed the freedom that only having one child brought. I could progress my career without having a massive gap on my resume. Finding a babysitter was easier. Daycare fees were lower. Everything worked.

I guess I should count my blessings that the little bean currently growing inside me will arrive right as Maisie will be starting primary school. Although juggling drop offs and pick ups around naps and feeds will probably be a nightmare. In truth, there's probably no *right* time to have a second child. Doing it all alone only adds another layer of complexity, and the thought of handling all the sleepless nights and never-ending days on my own gives me a headache.

There's probably a wrong person to have one with though. And it's not that I don't like Michael. It's just that I don't *like* him. Not in the way I should considering we are about to become parents. I can't even picture him taking proper care of himself, let alone a tiny baby. How would he go sacrificing his sleep, his sanity, his gym time, to put the needs of a child above his own?

Callum and I weren't right together, at least not anymore, but at least he is a good father. I wish I could say the same about Michael, but I don't see how it will work. Sure, he has his own way of showing that he cares: the little gifts he used to bring me and the way his touch always lingered on my lower back as we walked. But being a parent is so much more than that. It's giving *everything* for this little baby.

When I tried to tell him this morning, I clammed up, not knowing the words to say. I have no idea how to break the news that his whole world is about to change. What if he doesn't want to be a father? Technically, there are options for us, but not for me. I may be scared and confused and over-whelmed by the fact I'm having another baby, but somehow it also feels right. I can't bear the thought of Michael not feel-ing the same way.

When he laughed his way through our terrible catch up, I got the feeling he wouldn't be ready for this massive change. And that only made it harder to tell him. I know I should have; I know I need to. But the air was too sweet from the giant floral wall of the café, too warm from all the bodies trying to escape the harsh winter chill outside. I couldn't breathe.

My stomach clenches, a new wave of nausea crashing through me like a train. I heave over the waste bin, emptying my stomach of the apple I just finished eating.

I guess I do actually vomit after all.

Dropping to the floor, I curl my knees up to my chest, squeezing my arms tight around my legs. I was never this sick with Maisie. So sick it hurts.

I wish I had someone to rely on in times like these. Even when I finally tell Michael about the baby, it hurts knowing that he still wouldn't be here when I need him to be. He would still always be a phone call away, never around to rub my back or fetch me some ginger ale.

Stretching back up as the nausea begins to wane, I head to the kitchen to get my own fizzy drink. The bubbles tingle their way down my throat, settling below my ribcage and mas-saging my twisted insides.

The steady thumping of a hammer next door has

quietened, replaced by the occasional screech of a power tool and laid-back laughter of a dad and his sons. Through the noise, the crunch of tires on gravel drifts in the open kitchen window. Looking out, down the driveway, I see Callum returning with Maisie from their extra day together. His new girlfriend still cowers in the front seat, pulling her hair up as Callum parks the car behind mine. I don't blame her for being cautious of me. I wasn't exactly friendly for a while.

Now that I can appreciate what the two of them share—meaning, now that I'm over my initial jealousy—I'm happy for them both. I hope we can fall into an easy co-parenting team, and more than that I hope we can even consider each other friends. She seems nice, and Maisie adores her.

I step out to meet them, painter's apron still wrapped over my clothes and ginger ale still firmly clasped in my hands. The small porch is surrounded by roses planted by Callum's sister, with fruit trees lining the long narrow driveway. The block and house are small, but when Callum and I first found it, we fell in love with the little cottage propped in between townhomes. A little slice of the suburb's history that we wanted to claim for ourselves. It's all mine now, after the divorce, but I still see little bits of Callum everywhere. Even after I changed the photos on the wall, and the pillows on the couch. I bought a new bed and changed all the linen, rearranged the living space and spread my paints further into the sunroom. But the ghost of our relationship still hangs around.

I'm not sad about our marriage breaking down, at least not anymore. We were good, great even, until we weren't, and then it was time to move on. Living in this house, though, is like being trapped in time. I had been planning to find something else eventually, but with a new baby coming it feels like all too much, all at once.

"Mummy!" Maisie runs from the car, colliding with my

legs before continuing into the house. I'll have to figure out what to cook for her dinner soon.

"How was your date?"

Callum and Cassidy walk hand in hand towards me. My face crumples as a thick lump forms in my throat. Clutching at my stomach, I attempt to stretch my expression back into something that oozes comfort and friendliness. I'm sure I fail.

"Yeah, um, it was … great." My voice pitches unnaturally.

Cassidy steps away from Callum, eyes wide, folding her arms across her chest.

"Do you paint?"

Her change of topic catches me by surprise, and I stumble over my answer. "Yes," I croak as I finally form the word. "Well, kind of. Just for fun."

"She's pretty good," Callum's kind words surprise me. Although we get along now, I'm still wrapping my head around the whole 'being friends with my ex-husband' thing.

"I'd love to see them, one day." She turns towards the open door, calling through the house. "Bye Maisie!"

My daughter's voice echoes down the hallway, "Bye Cassidy! Bye Daddy!"

Cassidy's chocolate hair is swept back into the kind of messy mum bun I always longed for. My thin hair never co-operated though, so I gave up. In a way it forced me to always have my hair a little more styled than I have time for, but when I'm feeling as crap as I do now, I'd give anything for the quick easy throwaway style.

She tips between her heels and toes, hands on her hips. Eyes darting between Callum and me, she whistles under her breath. We might all be on friendly talking terms, but this drop off seems particularly strained. It was awkward enough when they came to pick Maisie up and Cassidy didn't want to get out of the car. I don't know if it's worse now that we are all left standing on the porch.

It's the first time I've had to call on Callum to watch Maisie on an extra day. The first time I interrupted their day in this way. But also, even though I know it's not the first time they have spent time together, it's the first time Cassidy has been here to drop Maisie off. Despite how I know Cassidy feels about taking on a motherly role—meaning she doesn't want it to have that kind of label—it still feels a little like that's what happened today. It's too much like the new mother figure in Maisie's life is dropping her back off with the old one. The lonely one.

"Well," I say, sucking in a deep breath and attempting to break the weird tension. "Thank you for having her today."

"Anytime." Callum's hands are shoved deep in his jean pockets. "We better go, let you get her dinner sorted."

"Yes, thanks."

Taking a step back, I pull my hand away from my stomach to wave an awkward goodbye before turning towards the house. Footsteps recede down the gravel driveway, but something stops me from going inside when I hear the car doors open.

"Wait," I call out.

As I spin on my heel to face them again, Callum steps a leg back out of the car.

"What's wrong?"

I jog a few steps towards them so they can hear me over the power tools next door. "Nothing, I was just wondering if you were still looking for a house?"

Callum turns towards his girlfriend. She tilts her head to the side and gestures to him.

"Maybe, why?"

"I found the perfect place for you."

Chapter Five

MICHAEL

"Oi Mikey, quit fucking around and bring me the nail gun. We need to get this frame up before the rain."

Taking a final, long swig of my sports drink, I throw up the finger to Brendan. His eyebrows pinch together in a scowl darker than the clouds rolling over. He slams his finger out towards the truck yelling, "Now."

Throwing the empty bottle in the rubbish cage, I hold out my palms in defeat. I jump down from where I was seated on the hood of the Ford Ranger and my work boots squelch in the clay that has somehow spilled off the site and onto the newly constructed road.

"Alright, alright."

I don't have the energy to deal with Brendan's bullshit. The bloke gets made site manager for one job and he thinks he is the king. Walking around with his shoulders back like he owns the slab of concrete we are building on today. But I love him anyway, I'd just never tell him that.

After grabbing the gun and a box of nails from the toolbox secured to the tray of the ute, I step onto the concrete slab. Baxter follows close behind me. He likes to pretend he is some big working dog, but the truth is that he'll find the sunniest spot on the slab and lie down to snooze the whole day through.

It'll be a big house, this one. Fancy too, from what I could tell from the blueprints. Wide open hallways, more living spaces than bedrooms, and what I'm sure will be a beautiful outdoor living area. But right now, it's just a slab on a pile of dirt and clay.

With the nail gun in hand, we go about fixing the pieces together like a puzzle. A connects to B, nails where everything joins together, and support posts for each section.

It's easy, thoughtless work. At least with Brendan calling the shots.

The overcast sky has turned dark by the time we call it a day. The low sun fights to give light, and the air has a wet mossy smell. The ground floor frame is complete, and Brendan pulls out his phone to check the weather radar. I don't need a fancy image to tell me the rain is coming. Plus, we all know the second story isn't getting finished today, even if it wasn't about to pour. We've been here since the crack of dawn, and there's no chance Dad would approve overtime when the job is so far on schedule. Besides, the scaffolding hasn't been delivered.

"Brendan, we're done mate. Let's pack up." I throw my shoulder against his as I walk past.

He shoves his phone in his pocket and clears his throat.

"Alright boys, let's pack up," he calls out.

I ignore the uncomfortable itch that spreads along my back, the one that wants to call him out for following my lead when he is meant to be the one in charge. Never mind the fact he called the shots all day, a grumble rolls through my throat that he took the credit for ending the shift. I don't want to be the one in charge, but it feels like crap knowing it's Brendan who is.

We started as apprentices at the same time and have been mates since the very first day we were asked to fetch the left-handed screwdrivers. It's great that he is stepping up and taking on some responsibility, he should have done it years ago. But I don't like feeling as though I'm being left behind.

Rolling my shoulders, I pack the tools into the box on my truck. The only person to blame here is me.

I check Baxter's feet, wiping away as much of the mud and clay from the fur around his paws as I can. Satisfied they are as clean as they are going to get without giving him a bath, I force him into the passenger seat before walking back around the car. I'm about to climb in, drive off without a hint of a goodbye when Brendan slams a palm on the passenger roof. Baxter gives a friendly growl through the half open window, and I jump a little at the clang, searching the sky for hints of thunder before I realise my mate was just being over enthusiastic.

"So, did you see that bird again? The mum?"

I suck in a breath. "No. I mean, yeah but it was terrible."

"You fucked up?"

"I think." I gesture to the door, pulling myself into the car and pushing the seat all the way back so I can prop my legs on the dash while we talk. Brendan climbs in the other side, shoving my dog onto my lap.

He's too big to be a lapdog at the best of times, let alone squished in the front seat of the car, but that has never stopped him before. Baxter's weight settles on my thighs, his leg resting on my knees. Once he's comfortable, I turn my attention back to Brendan.

"She didn't look great. I was worried, but I think I brought it up the wrong way? Maybe? Now I can't stop thinking about how I should have just said she looked wonderful anyway."

Although most of me knows that probably wouldn't have helped. It's been over a week since I saw Audrey and deep down, I know something is up. She wasn't just feeling unwell, there was more to it. There had to have been. Otherwise why would she have called and tried to organise the date. I need to get to the bottom of it, but Audrey is back to not returning my calls. There has to be a point where I come at this from a different angle, but I have no idea what that angle is. I have no clue how to make a girl who won't respond to my texts tell me what's going on.

My foot wriggles to the beat of the low bass from the radio and my mind races through all the possibilities. Despite my initial freak out, she can't have caught something. I double checked the date of my test and it was right before we were together, but even so we used a condom every single time. Except for that one time it broke, but she said it didn't matter. I assumed she meant she was all good too, unless she found out afterwards that she wasn't. I never thought to ask. And I saw her taking her pill. My mind flicks through our short-lived situation-ship, wondering what could be causing her as much grief and discomfort I saw on her face at the cafe.

Maisie. Shit, I hope it's not something to do with Maisie. I might have freaked out about the little girl being around, but that certainly doesn't mean I wanted anything to happen to her. She's a wonderful little kid, so full of life and laughter.

Audrey and her ex had still been figuring out all the logistics of their joint custody. Could something have happened there?

Pulling out my phone, I pull up the one-sided text message thread. I have to scroll an embarrassing amount to find the last message from Audrey. When I told her the name of the cafe and all she said was 'see you there'. Since that day it's been radio silence, again.

"Fuck mate." Brendan's voice shocks me out of my self-wallowing. "It's time to let it go."

I let out a deep, grumbling sigh. "Yeah, I think you're right."

I hate acknowledging it. It hurts a muscle I forgot existed, somewhere deep in my chest.

For so long I spent my time playing the field, breaking

hearts because I was never ready to settle down. I guess in some bullshit way this is my actions coming back to bite me on the ass. Because the one girl I always wanted to hear back from, won't return my messages. Or my phone calls. All she does is send back a thumbs up or a 'ha ha' against the messages I send.

But from the aching stab in my chest, I can't help but wonder if Brendan is right. Maybe Audrey and I were never meant to be.

Even still, I fire off another text, because now that the God-awful thought has entered my mind, I can't shake it loose.

Michael: Just tell me you and Maisie are okay.

Once the message is sent with a whoosh, I throw my phone onto the back seat, desperate to ignore it. Determined not to watch it like a hawk while I wait for a response.

"You've gotta pull your head in."

I turn my attention back to Brendan. Outside the truck, thunder rumbles. The sky is somehow darker than before, lightning crackling in the distance.

"You should get in your car before the storm hits."

"You should shut the fuck up and listen." Brendan snaps back. He's always been like this. The voice of uninvited reason.

"You know your dad wanted you to take on this job, right? He needs you to show some responsibility. And pining over a chick you barely know is not the way to show him you're on your way to running the business."

"And I told him I don't want to run the business."

He punches me square in the bicep. I barely register his knuckles grazing against the muscles I tense in anticipation. Baxter cocks an ear at the sudden movement, but quickly settles back down when he realises there's no threat.

"Fuck, do you ever not go to the gym?" Rubbing his

hand, he shifts his body to face back out the front of the car. Loaded raindrops start to fall. "Fuck," he sighs.

"I'm serious." Reaching up, I pull my hair from the loose bun I had it tied in while we worked. "He has these grand expectations of me, but I'll never meet them. He needs to stop hoping and praying that I'll change my mind. I told him I'd *consider* taking on one job. Not the business."

"Or, you need to get over this idea that you're not good enough. So, one job was a disaster. So what? You were fresh into your twenties and your old man was dumb to put that much pressure on you so soon after your apprenticeship finished. I couldn't have handled it then either. But you're not that kid anymore. You know what you're doing. I've seen you correct deliveries and boss around the lackeys. You've got more skill than any of the rest of us. You just don't have the confidence."

I stare out the window, past the heavy rain, to the frame we built today. I barely had to think, following Brendan's instructions, and I'd never tell a soul, but it was a little boring. I never thought I'd get sick of the simplicity of building a frame, but maybe some tiny part of me *is* ready to take the next step. It's scary just thinking about it. Scarier still to think that maybe after all these years, my dad was right.

"You were bored today." Brendan's acknowledgement of what was just running through my mind shocks me. "I saw it," he continues. "You were yawning, checking your phone constantly. You didn't even laugh when I asked Freddie to grab the left-handed screwdriver."

"Because that's a lame joke. It stopped being funny when my dad played it on us. Remember how embarrassed we were when we couldn't find it?"

"Sure, but Freddie fell for it too. And *that* is what's funny. But you were half asleep and didn't even realise."

"Okay fine, say I was bored. That doesn't mean I can run the whole goddamn business. It's a big jump."

"He doesn't want you to run the business right away Mike, he just needs you to take a step."

Brendan pauses, his hand on the door, ready to make a run for it. "Gym?" he asks.

"Does a bear shit in the woods?"

With a sharp nod, Brendan sucks in as much dry air as he can before running through the rain to his car.

The whole conversation has been too much for me, and I hate the way Brendan has gotten under my skin. Goosebumps erupt down my arms, leaving a crawling feeling in their wake. I don't want to think about how perfect Audrey is but how it's probably time to let her go. And I don't want to think about the next steps I might take towards running the business. Because both those thoughts hurt too fucking much.

I hold them in as I drive to the gym, ready to let them out on the weights.

Chapter Six

AUDREY

"You did *not*."

I turn away as Cassidy slaps Callum in the chest with a grin bigger than the sun. Despite how happy I am for them, it still hurts. I still remember how happy I was when he did the same thing for us, how bittersweet it felt when he signed the whole thing over to me in the divorce.

Just like I knew he would, Callum adored the showy town house and all its modern architecture. From the moment he stepped out of his car and into the shadow of the steep pitched facade, he fell in love. Cassidy loved it too. I'd barely finished locking up after showing them the place last week when Callum sent me through an offer well above asking. I hadn't realised Cassidy wasn't aware until we came for a final walkthrough today to sign all the remaining paperwork.

"You said you loved it, I love it, Maisie loves it." Callum replies, earning himself another slap. "Maisie stop running up and down the stairs."

Jumping the final step, Maisie lands with a clack on the tiled floor. She drops down to sit on the lower step with a thud, scoffing. Just to make sure none of us miss her displeasure, she crosses her arms over her knees and grumbles. I turn away from her little outburst, determined not to laugh. She's full of them lately, and the less I interact, the sooner she moves on from her miniature catastrophe.

"That doesn't mean buy it." Cassidy says to Callum, and I'm beginning to feel like it's time to remove myself from the conversation. I take a step back, towards the wide arched hallway that leads to the front of the house.

"Cassidy, I've wanted to buy a house since before I moved into the apartment, you know that."

"I can't afford this." Cassidy scoffs.

Bile rises to my throat, threatening to spill out all over the large tiles on the floor. At the happiness of it all. At how easily everything is coming for them.

"I don't need you to. I'm buying it for you, for us."

And here it comes.

"Excuse me," I choke out as I rush past the happy couple towards the bathroom on the main floor.

The contents of my stomach upend themselves into the toilet.

Cassidy, Callum and Maisie all fall silent as I succumb to my all-day sickness. I'd hoped it would be gone by now, but I've had no such luck. If anything, it's only gotten worse. What started as a lot of dry heaving has progressed into full on vomiting attacks that are impossible to hide. If I hadn't made it obvious by sprinting to the toilet, the noise has definitely given it away. The small bathroom has floor to ceiling tiles and my splutters echo all around me.

"Let's go outside," I hear Callum whisper. The screen door slams behind them.

After I finish coughing up my breakfast, I rinse my mouth and splash my face with cold water. Propped against the sink, I glare at myself in the small round mirror. My normally blue eyes are bloodshot and the loose hair framing my face sticks to my shining forehead. The rounds of my cheeks are red, and I swear they look puffier than they did a week ago. Not wanting to dirty the perfectly folded hand towel hanging on the rack, I dry my mouth with my sleeve.

I did the math. I wouldn't even be through my first trimester, and I've been vomiting multiple times a day, but I swear I've already gained weight. Tearing my gaze away from the sweaty face in the mirror, I glance down at my belly. The soft curves of my stomach and hips still mask the appearance of my tiny bump. Even so, my hands cradle my front as I remind myself that all the heaving, all the nausea and coughing and illness, will be worth it once this little bean is born.

"Audrey?"

I jump, despite Cassidy's gentle tone. The bathroom door sits open where I failed to close it. Cassidy's face pops through the gap. Her eyes tilt down as she takes in the scene. The room clearly smells like vomit, and I *look* like I've just emptied my stomach. And my hands still hold my invisible bump.

She opens her mouth a fraction, but closes it again with a slight shake of her head. Her hand reaches out towards me, but pulls back to rest on her own stomach.

"Never ask," she whispers to herself. Looking back up at me, she speaks more clearly. "Are you okay?"

I stand a little taller, pulling my shoulders back and dropping my hands from where they were resting. But the movement creates a new tsunami through my gut. Falling to my knees, I crouch around the toilet, but this time, nothing comes. My stomach is already empty.

"No," I finally choke out. "No, I am not."

Cassidy drops to the floor beside me, squeezing herself between the toilet and the wall. I can't comprehend how she fits in the tiny gap, but she does. One knee squishes against her chest and the other stretches out along the floor towards the sink.

She's so … little. No, that makes her sound like a child. Petite. The delicate features of her face match the gentle, natural wave in her hair, which gives way to her dainty frame. So unlike me. I'm all sharp and pointy in the face. Thin eyebrows thanks to the combination of my pale hair and spending my teenage years plucking them into spindly lines. Pointy nose, sharp cheekbones. I used to have a defined collarbone and a figure like Cassidy's, but motherhood had other plans. It took me a long time to find comfort in my new column shape.

Eventually I grew to accept it, just like I'm sure I'll grow to love whatever shape my body ends up in after this pregnancy too. But I can't help wondering if my marriage would have failed so easily if I'd managed to get back to my pre-baby body.

It's a pointless thought. One I know has no standing. But I can't help thinking about it anyway. Damn hormones.

"Do you, ah, want to talk about it?"

I pull my head away from the toilet to rest my cheek on the cool tiled wall. "Not really. Kind of."

Cassidy just shrugs, reaching a hand across the toilet to rest it on my shoulder.

"I know it might be weird, considering, well everything. But we can talk."

Yeah, it would be weird. But strangely, I do really want to talk to her. There is something about her kind green eyes that calls to my sorrows, promising me everything will end up okay.

"Maisie is going to be a sister." The words fall out of my mouth on a bated breath, and I realise it's the first time I've acknowledged the fact out loud.

Sure, I made appointments with doctors and ultrasound facilities. But it was somehow different. I was simply stating that I was pregnant, as though my subconscious knew I had a choice to make. Never mind the fact the choice was already made.

Cassidy remains silent, her thoughtful expression twists uncomfortably. Pressing her lips into a thin line, she toys with the ring on her forefinger. The flower spins against the pad of her thumb, filling the tiny room with its gentle hum.

"You're …?"

Her question fades away before she has the courage to voice it. I nod as I push my hair off my face and lean against the opposite wall.

"It was, well, it was a bit of a surprise. I'm still gathering my thoughts, but the morning sickness doesn't care if I'm still coming to terms with it."

"Who's the … wait no sorry, don't answer that. It's not my business."

Her voice shakes, and her eyes begin to glisten. Before a single tear can fall, she blinks away the moisture with a deep inhale. Cassidy presses her thumbs to her temples, then brings a hand down to tap at her chest. Just the same way Callum does when he feels overwhelmed.

"Can I help? Can we help?"

At her kind offer, my own tears erupt. They rush down my cheeks, dripping tiny wet patches onto my white blouse. I bat away the streaks as I swallow down the hard lump forming in my throat. For the first time since I saw those two little pink lines, I feel seen. Just a simple offer of support, and I no longer feel alone. An overwhelming sense of relief rushes through me and I fight the urge to lean across the toilet to hug her. My ex-husband's new girlfriend. The woman who, by design, I should not get along with, has somehow become the first person I confided in.

But truthfully, she's the only person I feel safe talking to. As though I knew, deep down, somehow, that she wouldn't judge.

Unlike the women from Maisie's Mother's Group, or the other parents from Maisie's kindergarten. The so-called friends who love to bitch and gossip as soon as someone leaves the room. The mothers who flit around in happy couples, celebrating the arrival of their second and third, and even fourth, children. I can't stand the pity in their eyes on Friday mornings when they overhear me tell Maisie her dad will pick her up. It's almost as bad as the way they pat my shoulder when I come to pick her up after she has been with Callum for the week. "Oh, you must have *missed* her so much," they whine. Or, "I just *couldn't* be away from my kids for a whole week," as though I chose this. I hate this, but they don't care. As long as it's not them.

I can't imagine telling any of them that I'm pregnant. That I'm not with the father and that I'm not sure he would ever want to be a father and I have no idea what the future looks like for us.

"Thank you," I whisper to Cassidy, reaching a hand towards her.

She takes it, squeezing my fingers between her own as we push ourselves to stand.

"I feel like I'm failing," I admit. Because I do. I had everything planned out, and one by one, all those plans are crumbling. It started with my marriage to Callum, then it was my fleeting relationship with Michael. And now this.

This feels like the biggest failure of them all, to fall pregnant when I'm not in a relationship and I didn't want a second child.

"I usually hate when people tell me that everything will be okay," she says. "Because really, who the fuck knows that? So, I won't say it. But I will tell you that you are not alone. In some weird way, we're family now."

Straightening my cardigan across my shoulders, she smiles at me. Her mossy eyes glitter with golden flakes, squinting together as she sees through my pain and into my deepest dreams.

"But I can see, somehow, that you want this. And that's all that matters right now. Everything else, all the nitty gritty details are white noise. Because you are going to love that baby so much. And I already know you are an incredible mother who only wants the best for her children."

My shoulders shake at her words, at the kindness she has shown me. And I believe everything she has said.

"You're not failing, Audrey."

Sucking in oxygen and courage, I straighten my posture as much as I can with the permanent twist in my stomach. "Cassidy?"

She responds with a gentle hum.

"Thank you," I tell her.

When I go to turn away, her grip tightens on my shoulders, forcing me to look back up at her.

"What are friends for?" she says with a coy grin.

Chapter Seven

AUDREY

The room smells clinical; bleach burning through my nostrils with a subtle citrus scent that tries to force its way into the aroma. It's sterile in a way that reminds me of the day Maisie broke her collarbone. I realised that day, how different our future was going to be from the one I had planned. I was no longer in charge of her every movement, I was no longer always going to be there for her. It broke my heart, but it was also a weird turning point for me.

Sitting on the floor of the waiting room, my arms wrapped around her legs, I realised that the three of us would be stronger apart. And that for this to work, Callum and I needed to get along, properly, not just a little bit. By default, I figured that meant Cassidy and I had to get along as well.

I vowed then to never be the clichéd evil bio-mum, trying to stop my daughter from having a friendship with her eventual stepmum. Because I have no doubts that Callum and Cassidy are racing down that path at breakneck speed. Maisie adores Cassidy, and the two have a lot of shared interests. I came to terms then with the fact that I was no longer the only woman in my daughter's life. That in a roundabout way she would have three parents, not just two, and certainly not just one.

That thought flings me back to the present at the same time the ultrasound technician turns back toward the waiting room with a furrowed brow. Her lavender scrubs compliment the deep purple of her hair but are contrasted by the bright red glasses framing her face.

"Are you by yourself?" she questions.

I'm sure she doesn't mean for the words to cut as deeply as they do. But I am. I am by myself, and this baby will only have one parent, so unlike Maisie with her whole team.

I could call Michael.

I *should* call Michael.

But I'm afraid of what he would say. Too scared he would ask if we should keep the baby I've already grown to love. Terrified that he might want nothing to do with his child. His actions have shown me that he isn't ready to become a father, so I've kept this secret. Because if he doesn't know, he can't hurt us by walking away.

Michael is outrageous and fun, there's no way he is ready to become a father. I've been clinging to that thought, as though it justifies my decision not to tell him. Even though he has a right to know, I'm choosing to protect myself, and this baby, first.

I give the technician a sharp nod and climb onto the re-clined chair. It's easier to let her comment slide than to open my mouth. If I do, the can of worms might spill open. I choke a little, hoping I can hold my nausea at bay at least until the appointment is over.

I pull up my shirt as she dims the lights, and I squeeze my own hands when she dumps cold gel on my stomach.

"That's fine," she chimes. "Lots of dads can't make it to appointments. We will take lots of pictures for you to show him."

Her bold assumption shocks the polite grin off my face. She cracked open the can of worms all by herself. Sure, most women that come in for pregnancy ultrasounds would be coupled up. Most dads would at least make an effort to be there, or care enough to want a printout—but then again, most dads also *know* about the baby.

My fingers squeeze against my thumb as I consider all

the possible reasons her words might have cut open an unintended wound. What about the women who choose to have a baby on their own? The ones who don't know who the father is? Or the ones who know exactly who it is but are desperately trying to escape him? What about the women having babies with other women, thanks to a generous donation from a friend or a stranger?

So many scenarios that don't fit the life she assumed I lived. For a moment, I consider pretending to live one of those lives. Anything to escape my own fucked up situation.

But I remain silent, choosing to avoid the awkwardness altogether.

Without another word, she presses the wand into my stomach. Forcing my flesh to descend and twist, she wriggles the receiver around while examining her computer. The screen above the chair remains blank, and her monitor is directed away from me, but the subtle woosh of my insides rings in the air.

Until another sound is added to the mix. One that makes my eyes unexpectedly swell. A piece of my heart tears away, floating down my abdomen and settling itself low in my belly. And it will stay there, I'm sure, until this little baby is born. Then they will carry it around with them forever, just like Maisie does with her piece.

Dub-dub, dub-dub, dub-dub.

It's faster than I remember, but the sound is unmistakable.

My hand clutches around my throat, my mouth falling open. Without intention, I reach to the table next to me for my phone. I want to record this moment. I want to be able to show Michael.

Because God, it doesn't matter if I don't think he is ready. It doesn't matter if he is immature and inflated, and it doesn't matter that he has no clue what he is doing with his life. Because what I realise now, is that he is also kind and nurturing. He cares more than his actions show and I know that because he still checks in, making sure I'm okay, even though he has no clue what might be wrong.

"Oh, you can't use your phone, sorry. I can print some photos, and take a recording if you like?"

The technician's voice cuts through the echoed heartbeat. I open my mouth to speak, but the words get stuck in my throat.

"Please." It comes out on a cough, spluttering its way into the air as I choke on the rush of emotion.

She clicks a button to turn on the screen above me. The display flickers to life, full of tiny words and numbers so small and blurry I can't make them out. As she presses the wand into me again, she also clicks on her computer. The image flashes onto the screen, a greyish wedge of lines and swirls.

Then, as she wriggles the wand, the grey seems to crack. A roundish shape of black emerges and there, nestled against one side is a tiny bean shaped baby. It throbs in time with the heartbeat still playing through her speaker.

"That's it?" I press up on my elbows, drawn towards the screen as though I could reach out and touch it.

I forgot. I don't know how but I forgot just how magical this moment is. Seeing my baby for the first time, I bat away the moisture trickling down my cheeks. More than anything, I wish I had someone to share this moment with. It's tainted almost, knowing that I am alone. Knowing that I might not have been if I had been able to see past Michael's flaws and tell him about the little bundle of life and joy that's growing inside me.

"Yep! That's your little baby. You're measuring ten weeks and three days."

It lines up with my own calculations. Almost perfectly.

"We've got your email on file, so I can send you the

digital files, but here are some printouts." She hands me a stack of photos before wiping the remaining gel off my stomach with a paper towel. The image on top steals my breath. My little bean, or is it a strawberry? I had an app that told me each week how big Maisie was, but I can't even remember what it was called now, let alone what fruit correlated to each week.

I brush the picture with my thumb, committing every millimetre of it to memory. I can make out the rough, oversized shape of the baby's head and the tiny arms and legs. The little button nose is barely formed, but I already know it will be just like Michael's. It's too small and soft to be mine.

I flick through the stack, registering that the technician printed two of each image. My hands shake as I pull down my top. My knees wobble as I push myself to stand. My ears ring as I book my next scan. And I know it's time to tell Michael that he is about to become a father.

I call him as soon as I get into the car. The phone bounces on the passenger seat when I throw it down as soon as it connects to the Bluetooth. I count the rings, desperate to distract myself from my rapid pulse. I have to have this conversation, but I have no idea what I'm going to say.

One ring as I reverse out of the car park, another as I steer towards the exit, a third as I pull out onto the main road.

Halfway through the fourth ring, he answers.

"Audrey?"

Somehow, his voice calms me the second I hear it. Laced with concern and care and something else that I can't quite pinpoint. It sounds like love, but surely that's not it. That's just the hormones talking.

"Michael."

My own voice is a shaky whisper. I clear my throat, wiping each sweaty palm in turn. My grey skirt turns dark with the streaks.

"Sorry," I correct myself once I've gained a tiny ounce of

composure. "How are you? Are you good? It's been a while, I'm sorry I haven't responded to your messages. I'm sorry I wasn't well that day at the cafe. I hope I didn't make you sick." I couldn't have made him sick, not when the only thing causing my nausea was the toxic mix of hormones and anxiety.

Word vomit continues to tumble out as I try desperately to fill the silence, to talk about anything other than the baby.

"Audrey?" Michael cuts off my rambling. "What's wrong?"

"I … You're … We …" I try, but none of the sentences flying through my head seem appropriate. There's no right way to tell the man I had a fling with that he is about to become a father.

The car seat scratches against the back of my thighs. I take a deep, pained breath, fighting the urge to close my eyes. When a traffic light ahead of me turns red, I ease the car to a stop and take the chance to blink away the stinging. Under my closed eyes, tears swell and overflow.

Michael sucks in a deep breath, letting it out on a low sigh. But he remains silent while I process my thoughts, trying to find the words I know I need to get out.

Behind me, another driver punches on their horn, signalling that I missed the light turning green. I take off slowly. As the car picks up speed, so does the pounding in my chest.

"I can't do this." The words surprise me as they escape my lips, but once they are out in the open, transported via Bluetooth and phone connection, I know what I need to do. Rolling my shoulders back I sit a little taller in my chair, faking confidence in the way I always do. "Can we meet again? I'm sorry I ran off last time."

It takes too long for Michael to answer. I hear him fumble with the phone and his rough breaths. My heart continues to beat ferociously and my left knee shakes as I pull into my work car park. Turning the engine off and unbuckling my seat belt, I trace the steering wheel with a finger while I wait for him to say … anything. Even no, by this stage.

"Look sorry, you don't have—"

"I want to." He cuts off my attempt to take back the invitation. My shoulders relax as he continues. "Yes, please. Let's meet again. But I can't this week. Maybe next?"

I sink into the seat.

"I'll have Maisie, the weekend after?"

The idea of waiting two weeks to tell him is a kick right to my growing stomach, but it's better than the alternatives. I can't rely on my ex-husband to look after Maisie again, but I have no one else nearby to babysit and I'm not ready to bring her along. We could meet for dinner after work one night, but I have evening showings for a bunch of high-end houses I need to sell. Plus, lately I've been so exhausted afterwards that I doubt I'll be able to get the right words out.

So, two weeks it is. At least I'll have time to figure out what I'm going to say. And plan for the many hundreds of ways this whole situation is likely to go pear shaped.

Chapter Eight

MICHAEL

"Skinny latte?"

The barista blinks up at me through her fake lashes, tucking a stray curl behind her ear. With a coy smile, she pops her hip as she leans forward over the counter. I don't miss the way she pushes her chest together with her arms, but I ignore her blatant flirting and keep my eyes on her face.

"Two, please."

Beside me, Baxter barks a short response to my voice.

Jumping to stand up straight, the barista wipes her hands on her apron and punches the order into her tablet. Belinda, I think her name was. Or Melinda. I love this little coffee stand. They have the best roast and until recently I would come past every other morning on my walk home from the gym.

I'm not ashamed to admit that I've had more than a handful of harmless flirts with, um, we'll go with Linda. We got along well enough, and she is nice to look at. A few winks and suggestive glances, a bit of fun banter. It was all in good fun, and if it got me a free cookie with my coffee I wasn't going to complain.

And then one day, she wrote her number on my take-away cup. At first, I'd saved it to my phone with every intention of calling her. Maybe not for anything serious, but at least for a bit of fun. Back when I was meeting girls any way I could, trying to find the one that would change my ways.

The next day, I met Audrey. I deleted every random girl's number from my phone within a week. Meeting Audrey, and getting to know her, was like a light turning on above my head. I could finally see everything clearly and I knew then she was going to change my life. That was before I freaked out and ruined any chance of being with her I thought I had.

"Are you meeting someone?" Linda asks. She pops her head to the side and pulls her lower lip between her teeth. When I nod, she pushes her lower lip out.

"Oh. You never called me."

I really want her to just make the coffees. I promised Audrey I'd have one ready for her when she messaged to say she was running late. I've never been so excited to hear I'd have to wait for someone. Truth be told, until she sent that text, I was worried she wasn't going to show at all.

"No, I didn't," I admit. I rest my elbows on the counter, keeping my expression flat and leaning towards Linda in a way I hope is friendly but not flirtatious. Truthfully, I don't know how to separate the two, but I'm doing my best. "I was going to but I—"

"Michael?"

Fuck. I jump back at the sharp tone of Audrey's voice and Baxter takes a step between my legs. Spinning to face Audrey, I get tangled in the lead, nearly toppling over. My face begins to light up when I twist myself free, but the smile drops as quickly as it was forming when I see Audrey's scowl.

Okay, so leaning forward too much falls a little too close to the flirtatious line.

Reaching behind me, I drop my cash on the counter.

"Keep the change," I call over my shoulder, not daring to face Linda again.

Audrey takes a step back, tucking her hands in the pockets of her grey cardigan and wrapping the fabric around herself. Her mouth falls open, but when no words form, she snaps it closed again. Despite the way she shrinks away from me, all

I want to do is envelop her in a bear hug. The kind she once told me she loved.

Beneath the wide rips of her faded jeans, her silky skin looks paler than it used to. Her hair is pulled back from her face with a big green clip, but the mousey colour of the top half still contrasts against her grown out blonde highlights. Everything about her—how she holds herself, her thrown together outfit, the way her eyes have sunken into her face—is so unlike the Audrey I first met. She was so put together, so … perfect. But somehow, this is even better. She is Audrey, so comfortably herself in a way I don't think she understands.

I scratch at my neck, unable to put my awe into words.

Audrey shifts on her feet, bouncing her attention between me, Linda making our coffees, and her feet. "You and …?"

"No. No, not at all." Baxter rubs his nose against the back of my knee, and I step towards Audrey, pleasantly surprised when she doesn't shy further away. Although he may just have wanted my attention, Baxter's nudge encourages me to be completely honest with Audrey. About this and about everything, from now until forever. I'm probably reading too much into my dog's habits.

"I mean, she gave me her number once. She was asking why I never called. I was just trying to let her down gently because she makes a damn good latte and I'd hate for her to start spitting in them."

"Why didn't you call her?"

My insides flip uncomfortably. Telling Audrey why I never called Linda would mean admitting a whole lot of feelings that I don't think are reciprocated. I'm not sure I'm ready for them to be floating between us. But I chose honesty a moment ago, and I'm going to stand by that. I take another step closer, reaching out to rest my hand on her arm.

"Because I met you the next day."

Audrey leans into my hand. All the stiffness in her posture melts away as I pull her to me.

"Everything changed when I met you Audrey, and sure I might still be young and stupid, but I don't want the same things I used to any more."

"What do you want?" The warmth from her breath slips its way through my top as she speaks directly against my chest. I wrap my arms around her, holding her close so she can't step away when I tell her.

"You." I admit, whispering the words into her hair.

Her body stiffens the tiniest amount as she squeaks a tiny gasp. I hold her in place, too afraid to look at her, too nervous that if I let go, she will run. She had to know that I felt this way, after all my texts, *surely*. But maybe there is something about finally hearing it that made the truth sink in.

Standing here, with my arms wrapped around her, I'm glad I never took Brendan's advice. Glad I kept trying, kept reminding her that I was there, waiting. Waiting for her to be ready, waiting for her to open up about whatever it is that's going on.

"Two skinny lattes for Mike."

The barista's cold voice cuts through the air. Audrey pushes away from me to collect our drinks. Linda's scowl could melt ice, yet Audrey is nothing but fire and light.

"Thanks so much," she drawls as she snatches the cups from Linda's hands. There's a remnant growl in her throat as she pivots on her heel. Her hips sway as she saunters back to me.

Passing me my coffee, her nose scrunches. She pulls her hand away the second I secure my fingers on the cup. "You told me not to call you that."

"It doesn't feel right anymore. Especially not from you."

Mike is what all the girls called me. All the other women I flirted with, all the dates I went on trying to fill a void I wasn't fully aware of. Mike is what my father calls me when he coddles me, like the child he still thinks I am. Mike is what the guys from work call me when we fuck around on a site.

But Mike is not what the woman I think I could spend the rest of my life with should call me. She should call me by my name, not my nickname. I want to be the man who makes everything right for her, and that deserves a 'grown up name'. My mother always said they chose Michael because it worked for an adult, and Mike because it was cute. Audrey makes me want to be that adult my parents imagined.

When Audrey doesn't respond, I shrug away the silence and gulp down my coffee. The creamy liquid burns its way down my throat, but I'm thankful for the distraction. The burn in my throat is easier to manage than the burn in my chest. That one feels like it will never go away.

Together, Audrey and I stroll down the wide path that heads into the Botanical Gardens. Baxter trots along beside me, occasionally pulling the lead towards birds or other dogs or children. Surrounded by all manner of trees and shrubs, it's easy to forget how close we are to the centre of town. I imagine that's what the landscapers had intended when they planted the thick hedges around the perimeter.

The early spring sun is warm this morning, but sparse, fighting to be seen through the clouds. When it does push its way through, long shadows cast through the gardens. Dew still hangs off the leaves and the grass twinkles with moisture. I had imagined us sitting in the sun, soaking up its rays while we reconnected, but the longer we walk the less likely that seems.

Beside me, Audrey attempts to make small talk. Telling me about the house she sold to her ex-husband and asking me about my family. The whole thing is forced, but I fake my way through the pleasantries. Reminding myself that Audrey will open up when she is ready, I try to avoid the unknown elephant that follows us along the gravel track.

Deep in the gardens, our now empty cups hang loose by our sides. The clouds have started to clear and I wonder if we might sit in the sun after all. Audrey falls silent, finally done with the trivial conversation topics.

It's only when we both stop talking that I noticed her laboured breaths; the way she heaves in every lungful of air like she just ran a marathon.

"Should we sit?" I gesture to a picnic table under a large oak tree. It's not native, but it must be hundreds of years old, based on its size.

Audrey doesn't answer, she just turns towards the table and heads over to sit down. When her ass hits the seat, her whole body slumps over until her head is between her legs. She pants faster than Baxter and I inch towards her. Glancing around, I search in vain for a refreshments stand or a drinking fountain.

Baxter pushes between Audrey's legs. As he stares up at her with his deep brown eyes, his head cocks from side to side as though he is trying to understand what troubles her. When her breathing steadies, he settles his head on her lap. Lucky fucking dog.

I sit next to her, close enough that our thighs are touching, but I resist the way my arm twitches. It wants to be around her, and I want it there too. I reach up gingerly, grazing her far shoulder with the slightest of strokes. She sits up at the touch, leaning her weight into me.

"Oh Michael, what are we going to do?"

Tucking Baxter's lead under my leg, I reach across my lap with my free hand. Finding Audrey's hands clinging together, I pry them apart to wrap my fingers around hers.

"What's wrong?"

Her knee bounces against my leg.

"Remember that time when the condom broke?"

Yeah, I remember. I remember how warm and wet it was

inside her. How she'd wrapped her legs around me when we noticed, pulling me back inside her and telling me it was okay. How effortlessly my cock slid between her folds and how downright fucking incredible it felt when I came inside her. My pulse throbs against my throat at the memory, and my cock strains against my shorts. My *loose* shorts. Fuck. I shift against the hard bench, willing my growing length to calm the fuck down.

"Remember how I said I was on the pill and it didn't matter? How I told you to come inside me because you make me lose my goddamn mind and we both thought it would be really … I don't know, good?"

"Audrey, what—?"

"I didn't lie. I didn't lie but the next day Maisie got sick. And then I got sick. She was vomiting, I was vomiting. I didn't think."

My mind catches up with what she is trying to tell me.

"You're …?" I can't say the word. After so long doing everything in my power not to put a baby in a woman's belly no matter how hot the thought was, the word feels somehow naughty. Like a swear word you really want to say as a kid but you're too afraid of the consequences.

"I'm pregnant, Michael."

Birds stop chirping, kids stop playing. The distant rumble of traffic evaporates into the atmosphere. The only thing left in the world is Audrey, and the weight of her words settling on my shoulders. I should have expected it. Should have known that this moment was creeping up on me, no matter how careful I always used to be. But it hits me harder than a freight train.

I pull my hands back, clenching them into fists that rest against my temples. Uncertainty creeps up my spine, leaving goosebumps that spread over my skin. I'm five degrees too cold and ten degrees too hot all at once. The sun glares in my eyes. I turn away from it, unintentionally turning my back on Audrey.

Her saddened whimper rings in my ears as I build the courage to turn my body to face her again. I can't bring my eyes to meet her own, no matter how much I want to.

"And you … the baby …" I want to ask if she wants to keep it but the air has been sucked from my lungs and it's impossible to form words.

"Yes," she reads my mind, answering the question I couldn't get out. "I'm sorry, but I really want to keep it. I can't explain it, but it's like I know I'm supposed to be this baby's mother. He came to me when I didn't know I needed him."

"He? It's a boy?"

She shakes her head, tenderly taking both my hands in her own. Her tiny fingers link between my calloused digits, thumbs stroking tiny circles on the back of my hands.

"I don't know, it's just what comes out. She doesn't feel right. So, it's just he for now. Or Bean, although technically he's the size of a plum now so that doesn't feel right any more either."

"Bean." The nickname rolls off my tongue and even though I know it won't stick, it melts away some of the tension in my shoulders. "I don't know what I'm supposed to say," I admit.

"Neither did I."

Chapter Nine

AUDREY

Michael's voice shakes as he processes the news. I don't blame him; I've known for almost a month now and I'm still coming to terms with it. But when he turns away from me, my heart cracks.

I had two weeks to prepare for this moment.

Two weeks of worst-case scenarios consuming my every thought. One week of wondering why he wasn't free that first weekend, followed by a week of doggy photos as he babysat his parent's tiny cavoodle who 'simply cannot be trusted in the apartment alone, or in public with Baxter'. People and their damned dogs. "Sorry I'm keeping Michael hostage," one caption had said, and I tried really hard to laugh. But the joke didn't sink in.

So, the week that followed was full of thinking that maybe I should have called on Callum to watch Maisie for an extra day, so I could have treated the anxiety like a Band-Aid. As soon as we planned this meeting, I wanted it to happen sooner. I wanted to rip the Band-Aid off and move on, probably with a new scar.

I'd be lying if I said that I wasn't worried about what Michael might have been doing the whole time. If I said I didn't wonder why he hadn't invited me to his apartment since he supposedly couldn't leave, or who he might have been seeing instead of me. Every night for the past two weeks as I curled up in my empty bed, I'd close my eyes and see him lying with another woman. Flirting with another woman.

Kissing her, taking her clothes off, removing his shirt. And every night I wished it was me.

It's just the hormones thinking, surely. Hopefully.

I can't fall for this man, any further than I started to fall before his baby started growing in my stomach.

Even still, as we acknowledge our loss for words, I sink my shoulder a little further into his. I press my knee against his leg, twisting my ankle behind his own. Linking us together in a silent embrace. This news was hard enough for me to wrap my head around. I can only imagine how hard it must be for him.

In response to the movement, Baxter looks up from his spot on my lap. An ear pricks up and his tongue hangs out of his mouth, still panting from our walk. I scratch under his chin, clicking my tongue.

Beside me, Michael's body heaves with a sigh. He's been silent for a while now, and I let him sit in his thoughts while everything sinks in. It wasn't until that day at the clinic, when I heard the baby's heartbeat for the very first time that all the pieces started to fall into place for me. That's when I finally realised that no matter the crazy, unconventional circumstances, this was meant to happen. I don't believe in God, but this baby came for a reason. Something sent him when I needed him the most. I just don't know if Michael needs him too. If Michael even wants him.

Remembering the ultrasound photos, I pull my small crossbody bag to my front to pull them out. "I have something for you."

Michael looks up. The sunlight hits his amber eyes, making them glow golden in an almost supernatural way. They glisten with a moisture he seems too afraid to blink away. When he doesn't move to take the photos from me, I pry his hands apart and slip the stack between his fingers.

"From the … ultrasound," I say. Shame flows through

me as the word gets stuck on its way past my lips. My chin trembles, waiting for his reaction.

"Ultrasound?" The word is a barely audible breath.

As he flicks through the photos, a single tear manages to escape from the cage he tried to keep them in. I watch as it slowly descends his cheek. When it dots onto the white corner of a printout, Michael swears.

"Fuck," the whisper is hoarse as he bats away the liquid soaking into the shiny paper. "Shit," he adds, batting at his cheek.

My hand tremors, reaching out to stop him. "It's okay."

He stands in one swift movement, pushing Baxter with his legs. The dog yelps, cowering into my lap while Michael takes two long strides onto the grass. Michael keeps his back to me and turns his face toward the sun. His shoulders rise and fall with each laboured breath.

I reach down for Baxter's lead, twisting the rope in my hands while I wait for Michael to say something. Anything.

"How pregnant are you?" Michael demands as he walks back to stand over me. "How long have you known?"

My cheeks burn, but not from the sun now glaring down on us. Spring has only just begun, but the day has turned bright and warm, the perfect embodiment of the season. More families have congregated on the lawn around us and all I can hear are the hordes of children laughing as they play.

I try to imagine how Michael and I would look as a family. It looks perfect, but this moment is far from that ideal. Guilt eats at my insides.

"I've known for about a month. Michael, I'm sorry. I wanted to tell you, that day at the cafe, but I panicked. It's no excuse."

I expect him to berate me some more. To question why I waited so long to tell him or scream that he had a right to know. Instead, he closes the gap between us and nudges my legs apart so he can stand between them.

Placing his hands on my shoulders, Michael looks down at me. Sorrow lines his eyes and his lips tremble with the shaky breath he puffs out. "I'm sorry I wasn't there."

My mouth drops open. He has nothing to be sorry about. I'm the one who kept this massive secret from him. I shake my head, but he nods in response. His gaze drops to my shoulder, where the ultrasound photos are still clasped in his hand.

"I don't blame you for not being able to tell me. Don't blame yourself. What matters now is this little plum sized baby. *Our* baby. And I have no idea what that means for us. But I'm here."

He leans down, kissing the top of my head.

We spend the rest of the morning strolling through the gardens, occasionally stopping for Baxter to sniff at a plant or for me to sit and catch my breath. We talk about everything but the baby, as though we silently agreed that we need to figure out what we want from each other.

Michael flits between acting like my boyfriend, to acting like an acquaintance. We walk, arm in arm along the path, his fingers trailing up and down my arm. There's an odd spark in the air, but when we sit at a bench it extinguishes. Michael sits a foot away from me, staring ahead while Baxter takes a drink from the small tub below the water fountain.

"Are you okay?" I ask as we head towards the entrance. I'm out of breath, and my feet hurt. And my ankles have some-how disappeared, swollen directly into my calves. I should have known the walk home would be too much, but at the time it felt like a great idea. Keep active, stay moving, all that stuff they tell you to do without warning you just how ex-hausting it will be.

Michael stops abruptly, pulling my hand back and

spinning me to face him. He holds both my hands in his and steps closer towards me. His chest rises and falls against mine with each forced breath he takes. The movement makes my bra rub against my extra-sensitive nipples, sending the spark from the air directly through me and into my core.

I push away the memory of how our bodies tangled together. How he hovered over me while he settled between my legs. How he wrapped his arms around me when he pushed himself in, and how perfectly full and whole I felt at that moment. I can't think about that now. Not when I just pulled out the pin and threw the grenade, and he had no choice but to catch it.

"Honestly, Audrey? I'm okay I'm just … I'm scared this means more to me than it does to you. I'm scared that I'm too in my head about *us* now, even though I know our relationship isn't magically going to blossom just because we're having a child together. A baby doesn't create love between its parents. I know that's a silly thing to think, but a part of me still hopes it does anyway."

I close my eyes, leaning in and wrapping my arms around him. With my face pressed in the crook of his shoulder, I inhale deeply. He smells like wood chips and spice and … home. And maybe it's the hormones again but for the first time in weeks I feel at ease.

Baxter tries to force his way between us, demanding attention. When we ignore him, he trots a circle behind me, resting his head on the back of my knees.

"Audrey, my feelings for you haven't changed now that I know you're pregnant. But they are still there. I've tried for weeks to make them go away but they followed me around more than Baxter does. I need to know if I should keep trying to push them away."

I lift my shoulders to my ears, hoping he can feel the

way I shrug. Michael leans down, his lips grazing the soft skin behind my ear.

"Tell me to stop, and I will."

My mouth opens, but instead of the word, all that comes out is a gasp. Michael pulls away from my ear to rest his forehead on mine. Our noses touch and our mouths are so close together the warm air he breathes out tickles my lips. His eyes are dark as he gazes directly into my soul.

My body starts to act on its own. My tongue darts out to wet my lower lip. My fingers trace a path up his chest. My arms stretch behind his neck and my hands tug him towards me, closing that last little inch between us.

When our lips collide, Michael lets out a rumbling moan. His kiss is slow and tender, like he is testing the waters. I'm testing them too, especially when I run my tongue along his lips, practically begging him to open up for me. But he doesn't.

He holds me close to him, planting gentle kisses along my top lip, then the bottom, then he pulls back to plant the softest kiss of them all on my temple.

Immediately, I fight against his grasp. Stepping back, heat flares up my shoulders and across my cheeks. I want to run. All the way home to hide under my bed. I can't believe I kissed him. I can't believe he didn't kiss me back—at least not in the way I wanted.

"I … I'm sorry," I mutter, staring at my feet.

Michael closes the gap I created between us, but keeps his hands by his side. "Don't be sorry. New rule, you're not allowed to be sorry."

I close my eyes. My attempt to hide my tears is deemed futile when they escape through my lashes to stream down my cheeks.

"I'm not sorry you kissed me, Audrey," Michael says as he takes my hands in his. "I love that you kissed me, and I want you to kiss me more. But I don't want you to fall into me just because we are having a baby."

He squeezes my hands and I look up at him, all blurry through my tears. I *think* I see tears in his eyes too, but he doesn't let go of his hold on me to wipe them away. It's almost comforting to think we are both standing here in the middle of a public park, crying at our circumstances.

Crying because we didn't plan this but it happened anyway. And now we have to navigate down a road we had no intention of turning on to. Crying because maybe, just maybe, there is hope for us.

"Let me drive you home."

I let him, because my legs have officially clocked out for the day, and my lungs aren't far behind. The drive is silent as he navigates through the side streets and down the long gravel driveway. Finally, when the car is in park and I open the door to step out, Michael turns to me.

"I have no idea what I'm doing," he admits. "I have no idea how I'm supposed to act, or what I'm supposed to do. I have no idea if it's inappropriate to still like you so hopelessly or if I'm supposed to cool off and pretend I never fell. I have no idea what to expect, no idea how to look after a baby, or how the two of us becoming parents would even look. I have no idea, Audrey. But I know one thing and I hope more than anything that you'll believe me when I tell you that I'm not running away."

He leans across the centre console to plant a kiss on my forehead. I lean into his touch, wanting more but also knowing that more is not what we need right now. His words are chipping away at the icy walls I built around my heart, but I'm not sure I'm ready to trust him.

"I'm not going to run away again," Michael adds.

And maybe it's reckless—maybe it's setting myself up for heartache—but I believe him.

Chapter Ten

AUDREY

The week since I finally found the guts to tell Michael he was going to become a father has been an exhausting blur of long workdays and sweet goodnight messages. I stopped leaving him on read and a little of the easy banter between us has returned. When he asked if I was free, I found myself *wanting* to see him. Wanting to find a little piece of what we could have had. So here I am, completely out of my comfort zone, at Michael's gym.

Weights and machines clang all around the wide, open converted warehouse. The sound echoes around the high ceiling, with its exposed vents and wiring. Beneath my feet, foam mats mould against the soles of my years old, worn-down shoes.

Michael reaches down and holds my hand as we walk further into the space. Everyone stops and stares, but smiles at Michael before returning their attention to their own workouts. Weighted squats over here, cardio machines over there, rows of dumbbells and plates set up to work every inch of muscle in your body. My chest is heavy. I don't know how to use any of these machines. I end up out of breath after pushing the shopping trolley around for an hour. This was a dumb idea.

I've stopped walking, frozen in my place near the temporary lockers set up by the door. Michael squeezes my hand.

"We don't have to be here."

I shake my head, mustering up a little confidence. "No, I want to be," I tell him, even when my body protests.

I do want to be here. But not because I want to work out

with Michael. Honestly as we're getting ready to start, I can't think of anything worse. No. I want to be here just to be with Michael. Everything about us, from the first few dates we've been on, to everything that's sure to come with the baby, has been about me.

Michael took me to the epic science fiction movie I desperately wanted to see at the cinema, even though he has no interest in far off, imaginary, desert worlds. He suggested we go to the gardens because I told him I love being in nature when I'm stressed. And he came to *my* house to meet Maisie, even though it ended terribly.

If we are going to be tied together by this baby, it's time for me to put in an equal amount of effort.

"You'll just have to show me what to do," I say as I dump my handbag into a free locker. "And go easy on me."

Stepping towards me, Michael rests a hand on my arm. His other hand lingers between us, but he waits until I give my head a small nod before he spreads his fingers out over my stomach.

"Are you sure you should even be doing anything? Won't it hurt the baby?"

I lean in to his touch, pressing my not really showing yet stomach against his hands. "Exercise is good for me. Healthy, and I could probably do with a little movement. Plus, he's pretty cosy in there, as long as you don't make me deadlift my own bodyweight or something ridiculous, he'll be fine."

"Right, no deadlifts."

He kisses the top of my head and steps back to pull off his hoodie. Tingles remain in my hairline as I follow him towards the closest monstrosity of equipment. They slowly spread their way across my body and I have to remind myself to breathe. I focus on Michael as he sets up the machine, trying not to be too daunted by the weights he is adding to either side. His arms strain under the weight of the plates, veins bulging. In a loose singlet and tiny shorts Michael is … wow.

I always knew he was more than fit. That much was obvious just in the way he holds himself and how his arms would always strain against his tees. But seeing him like this is on another level. It's like muscle on muscle, covering every inch of him. I might as well be drooling.

A few women pause as they walk past, clearly checking him out. Their toned bodies are on show underneath their tight crop tops and bike shorts, and I cringe at the daggy outfit I have on. Old, faded, probably a little see through leggings, and a baggy old band T-shirt. I will never match up to the girls he is around on an almost daily basis, and the thought stirs inside me.

I'm not jealous of those women. I'm barely pregnant but I'm slowly accepting the changes my body will go through. Slowly coming to terms with how it might never be the same. Because it is doing something incredible and I'm damn proud of it. So, it's not jealousy that leaves an uneasy feeling low in my chest. It's fear.

Even if I come to terms with my new body, how would Michael? He cares, so much, about his body and his physique and he puts in the work to maintain the standard that he wants. If I don't … how will he look at me? Will he find me attractive when the baby is born and I still carry the extra weight around my stomach?

Michael notices the girls staring, which is easy to do really. I'm surprised they don't have their phones out taking pictures. As I open my mouth to throw out a snide remark, Michael's arm wraps around my middle. He twists me to face him, planting another kiss on my forehead. I tilt my head up and his eyes meet mine. Heat flares between us as Michael rests his forehead against mine.

"They still looking?" he mumbles.

I glance over his shoulder. The girls are gone, but I almost wish they weren't. My lower lip trembles with anticipation. "What if they are?"

Michael closes his eyes. "If they are, I might need to show them just who I'm here with. I might not be able to stop myself. But if they're gone? I might be able to hold enough restraint to give you a choice."

My heart flips down into my stomach, pulsing far below my belly. I dart my tongue out to wet my lips and Michael's eyes track the movement. His hand spreads across my lower back, pulling me closer until our chests touch and I can feel every hasty breath he takes. The other hand cups my jaw and he traces his thumb along my lips. I gasp.

"Are they still there, Audrey?"

Our mouths are so close I can almost feel the movement of his lips as he whispers directly into me. I wish the girls were still there, wish he wasn't leaving the choice up to me because *God,* I really want to kiss him right now, but it would be so messy. Good, sure. Fucking amazing, probably. But everything between us is teetering on the edge and I don't know which way we should fall.

"They're gone." I close my eyes as I say the words. Wishing, hoping, he would kiss me anyway. But he doesn't.

Michael groans. His fingers dip into my back as he squeezes me tight before stepping away. A chill runs through me as the cool blast from the air conditioner rushes between us. I curse internally. The low pulsing of my heart in my stomach is replaced by a twisting, nauseating wave and for a second, I search for the bathroom, worried my morning sickness is making a rapid reappearance.

Sitting down on the empty bench beside the machine Michael has returned to setting up, I rest my elbows on my knees and catch my breath. He finishes placing the plates and adjusting the heights and turns to look at me. With a smirk, he gestures for me to stand.

"I'm not doing that," I tell him. I don't even know what I would be doing, but he put three big plates on either side of the bar and that's six plates too many for me.

He drops his hands to his hips and looks back at the bar. "Come here."

I stand up but make no move to walk towards him. "I'm not doing that," I repeat. "You said you'd go easy on me."

Turning away, Michael shakes his head as a wide grin spreads across his face. He starts wheezing. "Jeez Audrey," he gulps. "Do you really think I'd make you squat that?"

I fold my arms across my chest and shift my weight.

"I want you to spot me." His smile drops into something far friendlier, and he reaches a hand towards me.

I don't take it. "How can I spot you if I can't hold that?"

"If I need you to hold all the weight, I'm doing it wrong. All you need to do is support it *if* I get stuck. You will never be taking all the weight, only a fraction to get me through the rep."

"What's a fraction of six plates?" I have no idea how much they weigh, but they look heavy.

Michael shrugs, scrunching his nose. "Can you still pick up Maisie?"

"Yes," I answer, allowing the corner of my mouth to turn up a fraction. It gets harder to lift Maisie by the day, but that's more because she is a five-year-old in the middle of a growth spurt than because I'm pregnant.

"Then you'll be fine, I promise."

I'm still hesitant, but the whole point of me coming to the gym was to show Michael that I was interested in getting to know him and his world now that he has been forced into mine. I drop my arms, letting a hand fall into Michael. He tugs me towards him, then directs me to stand behind the bar.

"I'll step forward when I lift it off, and you just need to stay close as I do the reps. If you see me struggling, give a little upwards pressure on the bar *without* trying to take the weight. Okay?"

I hum my agreement because I don't trust myself to form words. It all makes sense and I understand what I need to be doing, but also, nope, not okay. He wants me to stand behind him while he holds the bar and squats. And I'm supposed to be focused on making sure he can lift the weight back up, not the way his muscles strain against the weight or how his ass is going to pop out towards me.

I'm starting to remember exactly why I fell for Michael in the first place. There's sex, and then there's the fucking mind blowing 'he can throw me around like a ragdoll' kind of sex. The kind that's rough in all the best ways but ends with warm embraces and gentle massages. And when I remember the post sex bear hugs, I can't help but think of the 'I'm so excited to see you' bear hugs and the 'please stay a little longer' bear hugs.

All this time, I was remembering Michael as the guy who ran out in the morning because he heard Maisie call out for me. I'd forgotten the flirty and nurturing guy who swept me off my feet and made me feel human again. I'd forgotten how afternoons spent with Michael flew by in a haze of laughter and the kinds of fun I didn't remember how to have.

Maybe I was too harsh on him. I'm still sour that he ran out when he did and took a week to call me, but I guess some small part of me understands it, at least. Maisie was always going to be a big adjustment for him, and maybe there's a case there that says I shouldn't have expected him to play happy family quite so soon. I held that against him for so long, even after he apologised countless times and tried so hard to get us back together.

All I can do is hope that the next six months are enough

for him to get used to the fact he is going to be a father. There's no running out this time.

In front of me, Michael lifts the bar and all its weight off the supports and takes a step forward. I shuffle closer, ready to spot him if he needs me. He does his set of squats, dropping low, and just as I expected his muscles pulse under the weight. I bite the inside of my cheek, trying to ignore that heat pressing against my core.

After six squats, Michael steps back and I jump out of his way as he re-racks the bar. He turns to me, hanging his arms over the now supported bar and winking.

"See. Didn't need you."

"Do you have to do more?"

Michael grabs the bar loosely and swings under it, landing in my arms. He gathers my hair in his hands, then loops the hair tie on his wrist around it, pulling my messy strands into a low ponytail. "While I rest, it's your turn."

A firm lump forms directly in my throat and I try to gulp it down but end up choking on a tiny sliver of my own saliva. Coughing, I wave my hand at him.

"I said I'm not doing that."

Michael pats me on the shoulder and reaches past me to pick up a thin bar from the floor. He rests one end on the ground and leans on it like a cane. "You'll use this."

Right. That makes more sense, I suppose. This bar is far thinner than the one Michael was using, but I've never done any kind of weight training. Surely this is too much. I'm about to tell him so, when Michael rests one finger on my lips.

"It weighs less than five kilos Audrey; you carry more than that when you bring the groceries inside."

The lump in my throat doesn't magically dissipate, but I nod my acceptance anyway. Michael shows me where to stand and how far apart to hold my legs, then stands behind me to place the bar across my shoulders. He isn't touching me, but we are so close his singlet brushes against my shirt.

"I'm right here," he whispers in my ear. "Bend with your knees and keep your back straight."

With his hands on my waist, he guides me through the first squat, and the second. His fingers barely graze against my hips for the next and I'm already dying to call it quits. My thighs burn and the bar is heavy on my shoulders.

"Three more." Michael's voice is breathy against the back of my neck and I force myself to complete the set.

"I'm done," I declare as he takes the bar from my shoulders. "I tried. I'm done."

"We can go."

"You can finish your workout. I don't want you to call it early because I'm an unfit pregnant wuss."

Michael drops my tiny bar into a rack on the wall and steps up to the plates on his far larger bar. One by one he pulls them off, hanging them back on the side of the stand. Once all six plates have been put away, he hangs the bar in place with all the rest and turns to me.

"I love that you wanted to come here Audrey, and I appreciate it, but I don't expect you to sit around watching me. This was meant to be about getting to know each other, right?"

I wrap my arms around my stomach, looking down at my feet with a nod. Stepping forward, Michael tilts my chin back up to look at him.

"So, we learnt that you don't like the gym unless you're watching me. And I have my own set up at home, so if you really want to watch me, we don't need to be here. And there are other things we can do back there that we can't do here."

His eyes twinkle and I allow a smile to creep onto my face. I tap my temple with my forefinger. "I don't need to watch you, Michael. I've got it all up here forever now."

He wraps his arms around me and pulls me close. I'm

about to squirm free when his mouth meets mine with a firm but playful kiss. I tense against him at first, but he doesn't let go and I relax into his hold, and into the kiss. Planting a kiss on his lower lip I edge away from him.

Michael looks down at my stomach, his hand hovering an inch away from where our baby is currently stealing all my food. As if in response, my stomach grumbles. Breakfast was too long ago. I'm about to tell him but he heads for the lockers and rifles through his bag.

"I have something for you, before we go."

Turning back to me he holds out a small brown, furry ball, along with a little plastic spoon that has a serrated edge on the handle.

"A kiwi fruit?"

He nods, tipping on his heels. "Our little baby isn't a plum anymore. The app said at thirteen weeks he is the size of a kiwi fruit."

"You downloaded an app?"

Michael pulls our bags from the lockers, slipping them over one shoulder and placing his free hand on the small of my back.

"Come on, you can eat it on the way to the gardens."

Chapter Eleven

AUDREY

"**M**ummy, you have to dance too!"

I laugh with a wave, brushing off my daughter's persistent pressure to join her on the tiny disco dancefloor. Wrongly, it appears, I had thought Maisie's kindergarten having an all-out graduation party at a fully catered disco party centre was a wonderful idea. I mean, don't get me wrong, the kids are having a fantastic time, but I just sat down after making small talk with a group of other mums and my feet are aching in my boots. I also thought having her partner-in-dance, Cassidy, here would give me the slack I needed to stay out of the dance firing line.

It's an odd kind of comfortable, knowing that Maisie has someone to share her love of dance and ballet with. Although it started a little too close to jealousy, the feeling is now soothing, knowing that when Maisie is with her father she has a special relationship with Cassidy too.

I never had a village when Maisie was little, so I find it weird that one started to form after I split with her father. But it did. Which makes me feel even better about the decisions we made. Funny how they also led me here, pregnant after a wild fling with a younger man.

My hand gravitates towards my middle, cradling the bump that is finally forming. The small swell that pushes against the button of my jeans and has me living in leggings and dresses. Maybe, if I'm lucky, this village will help me with this baby too.

Clearly not taking no for an answer, Maisie skips over to me, sidestepping around her friends.

"Does your belly hurt?" She yells over the music and I cringe. This lack of filter is exactly why I'm still not ready to tell her about the baby. She has the social graces of a, well, of a five-year-old.

"No chicka, I was just thinking about how your teachers promised there would be cake." I smirk at my little white lie, proud of how quickly it rolled off my tongue.

"Oh my gosh, are we having cake soon?" She jumps up and down, the pink and blue frills of her dress floating around her.

"In a little bit, maybe. For now, you're stuck dancing with me and my two left feet." I push myself off the chair, shaking off the tension in my arms and gesturing to where Maisie's friends are dancing in the middle of the room. A handful of parents are scattered amongst the group, but most are lined against the walls, chatting away over the pounding music.

Maisie looks down at our feet, pointing her toes out to tap my own.

"Do you really have two left feet?"

Laughing, I grab her hand and lead the way into the middle of the room, right underneath the disco ball hanging from the ceiling.

"No, not really."

Taylor Swift blends into a Disney tune that blends into something poppy that makes all the kids scream but I can't quite recognise. The beat sounds oddly familiar but also incredibly distant and removed. If I had to place a bet, I'd say an up-and-coming superstar has sampled a song from my youth.

Maisie and I sway and spin to the music. After a while, I stop caring if I'm moving in time. I follow her lead, pointing my toes to the side, swaying my hips side to side, spinning— very wobbly—on one leg. Cassidy comes to join us, and we form a triangle of joy, celebrating Maisie. Her friends are forgotten, but I see them dancing around us. They laugh and twirl and skip. A young girl cartwheels, her oversized graduation cape tumbling around her.

"You're not as bad as you think." Cassidy leans in, and we link elbows, each holding one of Maisie's hands.

"I'm just pretending I'm not a thirty-two-year-old single mum and instead I'm young and fun and drunk at a club."

Cassidy leans her head down to rest on my shoulder. It's only there for a second, but the gesture spreads a light feeling through me. Callum made a good choice.

"How life changes," she muses.

Her circumstances are so different to my own, but her life is changing in unexpected ways, too. I've realised now how hard it must have been to hear about someone falling pregnant by accident when a pregnancy is something she will never experience. She'd messaged me the next day, apologising for acting 'weird' and telling me about her infertility. I couldn't convince her that she hadn't acted in an unusual way, and that I wouldn't have known she was feeling uneasy if it wasn't for her message. Even so, I apologised in turn for unloading my emotional baggage onto her.

We've spoken many times since then. She offered to take Maisie to dance class every week, and truth be told I'm grateful to get out of the evening trips. I will support Maisie in every way, with whatever she wants to do. But sitting amongst those other mums, with their perfect lives, while waiting for the ballet lesson to finish made bile burn in my throat. I didn't fit in there. I'm not sure that Cassidy would either, but she loves dancing so much that she doesn't seem to mind.

As well as taking Maisie to dance class, Cassidy drops off fresh flowers and leftover baked treats from her boutique every week. She asks about my painting, and for the first time in a long time, I feel like I have a friend who really understands the way painting makes me feel. I guess being a creative type herself, she can relate to the tranquil feeling that washes over me whenever I sit down at my easel.

We've somehow fallen into an easy friendship, united by the changes in our lives in the most unexpected way.

The song builds to a final chorus and when it ends, Maisie and her friends erupt into cheers and giggles. Lights flicker to life around us, and as the room grows brighter, the party host steps out from behind her little DJ desk.

"Who wants to play pass the parcel?"

Somehow, the squealing gets louder. As the party host, in her rainbow tutu and silver top, helps the kids form a cir-cle, Cassidy and I slink away.

"Here," a deep voice comes from behind me.

I turn as Callum stands from the chair he was sitting on. One arm gestures for me to sit, the other wraps around Cassidy's waist. He pulls her in to plant a kiss on her cheek.

"Thanks for the chair," I say when he finally comes up for air.

"Of course."

I relax into the seat, stretching my feet out in front of me. "I'm exhausted all the time. Already. I can only imagine how hard it's going to be when I'm in my third trimester. Or when the baby is actually born."

I realise after the words spill out that I've assumed Cassidy has told Callum. I figured it was a given. And, thank-fully, from the way Callum doesn't miss a beat with his re-sponse, it seems I was right.

"Whatever you need, we're here to help," he says.

Callum excuses himself to go chat with some of the other dads, and Cassidy finds a lone chair to pull up beside me. Pass the parcel has ended and the party host has directed the children to a game of musical statues. None of the kids are playing properly, but the stop-starting of the music is giving me a headache.

Leaning forward, I rest my elbows on my knees, holding my head in my hands to press my thumbs against my temples.

"You okay?" Cassidy asks.

I can feel the air from her hand hovering by my shoulder, like she isn't sure if she should put it down. I never imagined I'd feel such kindness from my ex-husband's girlfriend, but I want more of it. I want to be her friend, I want to be able to confide in her and I want her to confide in me. Every friendship needs a little shove, so I innocently lean back a little until my shoulder rests against her hand. Her fingers stiffen as she sucks in a sharp breath, but then she relaxes into the touch, rubbing her fingers lightly on my shoulder.

"Just thinking about all the open houses I have to run this week. I've got one on Wednesday while Maisie is at dance class, and then a whole heap over the weekend."

She pulls her hand back and twists in her chair to face me.

"You don't sound thrilled."

Sitting up, I sigh. I'm not thrilled. Not even a little bit. I've signed on as many houses as I can handle. Maybe a few too many, considering what the next week looks like. But all these houses will earn me a commission to go towards what I hope will be an extended maternity leave. It just feels so exhausting, and I'm not even halfway through my pregnancy. Thinking about keeping up this pace as the pregnancy progresses leaves an uncomfortable tension in the back of my neck.

"I'm worried I'm burning myself out," I admit. "After Maisie was born, I worked so hard to be in the position I'm in now, but with this baby coming, I can't help but feel it was all for nothing. My boss is already talking about the right time to have other agents shadow my sales, 'just in case' I go on maternity leave early. They're ready to kick me to the curb just because I'm having a baby. So, I keep adding more houses to my roster, thinking if I can prove myself now, I won't have to start from scratch again after my maternity leave."

A second party host wheels a tray of hot party food into the room and the music stops. The silence leaves a ringing in my ears. I rub firm circles against my temples with my thumbs, trying to steady the pulsing that keeps creeping into my head.

"The more houses I add, the more monotonous it feels. It used to feel amazing, selling all these unique high-end homes. But now, they all blend into one and I really don't care if it sells for a hundred thousand less than the house up the street. I think I'm done, but if I'm done, what then?"

I surprise myself, saying the words. I hadn't really thought them until now. But it's true. After years and years working my way up and up, becoming so close to being the top real estate agent in my area, being named one of the top women in real estate in all of the country, fighting to be seen and heard in a sea of male colleagues, I'm done. I officially want out of the rat race. And not just because I'm pregnant and tired, but because I'm just tired. Of the hustle, of the fight. Of forcing myself out of bed every morning to work a job that no longer brings me joy.

"Could you do something with your painting instead? You could start with my commission piece." Cassidy's voice surprises me, reminding me that I'm once again opening up to the woman I should dislike. But it's impossible to dislike her, and maybe I'm sick of following all the so-called rules of life. Mine never seems to go to plan anyway.

Not long after she found out I was a painter, Cassidy had sent a text outlining the artwork she wanted to commission for her floristry cross cafe. Australian native flowers with cof- fee beans scattered throughout the petals. Big, too. The size of a big theatre room TV. I never responded, still unsure if I should, if I could.

I've never sold a painting before. I've given them away to friends and family, I've donated them to charity auctions and kindergarten fundraisers, but I've never *sold* one. I wouldn't even know what to charge. Besides, it takes me months to complete a piece.

"You deserve a career that sets your soul on fire," Cassidy continues, her arm reaching across the small gap between us to rest on my leg. "Plus, you could work the hours that suit you, rest when you need it, and have more flexibility when the baby comes."

"I could, but it would also be so irregular and inconsistent. I don't know how I'd be able to make a living off it."

It would be fun though. To work for myself, doing something I've always found so much joy in. But look where fun has got me already. Pregnant, and stuck in some kind of baby daddy situation-ship that I can't make heads or tails of.

"It's hard, but plenty of people have done it before. Or if you're not ready to take the leap you could look at art studios or supply shops? They might need people, even something casual to boost your income while you build a name for yourself as an artist?"

I sit back, leaning against the dark curtained wall. Lights sparkle around me, reflecting off the sequins on the wall and enveloping me in a rainbow of stars. Cassidy's not wrong, but it's hard to admit she is right. I've spent so much of my life building my real estate career. Just because it's not serving its purpose right now doesn't mean I should give it up completely.

I do like the idea of having some more flexibility when the baby comes though. And painting. Painting unleashes a part of me that is otherwise held back. The part where I ignore the rules and the colour theory and I paint outside the thirds or go straight in with the paint, not worrying about sketching first. It's freeing, when I think and act that way. Maybe I need to take the same mentality with the rest of my life.

Picking up on my silent contemplation, Cassidy pats my leg before standing up.

"You don't have to decide now, but you deserve to be thrilled about what you do for a living," she says as she turns away toward a group of adults near the door.

"Wait," I call out before she is too far away and she pivots back to face me with a grin. "I'll do your painting."

"Yes! I knew you would." Her grin pushes into her cheeks and she lifts her hand in a small fist to pump the air before turning back to Callum and the other couples he is standing with.

They all step aside to welcome Cassidy into their circle and I long to be included. I know that I probably could be, too. But small talk grates on me, and lately everything has been feeling a hundred times worse.

I adjust my legs underneath the chair and reach a hand behind my back so I can use the seat to push myself up. I hate to think how heavy and exhausted I'm going to feel as the months go on. I've barely started my second trimester and I'm already struggling to stand. I blame the dancing, but wish I had someone here to help me all the same.

No, actually. Because as soon as the thought materialises, I realise it's a lie. I don't wish I had *anyone* to help me get up. I wish Michael was here to help me. Because he would, and I wouldn't even have to ask. As soon as I finally told him about the baby, he has been nothing but supportive and kind. After he got over the initial shock, of course.

But since then, he's been cautious without being overbearing.

I hadn't thought about inviting him. Maisie never asked about him coming, and it hadn't even crossed my mind that he might want to be here. And I hate myself for that. Because now we are about to watch our little kindergarten kid walk across an imaginary stage and collect her little certificate. It's all for show, but I feel beyond terrible that I didn't give Michael the choice to be here. All the uncertainty aside, he is part of this family now, which makes me not inviting him so much messier.

The music fades back to a lull, but this time the lights stay dimmed as one of the party hosts hands Maisie's teacher a microphone.

It hits me, finally, that my little baby will be in school next year. Sure, she has a few more months of kinder, but the whole idea with having graduation so early was to celebrate before all the kids went off for school orientations on different days. The last few months of the year always pass so quickly anyway, but I don't know how we have flown so swiftly into the next stage of Maisie's life. But we have. And I'm about to start it all over again.

The thoughts swirl and spiral against the mix of emotions that were already brewing. I smile through the presentation, hugging Maisie after she skips back to me with her certificate. I pose for photos, lips turned up, cheeks puffy with my exaggerated grin. But all the while, I'm somehow missing Michael and I'm worried what I'm falling into is going to mess everything up.

Even more than it already has.

Chapter Twelve

AUDREY

The driveway is full. Another car is parked on the nature strip and a third sits in front of the neighbour's garden. I hadn't realised Callum and Cassidy had invited this many people to their housewarming. But then again, I'm here, so I should have expected the invitations to be wide reaching.

I'm still getting used to the whole concept of being friends with Callum. We share so much history, and our daughter, that the change in status from married couple to casual friends is jarring. It's weirder still for me to feel so close to Cassidy. But something clicked between us the day I opened up to her about the pregnancy, and every moment since then I've found myself leaning on her for moral support more and more.

"Will Cassidy be at Daddy's new house too?" Maisie asks from her place in the back seat.

I steer the car into the driveway to turn around and park across the street.

Michael unbuckles his seat belt, twisting around to face Maisie. "Isn't it your new house too?"

Her grin somehow reaches her ears as she bounces in the seat, waiting for me to reach over and unbuckle her harness. I twist my body uncomfortably, trying to reach. I wince as a sharp pain shoots up my spine at the unnatural way I'm trying to bend it.

"I've got it." Michael places one hand on my arm and stretches the other behind us to let Maisie out.

The weight of his fingers presses into the soft flesh below

my shoulder. I shudder at the unexpected feeling that spreads from his touch. It's laced with intimacy and care but charged with an explosive tension. I want to see what other feelings his touch could draw out of me. But I can't. Not here, not now. Not while I'm sure this attraction is being heightened by the hormones. Not with the way I know it will only make this whole situation messier. Not until I'm sure we could be something more than an easy—but incredible—fuck.

"It is my new house!" Maisie declares as she jumps out of her seat and tugs at her door handle. "Ugh, child lock," she moans when it won't open.

Michael's hand squeezes my arm as he holds in a laugh. "I still can't believe you didn't invite me to her graduation party."

There's a twinkle in his eye as he lifts one corner of his mouth up in a playful smirk. We've been through this, and the joke is starting to get old, but he keeps telling it anyway. My body curls in on itself and I force my shoulders to stop rolling forward. I push them back instead. Sitting up straight I glare at Michael with every ounce of apathy I can muster.

"It was two weeks ago. Will you please drop it?"

"Why didn't you invite Michael to the party Mummy?" Maisie's head pops between Michael and me. She climbs over the centre console and into my lap. I hold back a wince when she presses her knee into my stomach.

"It's because I told her I was busy," Michael says before I can answer. "She had no way of knowing I would cancel my plans to celebrate with you."

Is he … is he taking the heat for me? The air in the car grows warm, then hot as Michael's hand rests on my knee.

"Any plans?" Maisie asks.

"Yep."

"What if you were meeting the Queen?"

Michael scoffs. "Especially if I was meeting the Queen."

In my lap, Maisie jumps with a gasp. It's hard to breathe

but not because the baby is pressing on my lungs and not because Maisie has settled her weight against my chest. I stare out the window, willing the tornado of emotions to calm. *He doesn't mean it.* He's just saying it to entertain Maisie.

"You sure you're ready for this?" I ask as Michael reaches for the car door.

He squeezes my knee and withdraws his hand, leaving behind a persistent tingle. One that lingers even as we cross the road. One that spreads when his palm rests on the small of my back as we step up the front steps.

Maisie runs off through the open door to find her cousins, but Michael hesitates in the entry.

"You should eat this," he says as he holds out a pear. "So you don't start feeling sick."

I take it from him, spinning the fruit in my hands to break the stem.

"Technically, the pear is for last week. Sixteen weeks is an avocado, but that doesn't make for a very good snack."

The pear is juicy when I bite into it, filling my empty stomach and easing a fraction of the never-ending nausea I've grown accustomed to. "I want an avocado too," I say after swallowing a few hasty bites. "With a greasy roast chicken and a fresh roll and the saltiest chips you can find."

Michael wraps his arm around me and kisses my forehead. "Done."

We walk, arm in arm through the house. In the kitchen Callum greets us with an enthusiastic, but exhausted, thanks. Cassidy's eyes widen when she sees us. She squeaks when she takes the small housewarming gift—a plant I would kill in a week but that I'm sure will thrive in her care—from Michael. She spins back and forth on her heel, before settling to place the terracotta planter on the kitchen windowsill.

"To get the morning sun," she says quickly as she steps back, beaming. Her eyes dart from me to Michael and her mouth drops open, but she clasps her hands across her face and disappears outside before I have a chance to ask her if everything is okay. I assumed Callum would have told her I was bringing Michael, but maybe the message was lost along the way.

Callum hands us each a drink from the fridge and we head outside. Michael and I feel like the black sheep of this jumbled group of friends. Cassidy moves to sit on the grass with two women. One looks oddly like her, only blonde. Under her tight grey dress there's a gentle, but obvious, curve to her stomach. A giant rock sparkles on her finger and I clench my fists against the strange pulling in my gut. Sucking in a breath through my clenched teeth, I fight to relax my fingers and spread them against my stomach. It isn't round like hers yet. It's bigger than it used to be and on a good day in the right clothes I almost look pregnant, but I'm still waiting for my stomach to really pop into that round, obviously pregnant shape.

As though sensing my discomfort, Michael leans close to me and whispers, "You look beautiful."

The warmth of his breath settles behind my ear and spreads down my spine leaving a new feeling deep in my core. The same one I've been trying to fight off since that moment in the car. I take a small step forward, ignoring the low grumble in Michael's throat when I do.

He's full of moments like this lately. Offering me a hand up, but not forcing the help on me. Standing protectively at my side when I need it, whispering words that give me confidence and simultaneously make me want to melt into his arms. And it feels good. Trusting him, knowing he is always there. And especially the melting into his arms. But it worries me too, these feelings I'm suddenly recognising. The way I want more.

The other woman sitting with Cassidy and her sister has long brown hair tied in a braid and wears a knitted jumper over her ankle length blue dress. She leans back on her hands, tilting her head up towards the sun and soaking in its rays. I don't know her, but something about her makes me want to. Snapping her head back to Cassidy and Madison, she opens her mouth in shock before letting out a wicked laugh. *Yep, I definitely want to know her.*

Rolling my shoulders back in an attempt to muster up the courage I need to join the small group of women, I notice Michael has disappeared from my side. Maisie has run off back inside to show her cousins her new room. Callum leans against the brick wall, chatting with a tanned man I do not know. His sister followed the kids upstairs.

My choices are to stand here, drinking my lemonade alone, waiting for someone I know to return to my side … or sit on the grass with the other women. I choose the latter, but I gnaw at the inside of my cheek as I make my way across the grass.

"Audrey!" Cassidy cheers when I'm close, pushing up from her laid back position. "I'm sorry we don't have chairs."

I brush it off, awkwardly dropping to the ground. I sit with my legs crossed and my hands in my lap, and feel oddly like I'm the new kid at school. Whether she notices my discomfort, or just realises her manners, Cassidy nudges my knee with her own and turns to the brunette.

"Audrey, this is my old roommate, Amira."

Amira smiles, nodding her head in my direction before laughter from the guys distracts her. She tilts her head back up to the sky, but from this close I can see her gaze fall on the unknown man now talking to Michael.

"And this is my sister, Madison," Cassidy continues. "She's pregnant too … she's pregnant." She over-enunciates the 't' sound the second time, trying to hide her slip.

I brush off her concern and turn to Madison. "It's okay. I'm sixteen weeks pregnant."

A weight I hadn't realised I was carrying falls from my shoulders. Other than Michael and Cassidy, I haven't told anyone other than my medical team. Not even my parents, not even …

"Maisie doesn't know," I quickly add. I jerk my head around, to see the kids running back into the yard.

"Your secret is safe with us," Amira chimes in.

I suppose I have to tell Maisie soon. But I'm not ready for the questions I'm sure will follow. She's asked how babies are made in the past, back when she used to beg Callum and I for a little sister. We brushed it off with the cliche 'when a mummy and a daddy love each other they can choose to have a baby.' How am I supposed to tell her that this baby was an accident, but that we love it anyway? What do I tell her about my relationship with Michael? I stare at him for a while, thankful that he has slotted himself into the group of guys the same way I did with the women. A slightly older man has joined them, the salt and pepper of his hair obvious even from across the yard. They talk and chat and laugh, Callum is gesturing around the yard while Michael nods along aimlessly, pulling at the label of his beer.

I'm glad he is getting along with the men. No matter what happens between the two of us, he will become intimately involved in this thrown together family circle we have going on. That's why I invited him to Callum's housewarming in the first place. He is the only reason I'm here. But I'm glad I am. Something about this group of women feels nostalgic and comforting. We've barely shared a conversation but I'm instantly welcomed into the group, as though we've all been friends for years.

"So, you and the golden retriever?" Madison asks.

For a second I dart my eyes around the grass, wondering if I somehow forgot that Baxter came with us. When I don't see the dog anywhere I turn back to Madison, eyebrows pinched. She rolls her eyes. "Long blond hair, adorable smile, sexy as fuck muscles?"

"Michael?"

"Mike?"

My head jerks to Cassidy. "You know him?"

The mid-spring air grows thin around us, a heaviness settles inside me. I know her answer before she says it.

"Yeah, I … uh … we … look we went on one date. But it was *one date,* and nothing happened and I don't want it to be weird."

I take a minute to react. *It doesn't have to be weird unless I make it weird.* We'd never spoken about it, but I *knew* about Michael's past. Mike's past. It didn't matter, because what matters is the future, whatever that might look like. I'd just never considered that Michael might have dated someone I knew. Someone whose life has ended up so closely tied to mine.

I need to say something, but the moment has dragged on and I still don't know what to say. It's been so long that it's probably even more awkward for me to say something now. It'll seem too forced. Probably because it is.

As though sensing my unease, Madison leans over to nudge Amira. "And you and Noah? How was the wedding?"

Blush rises from Amira's neck, leaving her face a bright shade of pink.

"The wedding was good. But no. No me and Noah. Nup." She stands in a rush and shuffles her feet in the grass while she fixes the skirt of her dress. Once she's satisfied with how it falls, she turns her focus to Cassidy, glaring down at her friend with fierce lividity.

Madison and I share a confused glance, she shrugs her shoulders as Amira stalks off towards the house.

"I think something happened at the wedding," Cassidy snickers.

It's late in the afternoon when Callum finds me resting on the couch inside. My back started to ache from sitting on the grass, then my feet started to hurt from standing. My ankles were starting to disappear again when I slipped away from the group.

"You okay?"

I let out a long sigh as I push myself to a seated position. "Yeah, I was just trying to think of how to tell Maisie about the baby."

"No 'mum and dad fell in love' this time, hey." He gives a gentle chuckle as I shake my head.

"Let's ask your mummy if you can have a sleepover!" Maisie's voice echoes down the steps, followed closely by three sets of heavy footsteps.

"Maisie, come here," Callum calls out to our daughter. "Like a Band-Aid," he adds as he sits next to me.

Maisie skips over and her cousins dart outside to their parents. She jumps onto her dad's lap, stretching her legs out until they push against my thigh. Callum hugs her, then looks up at me. I glare at him, trying to tell him silently that I have no idea how to approach this.

I feel trapped, forced to have a conversation that I'm not ready for, no matter how necessary it may be. Only, I don't think I'll ever be ready. I need Callum to pull the Band-Aid. I shift my gaze from Maisie up to her dad, nodding my head in his direction. He cocks an eyebrow, but sucks in a breath and turns Maisie to face him.

"You know how when a mummy and a daddy love each other, then they can have a baby?" She nods, her toothy grin growing over her cheeks. "Well sometimes it gets a little mixed up, and two people who aren't in love end up having a baby."

Maisie nods, but her eyes squint as she tries to make sense of what Callum is saying.

Band-Aid.

"That happened to Mummy and Michael," I say with one quick breath. Maisie turns to me, lifting a hand to scratch at her chin. "Mummy is going to have a baby, and Michael is the daddy, even though we aren't married or love each other that way."

"But you like him enough to have sleepovers?"

I choke on my own saliva. "Yes."

"Will he have more sleepovers?"

I don't know, but I might want him to.

"We haven't really talked about that. But the baby won't be born for a while so we don't need to figure it out right away."

"Is it a boy baby or a girl baby?"

"We don't know yet, chicka."

"Okay!" She bounces off Callum's lap and turns to face him. "So can Jackson and Halley have a sleepover?"

Just like that, she's moved on, and I'm left wondering if I was overthinking the whole conversation. It's good, now that it's out in the open and I don't have to hide my pregnancy from her. But I'll have to call my parents to tell them before Maisie sees them next.

"No honey, you have kinder tomorrow. If it's okay with mum you can sleep here though." Callum turns to me to add, "I'll drop her there in the morning, if it's alright with you? Then you can pick her up as normal for the rest of the week."

Maisie presses her hands on one cheek, tilting her head and pouting her lips. "Please mummy? Please, please, please?"

Like I could say no to that face.

Chapter Thirteen

MICHAEL

Callum's new house is nice, although bare. A solitary grey couch sits in the centre of the living room, a table three times too small for the space has been left to the side of the kitchen, and the whole front room of the house was empty when we walked past.

It leaves the clean lines of the architecture exposed and my mind begins to tick at all the finishing touches. The exposed woodwork hasn't been hidden behind plasterboard or paintwork, and combined with the large tiled floor it oozes modern sophistication.

Making our way towards the back of the house, my shoulders curl forward. This isn't just meeting some of Audrey's friends. This is meeting her ex-husband, her daughter's father. Callum is friendly enough as he welcomes us in, but I'm frozen in my tracks when his girlfriend steps in to say hello.

I recognise her instantly, and any ounce of confidence I might have been faking slowly trickles away. I pass her the small houseplant without a word, dropping my gaze to the floor. I want to show Audrey that I can be the man she deserves. The man they deserve. Her and the baby. But I don't know how to do that with Cassidy here.

She squeaks as she takes the plant and spins around, finding somewhere to place it. There's no doubt she recognises me.

Fuck.

I look up to see the back of Cassidy's hair as she steps

outside. I knew my past would catch up with me at some point, hell it already has considering a little mini me will be running around my feet this time next year. But to have a girl I treated so poorly show up right when I'm trying to prove myself is more than a kick to the guts. It's a twenty-five-kilo plate straight to the balls and a nail gun to the chest. Should I talk to her? Apologise? Or would it be better to leave the past in the past?

Callum pulls back my attention, shoving a drink into my hands, and I follow him and Audrey out of the kitchen. I freeze after taking a step through the sliding door when I finally look up. I was expecting … something … from a house so grand. A nice decked area or a landscaped garden to match the front facade. But the backyard is completely bare save for a large gumtree in the far corner.

Cassidy has retreated back to her small circle of friends, all seated and laughing on the lawn. I decide to leave it be, for now at least.

Beside me, Audrey stands awkwardly, gazing at the small group of women sitting on the grass. In her linen pants and signature grey cardigan, Audrey is the perfect vision of a pregnant woman. She might not feel it through the morning sickness she said she still goes through, but she glows. It's fucking stunning.

I lean into her to whisper in her ear, "You look beautiful."

My stomach flutters in a way it never has before. She is more than beautiful, and I will tell her every day until she believes me. Then I'll remind her every day after that.

My fingers twitch next to her hip, but I hold them back. Not wanting to push the boundaries of our … whatever this is between us. I want to pull her into me, claim her mouth and hold her close. I want her to brush her hand along my back when she walks past, and I want to be able to go back home later and do all the unspeakable things I've been daydreaming about. Something sparks in the small space between us, and I back away slowly before it explodes. But I don't turn away until Audrey sucks in a breath of courage and heads over to sit with the women.

Callum calls me over, introducing me to a tall man he says is Cassidy's cousin.

"Noah," the bloke introduces himself. He barely glances my way, eyes focused on the women on the grass. One girl lies back in the sun, kicking at the long skirt that covers her ankles.

Audrey is like the sun, bright and warm and she pulls my attention away from the group. I pick at the label of my beer, distracted by her presence across the lawn. The conversation barely registers, not keeping my attention the way I know it should. I just can't stop thinking about Audrey and how *right* this feels. Us, being at this small family gathering, together.

I'm getting ahead of myself, I know that, but I can't help it. Everything about Audrey screams at me to be a better man. It has since the moment I met her, and I'll do everything I can to convince her I'm worth keeping around. I don't just want to be the baby's father. I want more. I want Audrey to be mine and I want to be hers. I want the three of us to be a family. No, the four of us, because Maisie counts too.

I'm in way over my head, because Audrey has made it clear that she doesn't feel the same way. That she isn't in this for us, but because of the baby we are having. I crave the thought of convincing her to give in to the chemistry that still drips from us. To remind her just how perfectly we were made for each other and just how good it feels when our bodies move in sync. But that doesn't mean I don't desperately want more. And some previously unknown part of me is holding back, protecting my heart until I know she is in this just as deep as I am.

"Audrey said you're a builder, Michael?" Callum turns to me, and I have to drag my attention back to the group. A slightly older man has joined us, but I was so transfixed on watching Audrey that I hadn't noticed when.

"Oliver," he says, jerking his thumb to his chest. I give him a polite nod before answering Callum.

"Yeah, I uh, do framework at the moment," I start. An uneasy prickling crawls along the back of my neck. I lift my hand to scratch it away, sweeping my hair out of the way.

Callum is so successful and I am … not. I had my chance to be and I ruined it. No matter how many times my father asks me to take the reins, I'll never live up to his expectations. And I'd never forgive myself when I screw everything up.

"I was thinking about building a deck, but I know nothing."

He gestures around the yard as he goes through his grand plans for the space. His plans would be easy enough to execute, the biggest issue would be time.

"I could help?" I surprise myself when I say it, and quickly work to take it back. I don't really want to spend every weekend at Audrey's ex-husband's house. "Or I could get some guys over. They'll probably be quicker. And it would look nicer. I'm used to working on the stuff that doesn't need to look pretty."

"That would be great, thanks mate."

I let out a long breath and the heavy feeling of my chest floats away with it. Callum excuses himself to check on the kids. Oliver follows him inside, mumbling something about needing chairs.

"Do you have a building company?" Noah asks once we are alone. "I want to build some new accommodation at the winery. It'll need to be from the ground up though."

I shove my hands in my pockets, shoulders slumping down. I hate that he assumed it was my business, as though it should be. As though working for my father is something to be looked down on. I bet this guy is just as successful as Callum is.

"I just work there, but I can ask my dad about getting a project set up. Would have to come and see the site." I speak the words to my chest.

"It's your dad's business?"

I huff in agreement. "He wants it to be mine."

"You don't want it?"

There's something about this guy, with his sun-bleached hair and his tanned skin and his casual shirt. Something that makes me want to talk to him. I don't get it, but the words fall out of my mouth all the same.

"Nah, not really. Maybe. It could be cool, but I'm not cut out for that shit. All the admin and coordination is not really me, you know?"

"Wasn't mine either." Noah shakes his head with a gentle laugh. "Can I tell you something?"

When I nod, a knowing grin spreads across his face. "I haven't told anyone here. Don't really know why I'm telling you, but something tells me you could use the pep talk."

He glances around the yard before leaning in towards me, talking in a low voice. "I don't just work at the winery. I own it."

My eyebrows pinch together. He owns a winery? Why would he keep that from the people he hangs out with? And why is he telling me?

Before I can ask, he holds up a hand to stop me. He laughs, leaning back against the brick wall and crossing his arms across his chest.

"I inherited it from my grandmother—not the one I share with Cassidy, my father's mother. I never met her, and she left me a whole damn winery in her will. Apparently, she always had some guy running the place, but he left when ownership was transferred to me. I don't think he wanted to work for some young kid from Sydney, especially not one whose only experience with wine was from a goon bag. Anyways, I was going to sell it but I fell in love. I can't explain it."

"So, you moved to Melbourne to run the winery? And you haven't told anyone?"

He nods, running a hand through his hair before letting it settle behind his head. "I was terrified I was going to screw everything up. So, I kept it a secret. It's going well, but it's too weird now to turn around and tell people. I think Callum knows because he did all this digging when Cassidy's business was struggling. But no one else."

"You didn't fuck it up though. You have plans to expand, it must be going well." It sounds like he is doing really well. The heaviness on my shoulders eases, allowing me to stand a little taller. Noah was thrown a whole damn winery and he made it work. If he can do that, maybe I could take on more responsibility from my dad. Just a little bit.

"That's just it." He smiles and pushes off the wall. "It's going really well. I didn't have an admin bone in my body, and I knew *nothing* about the wine industry. But it's going really well. And mate, if I can pull something as elaborate as this off? I reckon you could run your dad's business."

With a friendly slap on my arm, Noah's attention shifts back to the women. Looking over my shoulder, I see the woman he was spying on push herself to stand and storm back inside. Audrey adjusts her position, rubbing at her ankles.

"Amira," Noah calls out. He pats my arm once more before darting after her.

The rest of the afternoon is a jumble of awkward small talk and moments where I actually think I might get along with these people. Most of the time, though, I have to stop myself from talking right before I put my foot in my mouth. Like when I almost said the word 'baby' while Maisie was in earshot. Or when I offered to get Audrey one of the fruity alcoholic seltzers. I definitely put my foot right in there when I mentioned the age difference between Oliver and his—much younger—wife.

By the time the cockatoos are screeching their early evening song from the large gumtree in the backyard, Audrey has retreated indoors to rest her feet and I'm starting to feel like it's probably time to go.

"So, you and … Amy?" I ask Noah in one last effort to make adult friends.

"Amira?"

Heat flares through my temples, even though she wasn't around to hear me get her name wrong. "Shit. Yeah, sorry. I'm shit at names."

"It's all cool. But nah. Maybe? I don't think so."

"Sounds confusing."

He takes a long pull of his beer, emptying the bottle. Bringing it down, he spins the glass between his hands. "It *is* confusing. I wish I knew. But she needed a date for a wedding and so I went. Honestly, I thought maybe it could have meant something, but I don't think it did."

His eyes turn down, shoulders rolling as he loses the confidence he held all day.

"At least not to her, right?" I nudge.

"Yeah."

When he chooses not to elaborate, I opt not to pry. This guy is pretty cool. I might be a bit of an outsider between rich guy Callum, his lawyer brother-in-law, and distinguished Oliver, but with Noah, it's different. Sure, he owns a very successful winery, but he doesn't act like it. He acts like any other mate. And although I've only just met him, I feel like that's exactly what he is.

Audrey pokes her head outside, asking if I'm ready to leave. And I am if she is.

After we've said our goodbyes and made our way back to the car, the temperature in the air between us begins to spike.

When she pulls the car onto the road, her hand reaches across to rest on my knee. Fire burns from her touch, but I lean into it, placing my hand on hers to give it a tight squeeze.

"I told Maisie today," she says without taking her gaze from the road ahead.

"How did she take it?"

"She was more interested in sleepovers."

Audrey pulls her hand back, pressing her palm into her own lap before bringing it up to the steering wheel.

"I don't blame her, sleepovers are fun." They were fun as kids, and they are damn fun now. Just for very different reasons. And I don't want to 'sleepover' with anyone other than Audrey now.

A knowing smirk peaks through her tough exterior as Audrey shifts in the seat. Her grip on the steering wheel grows tight. "Yeah, they are."

"Do you want—?"

She chokes on a cough, cutting me off with a firm, "No."

"It *would* be fun, Audrey."

Because damn my heart straight to hell, I'd give anything to feel her body against mine again.

Pulling to a stop at a red light, she glares at me for a beat before she answers. Her eyes are dark and a crimson blush has forced its way up her neck.

"Fun is messy."

"Messy is fun, too."

Taking a gamble, I reach for her. My fingertips trail over her collarbone, inching lower. Her chest swells as she sucks in a breath. Behind us, a car beeps. Audrey draws her attention back to the road with a quick whip of her head.

As she takes off, I settle my hand against her stomach. I lower my voice, pulling the seat belt tight around me so I can lean closer to her. "And Audrey, I think we already made this as messy as it's going to get. We might as well have fun too."

Her exhale is shaky. But the "okay" that follows curls its way into my body, leaving a searing electricity in its wake before it settles in my lap. My cock twitches in excitement, and by the time she skips the turnoff to my apartment my erection strains against the zipper of my shorts.

Chapter Fourteen

MICHAEL

I'm out of the car before Audrey has switched the engine off. The air has chilled as the sun falls behind the trees, but electricity buzzes around us.

Anticipation floods my veins, arousal swells in my groin, making my balls ache. But a heavy feeling of dread settles unexpectedly in my stomach, freezing my feet to the gravel driveway.

I want Audrey, sure. But I want her to know that this is so much more than just 'fun' for me. I need her to know that I haven't been able to stop thinking about her since the day I let her down. I need her to know that I will spend the rest of my life trying to make it up to her. And I need her to know that the baby, my baby, has nothing to do with those feelings.

Finding out I am about to become a father was a huge shock, there's no denying that. When I first found out I was terrified. Then I was upset, disappointed in myself for making Audrey feel like she couldn't tell me. Now, I'm excited to meet my child, and grateful that it tied Audrey and me together in a way nothing else ever could. Our little avocado sized baby has given me a second chance with Audrey, and I don't want to ruin it.

"Audrey," I whisper as she steps out of the car and heads to the house. She pivots on her heel, wrapping her cardigan around her the way she always does when she is nervous. Her neck and cheeks are red with the same heat that burns my lungs.

Closing the gap between us, she places her fingers on my hips. They squeeze as she draws in a breath.

"Michael," she exhales.

Her eyes glow in the dying sunlight of the late afternoon. They still remind me of the ocean, but the golden, sand-coloured flakes sparkle against the deep blue. As she stares up at me through her lashes I see right through them, to where her true feelings rest.

She always tries to hide them, always so cautious and unsure. I want her to know that when she is with me, she can let them out. That she doesn't have to shy away, because I'm here, and I am hers.

"It's just fun," she whispers, mostly to herself as she looks down to the gap between us. Her voice shakes and she grasps my waist like she might fall without me to hold her up.

I close the gap, pressing our chests together and wrapping one arm around her back. With my free hand, I caress her cheek with my fingers and drag my thumb along her lower lip. Her mouth falls open with another shaky breath.

"Keep telling yourself that, Audrey."

And then I can't help but kiss her. The icy dread of what this could mean melts away, replaced with a burning need for it anyway. An understanding that we are well past the moment to talk right now so it will have to wait until later.

I tug her lower lip between my teeth, claiming her even though she might only be mine for this moment. Unease that this might be a one time thing still claws at my insides, but I push the sensation away.

She tastes too good. The sweet flavour from her lemonade mixes with the minty gum she chewed in the car. Running my tongue along her lips, I hold her tight against me as she opens her mouth to let me in. I explore her mouth with my tongue, savouring the moment because I have no idea how long it will last. We said it would be fun, but it will be so much more for me. How long before she grows tired of it? Will she end up wanting more?

"Michael," she moans into my mouth. Blood pulses below my belt. I don't think I've ever been this hard and I am desperate for some kind of relief.

"Inside, now," I growl, hoisting her up. She wraps her arms and legs around me as I carry her up the small path.

"Key. Pot. Rock."

I don't stop to tell her it's not safe to leave a key so close to the front door, I just reach for it in haste. One hand under her ass, supporting her weight, I fumble at the lock with the other and let us inside.

Audrey slams the door shut behind us and I'm done waiting. I need to feel her again, all of her. I need to feel the way she fits so perfectly laid out beneath me. I need to feel how fucking well her pussy clings to my cock while she comes. I thrust against her, and pull away from our frenzied kiss.

"Feel how hard you make me? Feel how my cock is just begging for that pretty pussy of yours?"

Audrey gasps, and I steal the sound with another kiss. I'd have her right here against the entry mirror if I had my way, but Audrey wriggles her way down until her feet hit the floor. She breaks away from me, grabbing my wrist and pulling me towards the bedroom. I fight the urge to scoop her up, instead following her like a lost puppy, waiting patiently while she closes the blinds. With a hand below my waistband, working to unbutton my pants and pull down the zipper, I reach behind me to turn on the light.

"Don't," Audrey whimpers.

She's removed her cardigan and top, but in the darkened room I can't make out her features. The delicate dimples in her hips, the freckles on her chest, the way they turn red when she blushes. I can't see any of it, and I hate it.

I drop my hand and take long strides towards Audrey.

With my hands on her cheeks, I drag my gaze up her body, pausing on all the bits I love the most—her thighs, her hips, her breasts—before looking her deep in the eyes. All the sand has gone, replaced with the darkest blue.

"I want to see you, Audrey. All of you. You are fucking beautiful and I want to appreciate every inch."

She nods the tiniest of nods and I reach down to flick on the lamp on her bedside table.

I guide Audrey back until her legs hit the bed, then lower her down. Leaning over her I kiss her, tenderly this time. First her lips, then her cheeks. I kiss her nose, her chin, the soft pocket of skin below her ear. I make my way down until I reach her chest, leaving a trail of wet kisses in my wake. My tongue teases her, licking along the top of her bra while I palm at her breast. Through the thin padding, I feel her nipple draw firm.

She reaches between us, undoing the front clasp of her bra. It falls to the sides and I pause to appreciate her beauty.

"God Audrey, you're perfect."

I tease her nipple with my tongue, savouring the tiny whimper she releases. My mouth closes around her breast, teeth grazing against her. When she writhes underneath me, I trail my fingers lower to toy with the waistband on her pants. The elastic band stretches easily and I dip my hand in. Her panties are soaked. Pushing them to the side, I run my finger through her hot, wet sex. With my thumb, I press on her clit.

"Is this okay?" I ask, hesitating at her opening. "For the baby?"

She doesn't answer, instead lifting her hips and guiding my finger into her. She gasps as I pull it out, adding a second finger and pushing deep to massage her inner walls.

"Kiss me," she whispers.

I pop my mouth off her breast, moving up to claim her

mouth again. With a firm kiss, I curl my fingers inside her, pumping in and out.

"Please, Michael."

She doesn't have to ask me twice. I will do anything and everything she asks of me, now and always.

I rub my thumb around her clit. Her muscles contract around my fingers as I move them ferociously, drawing the orgasm out of her. When she reaches a fierce peak, she grinds her hips up to fuck my fingers.

"Are you going to come all over my hand, Audrey?"

Her back arches off the bed. She moans into my mouth, and I continue to rub my fingers against her inner walls as she rides through her orgasm. She lets out a final whimper and collapses softly back against the mattress. Bringing my hand to my mouth, I lick my fingers clean.

God. Fuck, I forgot how incredible she tasted.

My cock strains, aching for relief, but all I want to do is bury my face between her legs and drown in her. She pushes against me, rolling us over until she is positioned over me.

Audrey kisses me firmly, then drops her hands between my legs. Her fingers unbutton my denim shorts but for some ungodly reason I reach under her shoulders and pull her up.

My balls scream at me, but I don't care. The relief I was craving is no longer important. Nothing could ever be more important than Audrey. I need her to understand this was not about me. Wrapping my arms around her, I hold her close.

"Not tonight. You don't owe me Audrey."

She hesitates, her fingers still twitching as she reaches between us.

"I mean it. Plus, there'll be plenty more of this if I have my way."

Her head drops to my shoulder and I hold her close, ignoring the intense throbbing in my balls. It's not exactly what I meant when I said not tonight, and I'll probably have to deal with my cock later, but it'll be worth it for this moment. To have been this close to Audrey.

To feel her completely relaxed in my arms. To get a glimpse into what our life could be like.

She lifts her head to look at me. "Should we get dinner then? I still want that greasy rotisserie chicken and hot salty chips."

"Not yet."

I kiss her forehead and she lays back down, snuggling into me. Her back glistens with sweat, goosebumps erupting where I caress her skin with my fingertips. We breathe in sync, soaking in each other's comfort.

There's something about this moment that is entirely foreign, but also intimately familiar. It's so different to all the one-night stands and short-lived flings. It's warm and comforting, the closeness filling a space inside me I didn't realise was lacking. It feels … right.

Until she wriggles free, snatching her bra and top off the bed. She holds them over her chest as she stands at the foot of the bed. Hair ruffled, eyes wide, chest heaving.

"Well," she squeaks. "That was fun."

And I think being called fun is even worse than being thrown in the friendzone.

Chapter Fifteen

MICHAEL

My knee bounces. Underneath me, the hard plastic chair works to slowly steal all feeling from my butt. The air is stale and smells so strongly of cleaning products that each inhale burns my windpipe.

Beside me, Audrey crosses one leg over the other. Her ankle flicks in tiny, rapid movements, as shaky as her breaths. The twenty weeks banana I brought bounces in her lap, untouched.

I lean across the armrest to nudge my shoulder against hers and nod towards the two kids playing in the corner. The smallest bites a book made of thick cardboard while the other runs in circles, holding a small plastic ambulance. It's seen better days, that ambulance, but the kid waves it around all the same screaming "nee naw nee naw." The brightness of the toys and books is a stark contrast to the rows of pale grey chairs and the dirty white walls.

"Did *they* get invited to Maisie's graduation party?"

Audrey tugs at her ear. Her shoulders round down as she folds into herself like she might be able to hide from the noise. With delicate fingers, she peels the banana, taking a bite and chewing slowly.

"It was weeks ago. Will you please drop it?"

I would. I should, probably. But there is something about the hint of guilt that flashes across Audrey's face every time I bring it up. The way she smiles to herself when she thinks I'm no longer watching. If I took a guess, I'd say she feels bad about it now, but there is some part of her that is happy about it. Not the fact she didn't invite me, but the fact I care.

She didn't think I would be interested, and I don't blame her for that. But I would have gone. Less for Maisie and more for Audrey. So that she knows I'm ready to show up for every milestone, big and small. Not just for the baby we share but for the family we are about to become. Even though she might not see us as a family yet.

Today though, the guilt is replaced by something that looks like a mild annoyance. Her gaze flips up to meet mine before dropping back to her lap.

"Audrey?"

I hesitate, my hand lingering over hers before I let it drop. She flinches at the touch, but doesn't pull away as I lace our fingers together.

"I'm sorry, okay. I'll stop bringing it up." And I'll add the fact that I kept bringing it up to the list of things I keep getting wrong here.

From behind the desk, a nurse calls out a name. A mother scoops up the youngest child, prying the book away and dropping it on the floor. Audrey watches as they walk past, the mother hobbling, belly swollen and with a toddler on her hip. She uses the arm rests of the empty chairs for balance as she goes.

"Thank you for coming," Audrey says, long after the woman has passed. "I'm glad I don't have to be alone again."

"I'm sorry I wasn't at the last one. I mean, I get why you hadn't told me then. I'm sorry you felt that you couldn't." I'll be sorry that my actions made her feel that way for the rest of my life. I'll try to make it up to her every single day.

She leans her head down against the crook of my neck and I squeeze her hand.

"What if the baby—"

"Shh," I silence her worries. Truthfully, I'm worried too.

But I know for the most part, we shouldn't be. We have nothing to worry about. All Audrey's check-ups have been fine. The baby's heartbeat has been steady at every appointment. Her stomach is growing—beautifully I might add—the perfect amount. Her other symptoms are easing.

"I just hope everything is okay."

"It will be."

The child in the corner finally quits the "nee naw-ing" and silence falls across the waiting room. The sound of doors opening and closing echoes down the corridor, and the receptionist taps away at her computer. Up on the wall, a mid-morning talk show plays on the TV; volume down, delayed captions on. I try to watch, but the delay makes the show impossible to follow. It looks like they are about to start baking, but the captions discuss a surfboarding dog.

Audrey keeps her head on my shoulder, her breaths deep and forced. The longer we wait, the more worried she becomes, wriggling her ankle again as she chews at her nails.

"Audrey Wilson?" A petite lady steps into the waiting room. Her floral, frilly top is so bright I have to squint my eyes. Not at all the pale blue scrubs all the nurses are wearing.

"Fuck." Audrey reaches beside her to grab her bag and I help her stand. We follow the lady in the bright top down the corridor, around a bend, and into a darkened room. Somehow, her shirt still shines fluorescent pink in the dim lighting.

"Before we start, I need to change my surname on the file," Audrey announces as she sits on the reclined chair in the centre of the room.

The ultrasound technician clicks away at her computer, not turning to face Audrey when she answers. "I can't do that here, but from what I can see Wilson is the surname on your Medicare card? The file has to match so that we can bulk bill the appointments."

Audrey's face drops. She closes her eyes to contemplate

before reaching into her bag and pulling out a pen. On the back of her hand she scrawls the word 'Wilson'.

"It's Callum's surname. You need to remind me to change it back to Baker. I keep forgetting."

I want to tell her it's not worth changing back to her maiden name when she could take mine instead.

I've never cared much for the name Bird, hated all the dumb nicknames that came with it at school. But all of a sudden, I wouldn't mind it on her and I'm starting to think of all the ways I could make that happen. Which scares me, thrills me, and has me wringing my hands together. This is not what Audrey needs right now. I've gone from ten to three thousand in the space of two minutes all because we started talking about her last name. But then, maybe that is what she needs, so she knows I mean it when I say I'll stick around. I can't get caught up about it now though, so I squeeze the thoughts back down as I sit in the chair next to Audrey's recliner.

"I'll remind you."

I suck in more air than my lungs should be able to handle. Push my shoulders back further than they should rest. Ignore the way my skin tingles where Audrey's hand rests against my forearm. Fun, she said. I might be the father of her baby, but I'm nothing more than a casual fling to Audrey. I didn't even get an invite to her daughter's kindergarten graduation, and I'd do well to remember that. After too long in silence, Audrey squeezes my arm before pulling her hand back to lift her top.

We don't make small talk with the technician as she deposits gooey gel onto Audrey's stomach. The soft purr of the ultrasound machine and the clicking of keys echo through the otherwise silent room. A tension has been added to the room at the mention of surnames, and all three of us know it. My knee bounces, as unsteady as my breaths and as rapid as my pulse.

Audrey pulls her lip back between her teeth and I fight to keep my eyes away. Fight to keep my mind off how she did the exact same thing when she was trying to be quiet. I try, with everything I can, not to think about the moans that escaped anyway, or how they reverberated through every bone in my body, perfectly in sync with the way my cock throbbed inside her pussy. Nope, definitely *not* thinking about that.

I shift in my seat, doing what little I can to hide the bulge growing in my pants.

"Sorry," the ultrasound technician murmurs when she reaches over to press the wand against Audrey's belly. She pushes hard against the soft flesh, creating a divot right on the side where I always imagined the baby's head to be. Audrey winces, wriggling on the recliner.

Dub, dub-dub, dub-dub-dub.

The heartbeat sounds irregular. Faster than a racehorse, but with just as many hooves.

Audrey looks to me, then to the technician, who's screen is still facing away from us. She clicks her tongue, wriggling the wand some more with her focus intently on her computer.

Then, the heartbeat settles. It's still fast, but it sounds more like I always assumed a heartbeat would. She moves the wand some more, and the steady thumps double. Moving across to Audrey's other side, the heartbeat sounds normal again.

All the while Audrey stares up at me, two thin lines between her brows. She pokes her tongue out to wet her swollen and cracked lower lip.

I cup her face, rubbing my thumb along her lip while my fingers caress her cheek. I have no idea what's going on, but I will *not* let her see my fear. Audrey places her hand over mine, closing her eyes and leaning into the touch. Her lip trembles.

"Has anyone ever mentioned the possibility of multiples?"

The technician's voice sends a shockwave through the room. Audrey's eyes snap open and I rip my hand back from her. We turn in unison to face the technician.

"What?"

Beaming, the technician turns her computer screen so we can all see. The display is a blur of static grey until she presses the wand back against Audrey's bump. The heartbeat settles to a steady rhythm and a tiny baby starts to form on the screen. An oversized head, sure, but two arms, two legs kicking away.

"This is baby number one." She moves the wand across Audrey's middle. The image on the screen returns to the grey static and the heartbeat doubles, not quite in time. "And from in the middle you can hear both heartbeats, I'm trying to get a shot of the babies together but the best I can get is this view of the top of their heads."

The screen shows two grey blobs, almost touching.

"And then, over here is baby number two." She stretches across to press the wand against the other side of Audrey's stomach, and a second baby comes to life on the screen. Two more arms, two more legs, another oversized head.

"Two," Audrey whispers on an exhale, staring at the screen.

"Two," I repeat, unintentionally pulling back.

"Michael?" Her voice is distant. "Is everything okay?"

"Michael?"

"It will be." I choke out. *It will have to be.*

So, I suck it up. I paint on the face of a man about to become the father of twins. A wide smile, a twinkle in my eye. I don't let on that the moisture there is out of fear, not joy.

The rest of the appointment passes in a blur. Two. Two babies. And I was only just getting used to the idea of having one. We drive home without words, only the rumble of the diesel engine and the faint midday radio show breaking the silence floating between us. I have no idea if Audrey is freaking out just like I am. If she is scared or worried, or maybe she is overcome with joy. *Is she worried I'll run?*

Pulling into her long driveway, I rest a hand on her knee. Her breath catches as a single tear falls from the otherwise impenetrable mask on her face.

"I'm here, Audrey." Because I am, no matter how much I'm panicking on the inside. I am here for her, for them. I doubt I have the maturity to be the best father in the world. I know I'm immature and forgetful and I can't take anything seriously. But I will always be there, with whatever they need. For those babies *and* for Audrey.

She scoffs, mumbling to herself as she gets out of the car.

I throw the parking brake on to follow her up the steps to her house.

"Audrey, I mean it. I am here, and I know this is unexpected and, fuck, it scares the shit out of me. But we are in this together and I mean that with every piece of my body. I might not be the man you wanted to have another baby with, if you ever wanted that, and I can probably never become that guy. But I will do everything to be the man you and those babies deserve."

Her shoulders shake as she pulls her arms around her front. I close the gap, enveloping her in my own arms as she sniffles into my shoulder.

"Hey, I look after two dogs all the time when my parents are out of town. I can handle two babies."

Audrey laughs against me. Her body relaxes into the embrace and she squeezes her arms out from between us to wrap them around my middle.

"Michael?"

I hum into her hair, enjoying the breathlessness in her voice a little *too* much.

"You know babies are *very* different from dogs, right?"

Chapter Sixteen

AUDREY

The phone rings out, but the second the vibrating stops, it starts up again with a new call. Same as it did two minutes ago. It hasn't stopped since I said goodbye to Michael, reassuring him that I was okay and he should get back to work.

I'm not okay though, and with each gentle whir from my bag the throbbing in my temple grows a little louder. The dread that began to settle in the dim light of the ultrasound clinic pulses through me. There's no way the person calling is bringing good news, and I know I shouldn't worry about the what ifs but they are the only thoughts left in my brain.

Is it Michael calling to tell me this is all too much? That he never signed up for one baby, let alone two, and he is done playing pretend.

Or maybe it's my mother, calling with good intentions to ask how the ultrasound went. She's been overbearing and smitten ever since I finally told her I was pregnant. The latest display of that, a giant hamper of baby goods, still sits fully wrapped on the entry table. She's probably ready to beg me to send her the photos of her precious grandchild. But if it is her, I'm not ready for that conversation. How do I tell her that instead of one surprise baby I'm having two? And I'm pretty sure my baby daddy is even more freaked out than me, and I'm freaked out *a lot*.

Most likely though, it will be my boss, calling to ask where I am, because I told him I would come in as soon as the appointment was over, but the appointment ran late and

I came home instead. He'd acted like a hero when he said I could have the morning off for my appointment, but the side serving of a passive aggressive reminder that I'll just have to work harder to clear my inbox in the afternoon gave away his misogyny. It grates on me, but right now I don't have it in me to care. I have no appointments scheduled and frankly, my inbox can wait.

Two babies.

Two.

My heart starts to gallop again. Walking to the kitchen and dumping my bag on the island bench, I stare down at the ultrasound pictures in my hand. Twin A written in tiny, bold font on the top photo. Twin B on the other. Which twin did we see in the first two ultrasounds?

Holding the photos next to the earlier one I keep on the fridge, I squint my eyes. The photos are far from clear and the profiles all look the same. To be expected, really, considering they are identical. I doubt I'll ever know which baby I saw first. I wonder if I'll be able to tell my babies apart.

I wonder if Michael will. I wonder if they will look more like me, or more like him. I wonder how often they will see their father, what kind of relationship they will have. Will he want to parent them the same way I do? Will he take them for weekends at a time, dropping them back loaded with sugar or emotional trauma? He said he will always be there, but for how long? When will he realise that his life has changed far too much, and he doesn't want it anymore?

When will he realise that being tied to me is not as much *fun* as it used to be?

Nausea hits me harder than ever before, squeezing my stomach and clawing at my throat. Dropping to my hands and knees, I rest my head against the cool stainless steel of the fridge. My body heaves but, thankfully, for the first time in a long time, I manage to keep the contents of my stomach where they belong. It takes an age for my muscles to recover, to loosen again. But my back continues to ache from the hunched over position, and my knees protest when I use the kitchen bench to pull myself up.

My bag vibrates all over again and I groan, conceding that I have to check who it is. At best, so I can ignore the call for a while longer. At worst, so I can tell my boss I'm not coming in today.

Brett Harper—Harper Smith Real Estate

His name flashes across the screen and Cassidy's words ring in my ear. *You deserve to be thrilled about what you do for a living.* But if not this, then what. Then art? But how would I pay the bills, how would I put food on the table? I don't want to rely solely on child support and single parenting allowances.

My hand shakes as my thumb sweeps across the screen to answer the call and I bring the phone up to my ear.

"Brett." The name comes out with more hatred than I intended, and I pray he hasn't picked up on my joyless attitude.

"Audrey, just checking in. Figured the appointment would be done by now but haven't seen you at your desk yet."

He speaks all snappy and sharp, and my jaw clenches at the way he drawls out my name.

"I was about to call you, actually. I just got home and—"

"Home?" He cuts me off and I want to scream at him that I deserve to be listened to. "I thought you were coming straight back. Your calendar looks empty but there is always work to do. I'm sure you have hundreds of potential clients in your inbox."

"I'm sure I do, Brett, but I had some … unexpected news at the appointment. I need to take the full day as personal leave. Just while I process and figure everything out."

"Unexpected? Ah well. I'm sure it'll be fine. Anyway, I guess if you aren't coming in, we'll have to chat on the phone."

I swallow down the rising anger. *How dare he?*

"About what Brett? I'm sorry but if it's not time critical, I'd really rather wait until tomorrow." I keep my tone flat, still fighting to hold down the burst of frustration that tries to bubble to the surface.

He lets out a quick, huffed, laugh. His lack of tact and his indifference to my capacity grate down my spine. One step lower and I'll jump.

"It's just about that house you sold. The big modern town home with the huge backyard that closed last month. You sold it to your ex-husband."

I hum, urging him to get to his point because I really want to get off the phone and go hide in my bed until I have to pick up Maisie from kindergarten.

"We've had some complaints," Brett states. I remind myself to breathe.

"Complaints about what?"

"Some buyers that missed out on the property seem to think the sale was conducted in a way that was deceptive. The complaint is that you enticed the buyer to reject offers, knowing that you wanted to sell the property to your ex. Now, if that's true Audrey, it's a major concern. And even if it's not, the fact we have had complaints is something we have to take very seriously."

I can't hold back the scoff. "Everything was done above board Brett. You know that because I had you sign off on everything *because* the buyer was my ex-husband. I gave each offer adequate weight when informing the seller. It's not my fault Callum offered a quarter of a million over the asking price."

"Yes yes, I am aware of how much he offered. Even so, Audrey, we need to take the complaints very seriously. We can't risk losing potential buyers of future homes, just because they aren't happy with how a sale went in the past."

"What are you saying Brett?"

Bile rises once more in my throat, burning through my neck.

"Nothing major Audrey, don't panic. But instead of having someone shadow you before your leave, we will be adding a second agent to every sale, to show buyers that we value integrity and honesty. All commissions will be split."

"What?"

"In an attempt to keep the situation fair, we will assign a different agent to each sales contract you currently have open. For their work in finalising the sale they will receive fifty per cent of the commission."

"Brett, that's not fair."

"It has to be done Audrey. I'm sorry we had to do this over the phone, but since you didn't feel like coming into the office it was needed."

I force out something that resembles, "thanks for letting me know," before ending the call and slamming my phone back on the bench. Tears blur my vision for a moment before one spills onto my cheek. I bat it away and wipe my eyes with the back of my sleeve. No. Brett doesn't deserve my tears. That stupid job doesn't deserve my tears.

I open the calendar app on my phone and count the weeks. I just need to make it to my maternity leave. Then I'll figure it out. Fifteen weeks. I can do this.

Callum's surname screams at me from the back of my hand. I want to scratch it off, but I wrote it there for a reason. No matter how desperately I want to wallow, now that I have an afternoon off, I might as well use it to get my name back.

In the small study nook, I open up the laptop and start making a list of all the organisations I'll need to contact. It drags on and on until my eyes hurt, but once I'm sure I have everything listed, I scroll back to the top to start the process. I'll have to physically go into most places, but it feels cathartic, finally leaving that piece of my history behind. Like I can finally start to think about what my future might be like.

Anyone would think a woman about to have a baby would have her future sorted, but I don't. I have no idea what it looks like. Especially now that I am questioning my career as well.

I wonder if I should feel scared. If I should be panicking beyond measure. But I'm not. I'm not scared or worried or nervous. I'm not excited or thrilled either. I just kind of am, and I guess right now that's all I can hope for.

Chapter Seventeen

MICHAEL

"Twins?"

Brendan's shocked tone screams at the part of me still desperate to run away and never look back. But I can't do that, I won't do that. Sure, a tiny piece of me wants to cling to my past and escape the future, but that part is tiny. Even if it is loud sometimes.

I rocked up to the latest job site hours later than I said I would, and the guys are already packing their shit away, ready to call it in. The main frame of another luxury townhome stands mostly complete, taking up almost the entirety of the block of land it sits on. This whole development suburb feels crowded and closed in. Large houses on tiny blocks, crammed together like sardines just for a slice of the Aussie dream that isn't hours from the city.

Not really my place to complain though, it's not my house we're building here. My house is waiting for me, kind of. I just need to build it. As soon as I was bringing in enough money to finance a mortgage, I bought land that was nestled right on the outskirts of the suburb. It's surrounded by other large blocks and right in the middle of a green wedge that means it'll never be developed further.

One day, I'll figure out exactly what I'm doing with my life and build a home on it. I guess that future in my head might be closer than I thought it was, even if it does look a little different to what I always imagined. Two distinct futures pass across my eyes.

I much prefer the one where Audrey comes to her senses

and realises we are more than just something light hearted and casual. The one where we build a house on the land together, where the kids grow up riding quad bikes through the paddocks. It seems so distant though, and I can't stand the thought of the more realistic future. The one where I'm never good enough for Audrey, and no matter how hard I try, I'm not good enough for the babies either. In that one, I probably never leave the apartment, my land stays empty and I only see my children on weekends, if I'm lucky. That future hurts and I will do anything to make sure it's not the one I'm stuck in.

I just need to figure out how to prove to Audrey that I'm here. I'm committed. To her and to the babies.

Stuck inside my contemplation, I nod in response to Brendan's shock. I'm still coming to terms with the whole twins thing anyway, so I don't exactly know what else there is to say. He stares at me, waiting for a response. Although the ultrasound technician had explained missed twins in early ultrasounds—how the babies had developed in a way that one twin had hid the other from view during earlier scans—I still don't quite *get* how we are only just finding out. Surely there's a test pregnant women can do to find out how many babies are growing in there. Or should we have picked up on the signs because of how sick Audrey was feeling?

"You there?" Brendan questions, clicking his fingers in front of my face.

"I don't fucking know," I snap. "I wasn't even expecting one kid and now I'll have two. Never mind the fact I don't mean anything to Audrey. She keeps saying it's fun, but it still feels like more than that to me. I want it to be more than that to her too, but fuck if a relationship wouldn't make things a hundred times more complicated than they already are. I don't blame her for trying to keep her distance."

It all spills out, and my shoulders are a little looser with each admission.

"I don't know what to do, man."

Brendan throws his toolbelt into the back of his truck and turns to lean against it. With a foot propped up against the tire he twists his hands together. "Maybe you should have kept it in your pants?" he jests, shrugging a shoulder. The words jab at me all the same.

I throw my empty water bottle at him. "Bit late for that advice."

A shiny black pick-up rolls to a stop on the street in front of us, interrupting us and looking entirely out of place amongst the muddy worksites.

"What's your old man doing here?"

My shoulders pull towards my ears. Whatever the reason, I suspect it's something to do with me. Brendan bails out as my dad's too clean work boots step onto the pavement, calling out that he'll meet me at the gym. I don't have time to tell him I'm not sure I'm up for it. Don't have the brainpower to figure out why that is.

My father strides over to me like he is the king of the world, but that's always how he has held himself. Even when he was a young apprentice, I still picture him acting like he was the most important person on the job site. It's a confidence that never passed down to me, and I hate the way he makes me want to cower behind Baxter.

My traitorous dog bounds towards his granddad, stopping short of jumping up to leave messy paw prints on clean jeans. My dad leans down to pet behind his ears. His mop of too long, rough curls fall over his face.

"Son." He nods in my direction.

"Father. What have we done for you to grace us with your presence?"

It's been years since he has stepped foot on a site, outsourcing literally everything until all he has to do is sit behind a desk making outrageous promises to customers and demanding we make it work.

"I was hoping to catch you before you packed up for the day."

"And?" There's something, I can tell.

"Can't a father want to come see his son?"

I scoff. "Sure, but there's always something else with you."

"Do you have to be so sceptical?" His smile fades, a firm crease forming between his eyebrows.

"I am how you made me."

He doesn't try to deny it. Doesn't do anything to prove me wrong either. Instead, he takes a step toward me, grimacing a little when his boot squelches into the mud. I pretend not to notice.

With a hand now firmly clasped over my shoulder, my father drills his eyes around the job site before turning to face me again. He shakes his head. I want to squirm under his scrutiny.

"You're worth more than this, Mikey."

Here it comes. I step out of his grasp, folding my arms across my chest.

"I've been thinking about that job you sent my way. Noel, was it?"

"Noah."

"Right, well it's a big job. But it was all you. So, I think you should take the reins. Have a little trial run."

Trial run? My face must mimic the confusion I feel. I agreed to take on a job, not one as big as Noah's hotel.

"I'm retiring at the end of next year. At least, I want to. You know the business is yours when I do, whether you think you're ready or not. It's time you started to step up and learn how to handle things."

My brain is stuck on his first few words. *Retiring. End*

of next year. That's only—I count the months on my hand—fourteen months. Shit. He's not that old. Is he? I try to remember how old he was at his last birthday, but the man has been adamant he is 'only twenty-five' for the past however many years. I've lost track.

"Why?" I cringe at myself, hating the way that was the best question I could come up with.

Shoving his hands into the pocket of his polar fleece jacket, he shuffles his feet, stirring up the mud under his boots. I watch as Baxter plays between his legs, slowly coming to terms with just how soon my father's planned retirement is.

"Your mother and I want to travel. Not just up the coast, but really travel. Buy a caravan, explore the country. See Uluru. And we want to do it while we are young enough to get around."

"You want to become grey nomads?" Dad and I used to laugh at the older couples whenever we would pull into a campground when I was younger. My mind races, trying to find the moment he decided he wanted to be one.

"It's always been a dream. And besides, I'm done here. I'm proud of this company, but I'm ready to move on. I won't sell it off, though. *Can't* sell it off. There's too much of me in every qualified builder that worked their apprenticeship by my side. Too much of my life in every contract the business holds. Which is why I need you to run it." His features slacken as he drops his gaze to the ground, shaking his head. "Please," he adds.

The back of my neck itches. Gnawing at the inside of my cheek, I swallow down the lump in my throat. Sure, I've known he wanted me to run the business, but he never really explained why before. At least not like this. It doesn't matter when he decided he wanted to be a grey nomad. It doesn't matter how soon he wants that to happen. He won't do it if I don't step up. For how many years did he push back his plans, waiting until I thought I was ready?

I still don't think I am, but guilt runs my veins dry. It's time for me to start trying.

A quick puff of air escapes my lips.

"Shouldn't I start with something smaller? The next town home, maybe? Something cookie cutter."

Dad stretches his arms out, gesturing around the site, towards the near-finished frame. "This? Whether you believe it or not, you could put this puzzle together in your sleep. You need to challenge yourself, and it's best to do that while I'm still around to help you if you really do get as stuck as you think you will."

"But—" I stammer, trying to come up with another excuse. I'm ready to start trying, but Noah's job is *full on*. The architects and engineers are drawing up custom plans, the framing will have to be done piece by piece, on the job site. No prefabricated walls ready to be propped up and nailed down. It's a big job. Too big to be mine. "But Noah is a friend," I stammer out. A stretch, calling Noah a friend, but maybe the excuse will work. "It would be a conflict of interest."

"You are not a bloody defence lawyer. We do jobs for mates all the time."

"But—"

He closes the gap between us, squaring me in when he places both hands on my shoulders. He squeezes firmly but with an unexpected kindness that throws me off guard. My spine relaxes.

"No more buts, Michael."

Chapter Eighteen

AUDREY

My stomach aches. Not in an 'I'm pregnant and I'm worried something is wrong kind of way', but in a dull, exhausted kind of way. In the way that it has since the day I found out there are two babies growing inside me, pushing against my organs and stretching my skin.

Annoyingly, it feels like my whole body has swollen with the news. I assume it's normal for my belly to be larger with this pregnancy than it was with Maisie, what with there being two babies in there and all. The midwives assure me that my weight gain—across my middle and everywhere else—is well within the expected range. Still, knowing it's 'normal' doesn't make me feel any better about how my bracelet doesn't swim around my wrist like it used to, or how I haven't been able to wear my grandmother's ring in weeks.

My feet hurt, too. Swollen and pressing against the usually comfortable fabric of my sneakers. Although that's to be expected.

"Can we sit?" I grab at Michael's arm, steering him towards the empty bench in the middle of the crowded shopping centre.

His forearm is tense from supporting our shopping bags. My fingers twitch against the corded muscle as I use him to hold my balance while I lower myself down to sit. Our bodies were always starkly different, but now, with my growing pregnant belly and the roundness somehow added to my face, the difference is startling. He's so … fit. But more. Toned, muscle on muscle in a way I never thought I would find attractive. But God, I do. I did. I shouldn't.

"I'll be back," he says before rushing off to the juice stand opposite us.

The very first time we met, long before we got ourselves into this … *delightful* … scenario, I thought Michael's physique was intimidating. I was overwhelmed by the strength in his size, taken aback by how small my hand felt in his. Those unsteady feelings were swiftly forgotten when he pressed a hand against my lower back and lent down to whisper in my ear. My heart raced; my core throbbed with anticipation at what he might be able to do with his body.

I was right, and the pure sexual chemistry was, at first, the only reason I kept going back for more. I craved a connection, and the physical one between us was something nothing, or no one, could measure up to. I knew it wasn't going to last forever, but I didn't care. I let the immature moments slide, I didn't let myself worry about how he had no ambition or how he still preferred being out all night to rest filled weekends. He's young, he has a right to those feelings. And it was just a fling.

Slowly, he started to show me that maybe we could be more than that. He traded a boys weekend with a winery lunch with me. He met Maisie. And sure, looking back I can see I was wrong to introduce him into her life when I did, but he *wanted* to be involved. Until he didn't.

I have to remember how much it hurt when he showed me that we were never more than casual to him. Something that could be so easily thrown to the side when the reality of my life became too much.

Fun. That's all I am. That's what we said after Callum's housewarming.

Even so, I can't help but slink down in the chair to rest my head against his chest when he comes back and sits next to me. His heart stammers, so much so I wonder if maybe he feels this new connection between us, too.

"Here," he says, placing a small cup of chopped mango in my hands. "They didn't have any forks."

I pinch a piece in between my fingers and pop the juicy flesh into my mouth. "Mango?"

"Twenty-two weeks. I just don't know if they'll be smaller, since there's two of them. The app didn't say."

"I suppose they might be, but it's okay. Thank you."

I work to catch my breath as I nibble at the mango. I've walked too far today.

"Do you think we got everything?" I ask once my little cup of food is empty.

Reading the list off his phone, Michael nods, his chin resting against my head. "All the big stuff is done: cots, pram, car seats. I'll come back with the truck during the week to pick it all up. A million tiny clothes, bottles. If there is anything we missed, it'll be stuff I can run out to get you when we realise we need it. Plus, we have time."

He's right, we do have time, but I feel like it's a train racing express down the track toward my due date.

"I'm sure we missed something." Like the whole fall in love, move in together, get married steps that usually come before having a baby.

"Audrey, it doesn't matter. We've done a lot. And my feet hurt so I can only imagine how yours must feel."

I relax further into his embrace. "They feel swollen," I admit. "All of me feels swollen, all the time."

"Then let's go home."

I'm too tired to question who's home he is talking about. As we walk back to the car I'm too focused on how he keeps an arm around me to care. Even as he plants a kiss on the top of my head before opening the car door and helping me in, I don't ask. Because ultimately, we don't have a home together and that thought hurts.

The tension in my shoulders drops when Michael pulls into my street. The familiarity of my own home, the babies' home, induces the deepest breath my squashed lungs can muster. And it's not that I want to rush into living with Michael when we are barely in anything that even resembles a relationship, but I don't like thinking about how he won't be here. I'll be alone, dealing with not one newborn baby, but two. Baby Maisie was hard enough, this is going to be … rough.

I shake off the shiver that runs up the length of my spine.

Leaving Michael to sort out all the bags in the back of his truck, I hobble up the hallway to flick the kettle on. Once I've made two cups of tea, I carry them to the couch and sit down, resting my feet on the coffee table. The coffee table with sharp corners and a lower shelf full of Maisie's books. My gaze flies across the room at all the little changes I made when Callum moved out. The fiddle-leaf fig growing happily in its giant ceramic pot in the corner, tiny pebbles covering the roots. The candle and dried flower arrangement on one side of the TV, and the Lego succulents on the other. The open entertainment unit with Maisie's games console and my outdated DVD collection. None of it is baby proof. *I knew we were forgetting something.*

I stretch forward, my back aching as I reach for the pen and paper Maisie left on the coffee table. 'Baby Proofing', I write at the top, followed by a list of all the things I just noticed. From my spot on the couch, I think my way through every room, jotting down everything a baby might get hurt on, choke on, or destroy.

"Did I ever tell you your house is beautiful?" Michael calls down the hallway after dropping the last few bags into the spare room I'll need to turn into a nursery.

I tap my pen against the paper. It is, as a real estate agent I can see that. But it's not me. It's not mine. "I'm trying to make it feel more like a home, but no matter what I do it feels stuck in the past."

Michael jumps down onto the couch beside me, startling me with his unnecessary force.

Keeping my feet on the coffee table, I turn my upper half to face him. The baby proofing to-do list rests in my lap.

"I wish it wasn't so modern. I can add as many coloured pillows or arty prints as I like and it still feels a little too much like a museum of recent history. You know?"

Of course he doesn't. He's never been in a serious relationship and still lives in a bachelor pad complete with a home gym system worth more than all Maisie's toys put together. He has no idea what it's like to feel like your house isn't your own.

"I get that." His response surprises me, and I wring my hands in my lap above my list.

"It makes me feel so ungrateful. As much as I appreciate Callum letting me keep it in the divorce, I wish I could move into somewhere new, something that feels like mine."

"So, why don't you?" he asks.

"What, move? I couldn't. I can't. Between trying to sell this place and looking for somewhere new, I doubt I'd have the time. Let alone finding a bank to finance the inevitable mortgage once I pay all the taxes."

He grumbles, deep in his chest. The sound brushes over my skin, leaving goosebumps trailing over me.

"You deserve to be happy, Audrey." He mumbles, leaning forward to rest his elbows on his knees. With both hands, he pushes his long beachy hair off his face.

"Unfortunately it's not that simple." I snap the words out, harsher than I intended.

Michael sighs, shaking his head in his hands. He pauses when his head tilts towards my lap.

"What are you writing?" Grabbing the paper he sits up.

"Another to-do list to add to the pile," I say, trying to take it from him. "There's so much to do and I'm running out of time."

Michael leans away from me, until the list is out of my reach. He scoffs as he reads through my messy handwriting.

"I don't think you need to worry about all this right now Audrey."

A heavy ball of stress hangs in my lungs, fighting against each breath I take.

"Michael, it's not a joke. These are all things I *do* have to worry about. I won't just have one baby crawling around, I'll have two. Plus Maisie. I need to make sure the house is safe so that when I'm inevitably in the other room with twin A I'll know twin B won't end up electrocuting himself or choking on a pen lid."

Reaching forward, he places the list on the coffee table and grabs my feet, pivoting me until my legs are across his lap. I squirm, fighting against the intimacy of our position. But it's comfortable, and he trails his fingers along my calves with just the right amount of gentle pressure until I'm falling back to rest my head on the arm of the couch.

"I know it's serious, but we have time. You're not due for another four months, and aren't babies immobile for like six months? I promise I will get all of this done."

I push my legs against his lap, the ball of stress growing until it presses against my stomach. A curse flies out of my mouth with my exhale.

"When though, Michael? I can't expect you to give up every RDO and weekend helping me sort my shit."

"What if I want to?"

He tries to still my legs, holding my feet and pressing his fingers against my soles. The tightness spreading through my body eases, but comes flooding back when I look up at him.

His cheeks are red, and he turns away from my gaze before I can read the look in his eyes. Stretching his hands above his head, he pulls his hair together, tying it into a messy bun at the nape of his neck.

"You don't."

"I do. Believe it or not, Audrey, I *want* to spend time with you. When you told me about the baby … babies … I promised I would be there. That I would help in every way that I can. I meant it then and I mean it now. And believe it or not, I like spending time with you. A lot."

He shifts, until my legs are no longer in his lap but pinned between his knees. My breath catches as he lowers his body over mine. Heat pools, everywhere, at the memory of him leaning over me. At how our bodies danced, at how he made me see stars, over and over again, every time we were together.

Fun. I have to remember.

"There's something here, Audrey. Maybe it started out as something casual. But it's not like that now. It's so much more."

His voice is guttural, sending the heat swirling through me right between my legs.

"You just think that," I choke out, my own voice husky and breathless.

"I don't, Audrey, I *know* it."

He crashes our lips together. I hesitate, torn between what my head says, my heart thinks, my body wants. I want the fun. I want the release. I want to believe his words. My head screams that it's just hormones and he doesn't really mean it, but I ignore it.

I kiss him back, twisting my arms between us until I can

clasp his face between my hands. He groans, pressing himself into me. His erection rubbing against my clit through the fabric of our pants. I run my tongue along his lips, and when he opens his mouth, I do the same, until our kiss becomes a frenzy of exploration and passion. He nips at my lower lip and a wave of pleasure rushes through my veins.

"Fun," I whisper, mostly to remind myself.

Michael growls in response, pulling away from the kiss to look down at me. "No, more."

With one hand still holding his body weight, he brings a hand down to skate up my shirt, pausing below my bra. I arch my back, urging him to touch me.

He brushes a thumb across my swollen nipple, his tender touch sending fire through me. But then he stops. He pulls me up until we are both sitting, panting shared breaths.

I bite my lip, scrunching my nose when he pulls back from our embrace.

"Fuck," he mutters. Sucking in a long breath he pulls my hands into his.

"I want so much more than some casual release with you, Audrey. For the first time ever, I want *more*. I want it all. I want to show you that first. Before we …" he trails off, but his unspoken words ring in my ears.

"I want to believe you." The words hurt me, and I can see the pain in his eyes, too.

"Then I'm going to do everything in my power, every day, until you know it's true."

And I can't explain why, but I believe that.

Chapter Nineteen

MICHAEL

The cool spring breeze whips through my hair and I curse when I realise I don't have a hair tie within arm's reach. There's usually a couple looped around one of the straps on my toolbelt, but that's safely nestled on the passenger seat of the truck, a few hundred metres up the gentle slope of the winery. The business shirt—fresh off the rack of the store I stopped at this morning—scratches at my neck.

Paperwork flicks in my hands as I try to find the printout I need. Finally finding the sitemap I printed three sizes too small, I shuffle the other pages, managing, only just, to keep a grip on them all. No one told me there would be so much paperwork. No one thought to say 'hey Michael, get a clipboard so you don't lose everything in the bloody wind.' No one knew I was so damn thick that I would print a site map so small I can barely read the font.

My eyes squint, from the sun casting rays so bright the white paper is glowing, but also in a vain attempt to read whether the gradient of the slope is eleven per cent or seventeen per cent, or for all I know, zero. It's not zero though, at least I know that much. I can tell by the way my right leg is bent from my position on the rolling hill.

With my eyes scrunched, brow furrowed, and shoulders so tense they might as well be touching my ears, I'm sure I'm the picture of cool, calm and collected. Just what Noah needs for our meeting. When he asked me to quote on this job, I doubt he realised he would become my father's guinea pig.

My big test. I wonder if it's too late for him to back out. How much of his deposit would he lose if decided not to play along with my father's games? Too much, I hope.

"You look like you need glasses."

His playful jab works, loosening the tension and somehow earning him a laugh. Well, a fraction of a laugh. A slight, raspy exhale of breath, followed by the corner of my mouth pressing into my cheek.

"We have two printers in the office, one for all the big sitemaps and architectural drawings, and one for your standard contracts and letters and stuff."

"And you used the wrong printer?"

My shoulders finally drop, resignation taking over my body until I'm drooping forward. "Can't even print something right," I mumble.

Straightening my back, I look across to Noah. His black pants and dark shirt look like they were tailored just for him, their boldness creating a contrast against the bright blue sky and green as paint grass. He stands with his sleeves rolled up, his hands propped in the pockets of his pants, and he looks … important. He might not have told his friends that he owns the winery, but he sure as hell looks the part. Guilt gnaws at my bones that he has to put up with me and my too tight shirt and too small paperwork.

Changing my grip on the papers so I can hold them with one hand, I use the other to sweep my hair out of my face, tucking it over to one side. The heat from the sun burns at my ears.

"Look, I'm sorry you got stuck with me. My dad wants me to … I don't know … see my own potential or some shit, but it's not fair that your massive project ends up with such a loose cannon of a project manager."

He shrugs, tipping his head to one side until his ear just about touches his shoulders. "Everyone has to start somewhere. Seems kind of full on that he would throw you in the deep end, but I guess he has his reasons. Let's go inside, we can look at the plans on the computer."

Noah's office is nestled behind the bar of the cellar door. The rustic wood and metal fittings from the open space carrying through into the small corner room. A wide steel framed window looks out to the sloping winery. Beyond it the sweeping hills of the Mornington Peninsula carry the view away towards the bay. It's beautiful, but the finite details inside the room call for my attention. Exposed wooden beams run the length of the slanted ceiling, and a barn style sliding door separates the room from the bustling restaurant.

"The architect designed something more modern for the hotel space," I muse out loud as Noah moves behind the large cement topped desk to turn on the computer.

"I think the words I used were sophisticated and classy."

"You don't think it'll be too … different?"

It looks good. The architect's drawings, even in their too small prints tucked under my arm, are clean, refined. Sharp lines and angles, smooth finishes, and not a hint of the rustic charm the cellar door building holds.

Noah's face scrunches as he sits back in his chair. His arms drape across the armrests and he stretches his legs up onto the desk.

"Sit down." It's an invitation, not a demand, but I do what he says anyway. My body tenses, on edge and fully aware that in this space, he is in charge.

Something sizzles in the air for a moment. I crossed a fine line I hadn't realised was floating between us. The fraction of an inch where this relationship cuts between being friendly to being strictly professional. I got too comfortable with Noah, stuck back when we were chatting in Callum and Cassidy's backyard instead of moving forward in a professional way.

'*Never tell the client they are wrong.*' I hear my father's words as clearly as if he were in the room. Remembering the last time I screwed everything up.

I hold my breath. Waiting for Noah to tell me I'm wrong or send me out or cancel the contract.

"Breathe you idiot." Noah throws a scrunched up sticky note at my face. "I will not have you panicking yourself to death in my office. I don't need to deal with that."

"Sorry I … um …" I stammer. "I shouldn't have said that. Do you want to look at the plans? The architect had you on the emails."

"You're right though. I probably used the wrong words. I want it to look sophisticated, but it still needs to be cohesive with the look of the restaurant."

"We can request changes. That's what this meeting is all about. These are just the first designs." I place my stack of paperwork on the table then lean back to settle into the leather armchair.

Noah turns his monitor so we can both see the site map now displayed. He clicks away at the mouse, zooming in on the image and cursing when he reaches into a drawer to pull out a pair of thin framed, square glasses. "Don't you dare tell anyone."

The air I'd been cautiously holding in my chest releases with a laugh.

"Shut up."

"I didn't say anything." I throw my hands up. With my eyes wide, I seal my lips, miming the action of zipping them closed.

"I hate them, but I can't read anything on this damn screen without them."

"They look … smart."

Noah rolls his eyes, turning back to the computer to pull up the plans.

We blunder our way through the confirmations together. Noah asks questions I can answer, and questions I can't. But there are things that he doesn't know either. For a moment, it feels like we are just two guys, faking their way through their big fancy jobs.

"It feels like that all the time," Noah tells me when I voice my thoughts. "Every day I learn something new. Or have to relearn something I forgot. But that's how everything goes. I just do my best every day. That's all you need to do, and if you get really stuck, I'm sure your old man wouldn't mind if you asked him a question. Hell, the guy's going into retirement, he will probably love feeling needed every once in a while."

Later, when we have a whole list of requested changes for the architects and Noah's signature is signed across every page, we head back into the open space of the cellar door. The lunch rush cleared away while we were scouring the plans, but a few groups remain scattered around the space. The wide folding patio doors have been opened, extending the space into the outdoor area and kids run around on the grass while their mother's sit sharing a plate of food.

Noah heads behind the bar to grab us each a drink, and I choose a table in the corner, as far away from the outdoor space as possible. Even still, the laughter of the children floats through the space and invades my ears. Cheerful chirps and squeals that sure, are pleasant, but also cause my fingertips to tingle and dig out a well in my stomach.

"You'll be fine," Noah says as he slides into the chair opposite me. "Both of you."

I furrow my brow and fold my arms across my chest. "I don't know what you're talking about."

He makes a show of following my line of sight before turning back to me and picking up his wine. "Cassidy told me about the babies."

I choke at her name, regret at how I treated her hangs

low in an empty space under my ribcage. "Did she say anything else about me?"

Noah picks up his drink, twisting the stem of the glass between his fingers to make the deep burgundy liquid swirl.

"She said you were a jerk, but that, as long as you're not a jerk to Audrey, the past doesn't matter. Something about hoping time has treated you well and that everyone is entitled to a second chance."

I nod. It's about as good as I can hope for.

"It's a Pinot Noir, by the way," Noah says, holding his glass up in a cheers motion before taking a precise sip. The wine lingers in his mouth before he swallows.

"I'm not drinking it like that."

"And I can't help it anymore."

I smell the wine before drinking it, uncertainty tingling my tastebuds. I've never been a fan of wine unless it was hanging in a silver bag from the clothesline. And it's been a long time since I've been quite *that* reckless.

Tentatively, I take a sip. It tastes like a lot, all at once. Cherry and wood and berries. The flavour sticks to my tongue even when I swallow the liquid. And I don't hate it. I take another sip, longer this time as I appreciate the full flavour as it swirls a little in my mouth.

"Not bad, hey," Noah jests.

Chapter Twenty

AUDREY

My stomach twists. Again.

This time, the pain comes like a wave. Nausea first, followed by a heat that flows through my body, settling in my belly and causing every muscle in my body to tense. Then, like the tide pulling the water back into the ocean, the pain recedes. Only I'm left crouched over in my chair, willing my throbbing heart to steady.

I'm just dehydrated, that's all. If I can just get to the kitchen and have a glass of water, then I'll lay down for a little before I have to go pick Maisie up from her playdate. I'll be fine. *Right?*

I repeat the words to myself as I use the windowsill to pull myself off my stool. The sunlight streams into the room, leaving bright angles on the far wall. My easel stands just outside the blinding ray, the almost finished painting for Cassidy sitting delicately on the stand. If I could just focus, I'll be able to get it done. If I can get it done, I'll be able to cross it off my list and start worrying about the next thing. And the next.

The mental to-do list I've been carrying around grows longer every day. Wash all the clothes we bought for the babies, put sheets in their cots, pack the hospital bag, get the car seats installed, practice folding the pram, remember how to swaddle a baby, buy zip up swaddles instead. On and on and on.

But right now, I need to find a tiny sliver of calm. I hobble to the kitchen.

Reaching over my head to pull a glass from the kitchen

cupboard, my stomach twists once more. Everything is tight and tense and painful. I try to breathe through the pain, but panic steals the air from my lungs. This can't be happening. Not yet.

The pain recedes, leaving a sweaty film over my skin. I reach to the counter for support, wishing I had someone to lean against. Wishing I had someone to whisper in my ear and tell me everything was going to be okay. Wishing Michael was here. Somehow knowing that he would know what to say.

Despite all my reservations, despite how immature he might seem at times, he has managed to surprise me over the past couple of months. He showed up, fully, after the shock wore off, and I'm grateful for that. Before I found out I was pregnant, I would have laughed if someone had told me Michael would make a great dad. He was goofy and spontaneous and flirtatious. Nothing like the nurturing father I would have wanted for my future kids.

I hate that my ex-husband set a bar so high, hate that I will always compare others to him. But little by little, Michael has proved my cautious nature wrong. He might not be the typical, settled down and ready to step up father-to-be, but that's okay. Instead, he works hard every day to be everything that I need. To learn how to be better. He's changed.

Pulling my phone from my cardigan pocket, I limp my way to the couch and call him.

"What's wrong?" He answers on the first ring, his voice two pitches higher than his usual timber.

"I think I'm having contractions." Saying the words out loud sends a new rush of panic over me. It's too early. I'm not packed. We didn't buy any premature sized clothes, only the 'tiny baby' onesies and not the 'born seventeen weeks too soon' ones. The car seats aren't in the car. *Fuck,* will the babies be okay. What's the survival rate for babies born at twenty-three weeks?

Michael asks questions but the line goes static in my ear. The room spins. My voice shakes when I try to answer him.

"Audrey? Are you home?"

My lips tremor as I hum an agreement, unable to form words.

"I'm coming."

My cheeks become wet as the tears pooling in my eyes spill over. I hum again, sobbing through shaky breaths.

Michael stays on the line as he calls out a rushed good-bye to whoever he was with. He stays on the line while the phone connects to the Bluetooth in his car. Even though I do nothing but sit and sob and quietly panic, he stays on the line, whispering reassurances I don't really hear.

He bursts through the unlocked front door, never breaking his stride until he drops to his knees in front of me. And only when he has one arm wrapped around my waist does he finally end the call.

"You came," I sob.

He lifts up higher on his knees, surrounding me with his arms and pulling me close. I relax into his embrace, clinging to his arms until my fingers tingle.

"How many?" he asks. "And how often?"

I try to count backwards in my head but lose track with each gasping breath.

"I don't know. A few. One earlier this afternoon but I thought it was just a cramp. A few more since then. Scattered, though, I think. It's too early. The babies."

"I'm going to call the hospital. Keep breathing."

With one hand drawing slow, gentle lines against my spine he calls the hospital. I focus on the trail of goosebumps he leaves behind with each stroke, following the movement with my breaths. My head falls against his chest.

He relays what I told him to the midwife on the phone, then stands as he hangs up.

"When was your last contraction?" he asks.

"While you were on your way over here."

"Okay, wait here." He squeezes my hand before walking away down the hall.

My heart begins to race as soon as he steps out of the room. Nausea rifles through me, but Michael returns after only a few minutes, bringing with him an unexpected calm, and a duffle bag over his shoulder.

He helps me stand and guides me to the front door, locking it behind us. With a hand on my back, he takes my weight as he helps me into the car and leans over me to do the seat belt up. Before closing the door, he cups my cheeks between his hands and plants a kiss on my forehead. He holds me still, lingering with his lips against my skin until another tightening in my belly makes me cringe.

This one is somehow less intense than all the others. The searing pain still slices me in two, but having Michael so close keeps me calm. His tender touch on my cheeks, his spicy wooden scent, his soft whispers in my ear. They swirl together, skating over me like the gentlest breeze and settle right over my heart. Then they seep in, along with every other emotion I'd been trying to deny.

I'm sobbing as the contraction subsides and I'm left to dwell on the love left in my heart. The love I have no time for right now.

Michael eases away from me, gently closing the door so he can step around to the driver's seat. When he climbs in, his hand falls right into my lap. Squeezing gently at my thigh.

I want to say something, anything. I want to tell him how I feel and I want him to remind me that he feels it too. Not just the undeniable attraction, but something *more*. I want to know if this is what he meant or have I romanticised each moment a little bit too much.

Before I can find the words—never mind build up the

courage—Michael pulls into the parking lot of the Women's Hospital. I hadn't even noticed us leaving the driveway. He rushes around the car to help me out.

We walk like a married couple would, his arm draped around my waist, a little too much of my weight leaning on him. I wonder if people will assume. I hope they do.

The same blend of bleach and citrus from the ultrasound clinic assaults my nose when we walk through the automatic doors. I cough it back and Michael turns to support me with both his arms. Another wave of tightening, somehow even less intense again, washes over me.

A midwife runs around the desk to help guide me into a chair. She asks questions and Michael answers, and then she leads us to a consultation room down a long hall.

She checks my blood pressure. I go to the bathroom to bring back a urine sample. I'm guided to the bed. It all feels like I'm watching someone else go into labour seventeen weeks early. This isn't my life; it wasn't the plan. But I have put all my trust in Michael. Trusting him to be my voice, trusting him to make the right decisions. Trusting him to be the adult when I'm not strong enough.

Tiny monitors held in place with a long elastic band are wrapped around my bulging stomach. A jug of water and a plastic cup are placed on the little bedside stand. I'm only half paying attention when the midwife tells me I need to drink plenty of water, and hands me a little remote with a solitary button.

"Any movement you feel, press here," she says with a smile. She turns to Michael to add, "And if she feels another contraction I need you to take note of the time, and how long it lasts, so we can match it to what the monitor shows."

She whisks out of the room with a promise to be back soon to check how I'm going.

The machine murmurs away. Michael seats himself at the

end of the bed. His muddy work clothes leave deep brown marks on the white sheets. Resting a hand on my foot, he sings under his breath. Something unrecognisable at first, but then I realise what it is, Twinkle Twinkle. The melody floats around the room, the deep rumble settling within me, adding another layer to this new feeling.

"Maisie is at her cousins' house." I remember, the guilt of forgetting sits heavily on my chest.

Michael picks his phone off the bed, and rifles through the duffle bag he packed to find mine. "I'll message Callum."

I wish I could hug Maisie. It wouldn't take away any of the fear, but there's a certain kind of comfort that your child brings, and I'd feel better with her in my arms. Michael wipes the tear away, humming the same melody.

The minutes tick by. I press the button once, twice, then a bunch more as the babies have a kicking match. My stomach tightens and just as he was asked, Michael makes a note of the time and duration on his phone.

"I don't know if you should include that one, it wasn't that bad."

He scrunches his nose, typing on his phone. "I made a note that it was mild."

When the midwife returns, she brings a doctor with her. I turn to Michael because if the doctor is here something *must* be wrong. He squeezes my ankle, then rubs small circles on the sole of my foot with his thumb.

The obstetrician explains that I'm not in labour, and my whole body sighs with relief. Michael looks up, pausing his gentle massage, no doubt to ask a question, but she continues before he has a chance.

"You were experiencing Braxton Hicks contractions. Probably pretty tough ones, by the sound of it. They can feel worse due to exhaustion and dehydration."

I think about how little sleep I've been getting; how

draining work has been and how I can't switch off at night, worrying about all the things I need to do. As a collective, all four of us look to the jug of water beside the bed. The still full jug of water.

"I want to give you a bag of fluids to get your hydration back up, but you need to stay on top of drinking water from now on. Having twins is incredibly hard on the body. You need to nourish it so that it can do the best job at helping those two babies grow for as long as possible."

I swallow down the lump forming in my throat. I hate needles. But I will do it. For them.

So, I squeeze my eyes shut and I squeeze Michael's hand as hard as I possibly can while the midwife inserts the drip. Once it's all set, she kindly covers my arm with a blanket, so I don't see the cannula.

"I'm sorry," I whisper to Michael once she leaves.

The cool fluid spreads up my arm, leaving tingles in its wake.

"You're not allowed to be sorry, remember?"

Chapter Twenty-One

MICHAEL

Slowly, as the fluid drizzles into her veins, Audrey gains a little of her colour back. But she still has a sorrowful look painted over her as we thank the midwives. She melts into the car seat while I drive us home, hugging herself and letting her head fall forward.

"I'm sorry I wasted your whole evening," she says as she steps into the house. Her hand rests on the door, as though ready to close it behind her after she says her goodbyes.

I step across the threshold before she has the chance. I take the door from her hands to close it, then twist the shutters to the entry window. The homey habit comes naturally, even for me, even here in a place that isn't my house but feels like home. Because Audrey is here. Because the babies will be too.

"It wasn't wasted."

She scoffs in disagreement behind me, pushing past me, towards the open layout of her kitchen and living spaces.

I follow her into the house. "I'm serious, I meant what I said about always being here for you."

Audrey pivots to face me and pulls her cardigan tight around her body. A flush creeps along her cheeks. "Well, thank you. I appreciate that you took me to the hospital. And I'm still sorry that it was all for nothing. I don't remember having Braxton Hicks contractions with Maisie." She pauses to take a long breath, leaning some of her weight against the island benchtop. Her head drops to look at her belly and a small piece of hair falls across her face. "Was Callum really okay with having her for the night?"

"He said he will drop her at kindergarten in the morning, you can pick her up like usual in the afternoon."

Closing her eyes, Audrey sighs. "I feel so bad for her. As if she hasn't gone through enough changes, now this? Now I can't even pick her up when I'm supposed to."

She runs her hands through her hair, tucking it behind her ears.

"Maisie is a bright kid, a caring one, too. She is already so excited for those babies, and there will be plenty of changes when they come, but for now I'm sure she was pretty excited to spend another night at her dad's, running up and down those stairs."

With her eyes closed, Audrey fights against the gentle smile on her lips. Her hands drop, pulling at the corners of her cardigan again.

"I feel like I should know what I'm doing this time, but this whole pregnancy has been so different."

"Well there are two in there, remember. I'm no doctor but surely that's going to make everything at least a little harder and more intense."

I step towards her, closing her in as I wipe my thumb over the tear that trickles down her cheek. I coast my fingers down her arm, settling my hand against her waist. The pink in her cheeks turns a brighter shade of crimson.

"Audrey?" I whisper, aware of the electricity that fizzles between us and the hesitation in her stance.

She pushes me back, moving to the side to turn the kettle on. Reaching above her, she pulls one mug from the cupboard.

"You don't have to stay. My stomach feels fine now."

In two short strides, I'm back in her space, reaching above her to take out a second mug. I place it on the counter beside hers and pop a tea bag from the canister in each.

"I know I don't have to, but I want to." I say the word with a shrug, trying—and failing—to keep my tone light-hearted and carefree.

"The babies are fine, Michael."

"I know."

"So, you can go. Isn't that why you're here? Because we thought something was wrong with them? But there's not. I'm just some idiot who can't drink enough water and worries over a little Braxton Hicks contractions."

Placing my hands on her shoulders, I turn her to face me. She keeps her gaze on the ground, so I use my fingers to guide her chin up. Her blue eyes sparkle, the wetness reflecting the light shining from the pendants hanging over the bench.

"You're not an idiot." I shake my head, pressing my thumb over her lips when she tries to rebut. "Is that really what you think? That I'm here because of them?"

She nods against my hand, blinking the tears out of her eyes. I wipe my thumb across her cheek.

"I'm here for you. And sure, because I am their father and I already love them too, but I came because *you* needed me. I'm staying because you had a rough day, and I don't want to leave you." I don't miss the way her eyes scrunch together when I say I love the babies. I hate the way the word 'too' slipped out after I declared my love for the babies, I wonder if she knows what I meant. I wish there was a way I could show her that wouldn't feel like jumping off a cliff.

"You don't need to stay, Michael. I'm literally going to have a hot drink, order a roast chicken and hot chips to be delivered, curl up on the couch, and binge watch repeats of Bondi Rescue."

"I love that show."

"Michael." She glares up at me. Her eyes are still scrunched, her arms still wrapped around herself, hands balled into fists holding her cardigan tight.

"Okay, I've never watched it. But I'm serious. I like spending time with you. I *want* to spend time with you. So, even if it is some reality TV show, I still want to stay. I meant what I said, every time I said I cared about you. That started long before I found out about the babies, and it will carry on long after they are born. And I know you want to fight it because you think it's just casual flirting and it's just hormones, but I know you feel something too."

The electricity buzzes, ferociously, like it's ready to split the house in two. The pendant light above us flickers, as though it somehow senses it too. I don't want to back down; I need her to understand. But … if she really doesn't want me here. I can't force that.

"If you really want me to go, I will." I pull my hand away from her chin, tucking it into the pocket of my work pants. With the other hand I pull the tea bag out of my mug and drop it back in the canister.

I take a single step backwards and turn on my heel to walk out of the kitchen. My shoulders roll forward as a deep stabbing pain cuts through my chest. "But you need to stop lying to yourself."

"What if it's too messy?" Her voice reaches me a second before she does. A gentle hand grabs my wrist, spinning me to face her again. "Relationships fall apart all the time after a baby is introduced, what if it's all too much and you walk away. I can't risk that. If I have to force down feelings and lie to myself, okay. But I can't risk an ending where my babies don't see their father."

My heart sinks. Is that really what she thinks of me? That I would walk away from my children? From her?

"I could never, ever walk away from those babies. Ever." I step so close our chests are touching, her stomach pressed into me. She looks up at me and I get lost in the ocean of her eyes. "And I would never ever walk away from you."

I close the fraction of a gap between our mouths, planting a firm kiss on her lower lip. I savour the moment. Waiting for her to push me away. When she doesn't, I kiss her top lip. Then each corner in turn. With a little extra confidence, I run my tongue along her mouth, groaning when she pulls her lips apart to kiss me back. It starts slow, building up like a steam train gaining speed and soon we are a tangle of lips and teeth and tongue. Exploring each other, understanding the unspoken words now floating between us.

The buzzing in the air recedes, replaced by a searing heat that radiates off us. Audrey pulls her cardigan off her shoulders, dropping it onto the back of a stool. She shifts on her feet.

I pull her body into mine, wrapping my arms around her waist and hoisting her up. Her legs wrap around me and I carry her back down the hall and into the bedroom. With more grace than I've ever managed, I hold her while I twist the shutters and turn on the bedside lamp.

Arms still wrapped around her, I sit on the edge of the bed. Audrey's legs fall over my thighs and she straddles me, wriggling as she gets comfortable between my legs. Her fingers stretch around the back of my neck.

"What are we?" The words tumble from her mouth on a deep exhale. Her chest heaves in anticipation or fear or worry or … something else I don't want to hope for.

I close my eyes, for once in my life thinking about the words I want to say before I say them.

"We are whatever you want to be. I will give you everything, all of me, all of my heart, my soul, and ask for nothing in return. But if you want to give me a little piece of you, I will cherish it for the rest of my life."

I swallow down the lump in my throat, blink away the tear that forms in my eye. It spills over, leaving a wet trail down my cheek. Audrey leans in and kisses it away.

"You can have all of me, too."

My insides flip at her words. I flatten my hands against her back, squeezing her somehow even closer. The small round of her perfect belly presses against me, a barrier between us but also, somehow, the glue that bound us together. Our foreheads touch and we breathe in sync, revelling in our confessions and soaking in the love that floats around the room. Neither of us said it, I know that, but I can feel it. And from the way she gazes longingly into my eyes and her deep, settled breaths, I'd guess she does too.

I plant another kiss on her mouth. Tender and caring and claiming. She kisses me back with a passion like never before, claiming me back and whimpering into me. I skate my hands under the hem of her tank top, pausing to caress her stomach.

"You're incredible," I whisper into her mouth.

Using my thumbs, I brush against the underside of her bra. She moans, arching her back and pressing her breasts into my hand. I run my thumbs over the thin padding, taking the soft mounds in my hands. Her head falls back, and she looks peaceful as I massage her chest, kissing down the front of her neck. I tug at the neckline of her top with my mouth, but lean back to pull it over her head when she moans. She reaches behind her to unclasp her bra and tosses it to the side. Her chest and cheeks fill with blush and her eyes widen. Hastily she leans towards me, hiding her beautiful body from me.

I kiss the top of her head, then nudge her back until I can kiss down her front again, pausing with my face between her breasts. I push her breasts together, enclosing my face in her cleavage. Her fruity perfume blends with the subtle smell of hand sanitiser from the hospital, and I soak it in. I could spend the rest of my life right here, and it still wouldn't be long enough.

Audrey shivers as I knead at her breasts, toying and

twisting her nipples until she is panting in my lap. She grinds herself into me. There's too much fabric between us, but the friction against my firm length has me groaning.

I turn my head and suck at her breast, wrapping my mouth around her firm peak. I tease it with my tongue, biting gently.

"Michael." My name is a moan on her lips as she arches her back, pushing her breast further into my mouth. I pinch her other nipple and her legs tense around my waist.

Heat pools all around us and my cock strains against the thick fabric of my work pants, aching to feel her.

"I'm going to …" she gasps, tipping her head back as a shudder runs through her body. Her mouth falls open in a tiny O and her chest heaves against my face. Rocking back and forth in my lap, she draws her pleasure out using the friction from our clothes.

When her legs relax, I wrap my arms around her back to pull her close again, kissing her forehead. She reaches between us to unbutton my pants, stepping off me so I can lift up and pull them off, taking my briefs with them. My erection bounces free and Audrey licks her lips at the sight. I tug her leggings down and she steps out of them slowly. Teasingly.

She pulls her lower lip into her mouth and … God, she is perfect. Every inch of her glorious body glows in the warm light of the lamp. Taking a step to stand between my legs, she grabs at my work shirt. There's no calm and collected or patience left in me. I rip it over my head. Tiny buttons snap away from their threads.

"Can we?" I ask, placing a hand back on her stomach while grabbing her ass with the other. I want to … God I don't think I've ever wanted anything more. But the babies …

"Yeah," she moans as she straddles my legs. "We can."

Audrey glides her pussy along my engorged shaft. The

motion spreads the wetness of her desire all over me and a grumble forms deep in my throat.

"Fuck, Audrey."

She freezes, positioning her entrance at the tip of my cock.

"I intend to."

As she impales herself on my firm length, I wrap my arms around her and pull her as close as I can. She kisses me furiously and rides my cock like she was made for me. Like I was made for her. My hands grab at her ass, her hips, holding tight to her. To this moment.

The gentle back and forth of her movements becomes frenzied, and when her lips start to tremble against mine, I take her weight off her. Bouncing her ass up and down in my lap, I slam powerful thrusts into her.

"Michael," she gasps, arching her back once more as another release flows through her. With her inner walls fluttering around my dick, my balls draw tight. My own orgasm comes hard and fast, sending me to oblivion and back.

It takes an age for our breathing to settle, and we remain in our firm embrace while our chests rise and fall as one. I brush my fingers along her back, and she tangles her own in my hair.

"Stay," she whispers in my ear.

So, I do. Because I will do whatever she asks, always.

Chapter Twenty-Two

AUDREY

The rest of November passes in a blur, edging closer to the end of the year. Creeping towards my due date; the date my whole life will be once again flipped on its axis. Maisie has orientation at her new school and I cry a thousand tears that she is about to become a big school kid. Spring gives way to a summer that already feels like it's going to make me roast.

And even though I'm slowly getting used to the idea of having not just one baby, but two, it still somehow takes me by surprise each time it comes up. The midwife giving me a separate flyer on positions to feed both babies at once, the old woman at the shops who meant well but commented on how big my belly was when I told her I was only twenty-five weeks pregnant, the unimaginable twisting and pulling when they start to kick against one another and fight for room.

Each tiny moment throws the reality of having twins back in my face until I'm hyperventilating.

My stomach feels heavier with every day that passes. My feet swell. My breasts fill out. My back aches. None of it is fun, but I suppose pregnancy never really is.

So, no, I did not want to celebrate my birthday. I did not want to go out for dinner and worry if I was allowed to eat the food. I did not want to sit uncomfortably in a restaurant chair, hating the way even maternity jeans dig into my waist after I eat a meal. I wanted to curl up on the couch, put on a movie, and fall asleep by nine p.m. pretending I wasn't another year older. No one cares when you turn thirty-three, and my birthdays have become more meaningless with each one I have.

Michael refused to let the day pass us by, though. It grated at my skin, the way he insisted we celebrate.

"Birthdays are the only day in the year you can celebrate you. You *have* to do something."

He had scrolled through event websites searching for the perfect—low key—way to celebrate.

I huffed, turning my back and calling for Maisie to come down for dinner, and I thought he had dropped the subject.

Only now, I'm sitting on my bed, waiting for him and Maisie to finish setting up whatever it is they have planned. The afternoon sun streams through the open windows. I follow a little sparkling piece of dust as it dances through the beam of light, wondering what it would feel like to be that carefree. To have nothing, and no one, depending on you, and nothing you ever had to worry about or think about or keep track of. What a life, to be a floating piece of dust, destined for the vacuum.

It's miserable, really, to compare my life to such a tiny, inanimate, speck. My shoulders droop. How did my life come to this? Is this baby blues coming early? Should I expect them to hit twice as hard since I'm having twins, the same way everything else has?

I'm probably overreacting. Turning my annoyance at Michael's insistence on making plans into a life-sized meltdown.

Maisie's giggles float their way down the hall, followed by Michael's low grumble.

"Can I come out?" I call.

Maisie's squeal of a "no" rings in my ears.

Those two are up to something, and as frustrated as I am, I'm also thrilled that they are spending time getting to know each other. Michael's plans for my birthday evening have been kept top secret. He wouldn't tell me what we are going to eat for dinner, or what activity he is setting out for us. He wouldn't even give me a clue.

The melodic *ding, ding, ding,* of the doorbell rings and I push off the bed to see who has come. If he planned a surprise party, I might kill him.

I'm still struggling to sit up when he barrels down the hallway to the front door. Before answering, he pokes his head into my bedroom.

"Soon," he says with a smirk, then blows a kiss and pulls the door shut.

I can't make out the conversation, but when he closes the door, only his footprints track back up the wooden floors. The smell of grease and salt wafts through the gap under my door.

"I'm hungry! Let me out!"

My whining is met with another squeal and a fit of laughter from Maisie.

"Almost done," Michael calls out. I fall back on the bed at his words, knowing I shouldn't lie on my back but doing it anyway. My eyes flitter shut to lessen the harsh stripe of light that cuts across the bed, and my face.

I breathe slow, the way the midwife showed me, and allow my tense muscles to relax against the soft pillow.

"Audrey?" I feel his whisper underneath my ear. By the time I coax my eyes open, Michael has stood up, and back. Maisie steps forward, one hand outstretched to help me up, the other clinging to a giant bouquet of fresh white lilies.

I roll to my side, then use the strength in my arms to push up to a seated posting.

"You have to come see!" Maisie bounces on the spot. I grab the flowers from her, then let her take my free hand to drag me down the hall towards the kitchen and living space.

Stepping out of the hallway, I freeze to appreciate all that they've done. The dining table has been covered with butchers paper, and three tiny easels are lined up on one side. A rainbow of paint tubes are scattered between the easels, and each 'place setting' is complete with a canvas, a paper plate, a cup of water, and a collection of brushes.

"Let me take these." Michael stretches around me, taking the flowers from my hands.

He unwraps them, then places the bouquet in the crystal vase sitting in the centre of the table. The *new* crystal vase.

Maisie wraps her arms around my leg and I lean down as far as I can to hug her. Looking up to Michael I beckon for him to join us. He envelops me with his arms, trapping Maisie between us. We sway a little, off balance in our three-way hug, but the moment is everything I ever wanted and more, and I never want it to end.

"Happy birthday." Michael plants a kiss on my forehead.

In response, a low grumble from my stomach cuts through the peaceful silence and we laugh together.

"Dinner first?" I ask.

Michael steps away, around the island bench to the platter of food. Fried chicken, hot chips, fresh rolls, and a decent side of gravy. And a cheesy cauliflower bake. The meal itself is nothing flash, but it means so much more.

"Hot chicken and chips," I mutter under my breath. My smile spreads wider. It's the one meal I've consistently been craving all pregnancy, and he remembered.

"Sorry it's nothing special," Michael starts as he serves our dinner. "I wanted something I knew you would enjoy and I'm not very g—"

"It's perfect."

He stands a little taller and the slight wrinkle between his brows flattens.

"I think we're running out of fruit," he adds, gesturing at the cauliflower bake. "At twenty-six weeks the babies are, apparently, the size of a cauliflower. I figured this might taste a bit better."

When he hands me the first roll, I devour it. But I take my time enjoying the rest of the meal. There's no need for small talk between the three of us, we just sit in comfortable silence as we eat my birthday dinner.

Maisie has only eaten half of her sandwich—and three servings of chips with gravy—when she declares she is full.

"Michael," she asks in her chirpy voice, "will you live here when the babies are born? Because you're their dad. Or will they go spend half their weeks at your house like I do with my dad?"

Michael and I pause, sharing a glance. He sucks in a quick inhale, letting it out slowly before he answers.

"The babies will need to stay with your mum while they are little. And I will be wherever she needs or wants me."

Here, I realise after he says the words. I want him here. I don't want to handle the sleepless nights and exhausting days on my own. But for him to live here … I don't know. It's like we've been taking baby steps this whole time, carefully adding layers to our budding relationship. But him moving in? I never wanted to fall into a relationship *because* of the babies and if they weren't a factor we wouldn't even be considering it. So, if he did, what would that mean for us? It would be a giant leap in our relationship that we wouldn't be taking if the babies weren't a factor.

He must see the thoughts racing through my mind, because he reaches past Maisie to hold my hand.

"But we haven't talked about it yet," he says, turning back to Maisie. "We can figure it out closer to when the babies are due."

I'm still thinking about it while Michael clears away the dishes, adding it to my list of things to do and figure out. When I sit down in front of one of the easels, my mind finally clears. I'm ready to get lost in the creative juices that flow as soon as I have a paintbrush in my hand.

Michael clears his throat before he sits down. "I thought we could all paint the flowers. They are lilies, which symbolise new growth and change. It seemed fitting for our lives right now." He twists a paintbrush between his fingers and adds, "I hope it's okay."

Reaching below the table, I place a hand on his bouncing knee. He stills the movement but continues to pull at the paintbrush in his fingers.

"Michael, it's perfect, thank you."

Maisie claps on my other side, demanding my attention. Using a paintbrush as her pointer, she gestures around the table at the paint tubes, spread in a perfect rainbow around us. "And thank you Maisie for putting all the paints out. I made a rainbow, see?"

"It's beautiful, Maisie," I say as I stretch my arm around her shoulders and pull her close.

Everything about this evening is perfect. I don't even care that Maisie stays up past her bedtime to finish her painting. We just sit and talk and joke and paint, and all my worries about what the next twelve months will bring slowly melt away.

Maisie drops her paintbrush into the murky water in her cup with a yawn.

"Finished," she sings as she jumps from her chair.

Squeezing her way onto my lap, she looks up at our paintings. Her's is full of abstract lines and paint that blends together in criss-cross strokes. There's a subtle hint of the bouquet's shape, blue resembling the vase and some white splotches in between the shades of green.

"I love it," I whisper in her ear. "I love how you chose to use blue for the vase."

"I love yours too, Mummy."

I hide my smile in her hair. My own painting is rushed, incomplete. I wish I had let the paint dry between layers to prevent some of the sections where the green has bled into the white flowers. But for something I created in only a couple of hours, I'm happy enough with it.

"How come you chose rainbow colours for the vase?"

Tilting Maisie to one side, I point at how the light reflects in the angles of the crystal vase.

"See there, how it shines like a rainbow when you get the light just right? That's what I was trying to show." I squeeze her tight adding, "Plus, I loved how you made a rainbow with the paint tubes and I wanted to use them all."

Maisie squeaks with a bashful smile and turns to Michael. His painting surprises me. It's far more refined and precise than I imagined. Taking no creative licence in his artwork, everything matches the bouquet in front of him perfectly. The exact number of leaves and flowers, the hints of white and blue forming the outline of the otherwise clear vase. Even the stray leaf that has fallen to rest on the table. It's good. Really good.

"Wow." Maisie's praise is a whisper as she stills in awe.

"Michael, this is …" I trail off in admiration, soaking in the beauty of his painting.

Shifting in his seat, Michael runs a hand through his loose hair. His chin tips down as the tops of his ears brighten to a sharp crimson.

"It's nothing. I messed up this flower here, and the vase is, I don't know, not right. And this leaf looks all wonky."

Using his paintbrush to gesture at all his apparent mistakes, Michael slouches down in his chair. I unwrap one arm from Maisie's middle and place it firmly on his arm.

"Stop it."

He turns to look at me, but keeps his chin low and shoulders hunched.

"Michael, mistakes are fine. When you look at the whole picture you don't notice them. This whole thing is incredible, you should be proud."

His chin dips in a sharp nod. "Art was always my favourite subject at school. But then I started working for Dad and I just never pursued it. It became something that a younger me used to do. I wish I had an art studio like yours." He gestures toward the sunroom where my easel and paints are permanently set up. "I'd paint every day."

"I thought you worked out every day?"

"Most days, less now than I used to. But I think I'd enjoy this more."

Maisie jumps in my lap, scrambling to climb over to Michael's knee. He lets her settle in place, then wraps a tentative arm around her.

"If you came to live here," Maisie squeaks, "you could use Mummy's painting room all the time."

"He could," I answer when Michael looks up at me for guidance. And after tonight, I think I kind of want him to.

Chapter Twenty-Three

AUDREY

I half expected Michael to leave once we had finished our paintings and I was in the midst of wrestling Maisie into bed. Thought he would take the opportunity to slide away and spend time doing whatever it is young adults do on Saturday nights.

But he stayed. No, he did more than stay. He helped. He convinced Maisie to brush her teeth, and told her about the time he wet the bed on school camp when she complained that she shouldn't have to use the toilet before bed *every* night. He brushed her hair for her and helped her straighten all the teddies in her bed. And he gave her an affectionate, almost fatherly, hug goodnight.

While I tucked her in and spun her dream catcher five times—and promised to spin it again before I went to bed— he cleared the dining table. He washed the paintbrushes and laid them flat on a towel to dry. He packed all the tubes of paint into their drawers in the sunroom. He even unpacked last night's dishes from the dishwasher, reloading it with everything that had accumulated through the day.

I walk out of Maisie's room with a yawn, pulling her door shut behind me and shuffling my feet back to the kitchen. Looking up from the dishwasher, Michael rakes his gaze over my swollen, exhausted body. His Adam's Apple bobs and his eyes darken as he beckons for me to come closer.

As though he can't wait for my waddling steps, he takes two long strides to reach me, wrapping me in his firm arms until I relax some of my weight into him.

"Thank you." I speak the words to his chest, not wanting to leave his warm, comforting embrace.

He pulls back, shaking his head. A grumble forms low in his chest.

"This was nothing. You deserved to do something special, but I know you didn't want to go out, I thought maybe—"

I stretch a hand in between us to put my finger over his lips. "It was perfect, Michael … this … everything."

I want to tell him that I love it all. I love how he thought about me and what I like and what I wanted when he came up with the plan for my birthday. I love how caring and protective he has become. I love how he thinks of me first and always acts with my best interests at heart. I love how he keeps his hand on my lower back when we are walking and how he wraps me up and holds me when I'm tired. I love how when he is around, I feel calm and safe and nourished. I love … him.

Shit.

Is that too much? Too soon? Is it hormones?

The words dangle on my lips, wishing to be out in the open. But Michael speaks before I have the courage to say them.

"Audrey, I have to tell you something."

Also shit.

My stomach drops and twists into an anxious ball of knots. I step back, wrapping my arms around my waist to try to hold the sensation in. I was about to tell him I love him. I was about to open my heart for him and now I'm terrified he's about to flee. I look down at my feet, only I can't see them past my ever-growing baby bump. I look at the vase of beautiful flowers. I look at the clean bench and the handmade card from Maisie stuck on the fridge.

I look anywhere but at Michael, waiting for the blow. Because of course it was just hormones and of course I'm reading into this more than I should have. Michael doesn't want what I have to offer, he's just here because he *should* be. And because it's fun. Only I'm starting to feel like it's more, and we are fast approaching the moment where the fun will be forced to end. My heart thumps so furiously I bet he can see my pulse in my temples. I pull my cardigan tighter.

"It's okay," comes out as a whisper as I nod to my stomach.

I get it, I want to say. I know.

But Michael laughs, a low chuckle that forms deeper in his chest than usual. He runs a thumb over the crease between my brows and wraps my face in his hands. Pressing my chin with his thumbs, he tilts my head up until I'm forced to look at him. His eyes are a deep chocolate brown, far darker than the amber colour the sun brings out, but they overflow with tears. He blinks the salty liquid away and I wipe his cheek with the sleeve of my cardigan.

"You went somewhere bad, hey?"

I nod, trying to hold back my own tears. My heart flips and races and stops and starts, and my hands shake.

"First, you need to know that this is not because of them, okay?" He places a hand on my stomach and the babies jump around underneath his touch. His face lights up at the feeling. "I love them. Already and always."

My silent tears overflow, hope blooming from the depths of my soul. A tiny seed of blackened doubt still floats somewhere in my gut, but it doesn't belong, so I will it away.

Michael wipes my cheeks and leans forward so our foreheads rest together. His shaky breaths become my own.

"Audrey, I don't just love them. This feeling started long before they came to throw us back together and even before I knew about them, I couldn't shake it off. And I know I messed up, again and again and again. I know I'm not the guy you would have chosen to be the father of your surprise babies, and I know you deserve so much more than some kid who can't seem to pull his life together, but I can't get you out of my heart. You're in my mind, my soul. You're everywhere. I love you."

He seals his final words back with a kiss. The hope that had bloomed through me erupts into the room, surrounding us in a cloud of overwhelming joy. My shoulders relax and I wrap my arms around Michael's neck to pull him somehow closer.

Our kiss is a tangle of lips and tongues and love. It's slow and tender and sensual and like nothing I've ever known or felt. We get lost in it, together.

Breaking the kiss despite Michael's whimpering protest, I rise on my tiptoes to kiss the soft spot behind his ear.

"I love you, too."

My admission unleashes something almost feral inside him. He doesn't hold back, scooping me into his arms to carry me down the hall. He places me in the centre of the bed, propped against the pillows, then stands back to admire me, laid out for him. Heat pools in my belly when he rips his T-shirt over his head and crawls over me. I run my hands along his firm chest and down his muscular arms. The veins bulge as he supports his weight over me.

"You're perfect," he growls.

I shake my head, pressing my lips together in a thin line. *I'm not.* The thought doesn't belong right now, so I don't voice it, but he hears me anyway.

He kisses my nose, my ear, my shoulder, the inside of my elbow, the side of my belly where the excess weight I've put on flattens against the mattress, my hips, my thighs. All the bits I don't like, all the bits I wish hadn't grown along with my baby bump.

"This is perfect," he says after each gentle peck. "This is perfect. This is perfect." And then, nestled between my legs he looks up with a goofy but charming grin, "You're perfect."

My core throbs at his closeness and my breaths turn heavy. "Michael," I moan, remembering what he can do with his mouth.

"May I?" His fingers dip below the waistband of my leggings. I push my hips off the bed so he can pull them down. He stares at what I'm sure is a very wet patch in the centre of my grey, boring, panties. Licking his lips he runs a thumb along my centre, pressing down on my clit until I'm trembling under his touch. Desperate for friction, I rock my hips into his hand.

He growls, dipping his head and using his teeth to tease me further. My hands reach to his head, fisting his hair as I grind against his face.

There's a tearing sound, a flash of searing heat, and then his warm tongue straight on my pussy. He tore my underwear clean off, but the thought only passes through my mind for the tiniest of moments. Because he devours me like a man starved, bringing me to the edge of oblivion. He swirls his tongue around my clit, flicking the sensitive bud over and over until I'm aching for more.

"Please Michael."

"My pleasure." He doesn't stop to answer, instead speaking the words directly into my pussy. His hot breath sending a fire through my veins. He strokes through my wetness, spreading it around before dipping his finger into the source. I gasp at the way he immediately curls up to find that delightful spot inside me. Teeth graze against the apex of my thighs as he pulls his finger out to add a second.

I'm trembling beneath him as he pumps his fingers into me, nipping and sucking at my clit until I'm soaring. Hot moisture pools as I tumble, releasing my grip on his hair to fall back into my nest of pillows. My head spins, my chest heaves.

Michael kisses his way back up my body, pulling my tank over my head as he does. When he reaches my mouth, the taste of my arousal on his tongue sends a new heat blooming through me. He kisses me the same way he devoured my pussy, like there is nothing on earth he would rather do. His hand is in my hair, his tongue exploring my mouth as he notches himself at my entrance. I lift my hips and he slides inside me, stretching me, filling me, owning me.

"I love you," he whispers as he presses in until I'm taking all of him.

I wrap my hand around his neck to hold him close. "I love you, too."

Our hips rock back and forth in sync. It's not rushed or frenzied, it's just … bliss, wrapped in each other's arms in the most sensual way. And when my orgasm builds, so does his. Until we leap off the cliff together.

"I want you to stay," I tell him later, after we have showered and curled under the blankets for the night. We lay on our sides, foreheads touching, hands clasped together, legs entwined.

"I thought that was a given when I brushed my teeth and got into bed with you?"

"I don't just mean tonight, I mean when the babies come. You deserve to see them, they deserve to be with you as much as they are stuck with me. And I want you here."

Michael nods his head against mine. "Then I'll stay."

Chapter Twenty-Four

MICHAEL

My father stands in his too-clean work boots, arms folded across his chest. The wind whips at the ends of his greying hair.

"Why am I here?" he complains, and I should have brought my mother for moral support.

Here is my block of land in Melbourne's South East outer suburbs. Close enough to Audrey's current house that the custody agreement she has with her ex would still be suitable. Maisie would still be able to go to the school they enrolled her in. *Here* is the place I want to build our future. *Here* is the land I bought when I was young and smart enough to know it was a good investment but dumb enough to not care about building on it. *Here* is exactly where the front door will be.

"Michael?" My father's grating voice snaps me out of the house I want to build and back to the mud I'm currently standing in.

"I want to build."

"It's about bloody time."

He's not wrong, but I shrug away the condescending tone.

"Start thinking about your floor plan and we'll set it all up," he adds. He throws his hand around in front of him before tucking it back under his arm and side stepping towards the car.

I'd bet he is itching to get back to his pristine office. When I first started working for him, he hated being confined behind a desk all day. He jumped at any chance he got to get outside and on the tools. Now though, he hardly ever shows at a job site unless things have gone terribly south. He prides himself on the way the business runs immaculately with him at the helm. All the right people in all the right jobs making sure every task is completed on time, and to the highest quality. Everyone except me. I still feel out of place at the project manager's meetings, despite Noah's winery build running seamlessly under my—somewhat questionable—guidance.

I still wonder if I'm cut out to run such a massive job, let alone the whole company. But Dad seems to think I'm doing alright, even with all the questions I've had to ask him, and Noah tells me I've done good. So, maybe there is hope for me yet.

Stepping onto a lone patch of grass still fighting the muddy sludge of the rest of the block, my father stares across the lot at me. His shoulders hunch against the wind. I shouldn't have brought him here for this conversation. Should have met him in his office where he is most at ease. Maybe the second and third parts of the conversation would go down a little easier.

My fingers twitch against the hem of my shirt as I try to find the courage to tell him everything. I shouldn't have waited this long, but the longer I put it off, the harder it gets.

"It's ah, not for me." I cough the words out before I can back out.

Unfolding his arms, Dad slips his hands into his pockets briefly before folding them across his chest again. His weight shifts between his legs and even with the distance he put between us I can see the wrinkles between his brow deepen.

Off at the back of the lot, Baxter howls. He runs back, tail between his legs as my parent's fluffball chases him down.

"Fuck, I knew I shouldn't have brought her here." My dad growls at the sight of his usually pristine white dog. Her fur is splattered with mud, just like Baxter paws.

"It'll wash off, I'll bring her back to your house in the tray of the ute, Baxter loves riding back there."

"She hates the tray."

"She'll survive."

He scoffs.

"So, if the house isn't for you … don't tell me it's for a girl."

I roll my eyes but my breaths come quick and my temples throb. Audrey is so much more than just a girl. She always has been. And I'm not dumb enough to imagine she'll never get sick of me. One day, when the babies are born and her pregnancy goggles are gone, she'll realise she deserves so much more, but I'll soak in every moment she lets me spend with her until then.

"Her name is Audrey." Hearing her name, even from my own mouth, helps chip away at the unease I had been feeling. My shoulders relax and I stand up a little taller. "She is … wonderful. She's ambitious and caring and thoughtful and she is the most amazing mum to the most incredible little girl and …" I trail off unsure how to say the next piece. The words get stuck in my throat so I push them down and let more of my love for Audrey spill out instead. "I wake up every morning and I think of her and I wonder what I did right for her to come into my life. Because honestly, Dad, I don't deserve her. She deserves so much more than I can give her, but at least for right now, she wants to share her time with me. I will count those blessings every day for as long as I have them."

My father tips his head to the side, a hand creeping out from under his arm to clutch his chest. A hesitant smile breaks through his stern gaze.

"You're in love."

My cheeks puff with my smile. "Yeah."

"Is she worth a house?"

"Dad, she is worth the world."

He steps over the mud towards me, throwing his arms over my shoulders. He slaps my back with pride, chuckling to himself.

My breath catches. "There's something else."

He leans back, his eyebrows rise towards his hairline as he jerks his chin for me to continue.

Now or never.

Sucking in a deep breath, I throw the words out in one long exhale. "She's pregnant. We are having twins. You're going to be a Grandad. Yes, it was a shock, and yes, I freaked out, and yes, I have no idea what I'm doing, but I'm *excited* and I'm ready."

They hang in between us, filling the air with my nervous energy and something cold coming from my dad. He closes his eyes, breathing deep into his lungs.

"Dad, say something."

He doesn't. He just nods slowly, eyes still closed.

When he finally speaks, it isn't good or bad or excited or angry. It just … is.

"Twins?"

I nod and he adds, "You're going to need a big house."

I'm late for my meeting with Noah, but it took longer to get away from the block, from my father, than I had intended. After the news he was going to be a grandad finally sunk in he was *almost* excited. Tentative, sure, but he didn't seem to hate the idea.

Birds chirp in the flowering gum trees that line the path from the carpark to the cellar door—and Noah's office. Children's laughter rises with the breeze—far gentler here in the hills than it was at the block—along with cheerful chatter and the clinking of plates and glasses. For once, I don't blame other people for having a good time. It's the perfect early summer day, one of the few weekends left before Christmas. Who wouldn't want to enjoy a delicious lunch paired with a succulent wine at what is fast becoming one of the most popular wineries this side of Melbourne? The crew has begun to prep the site for the hotel build, but even with the cordoned off jobsite there's still plenty of open space to enjoy the sun.

It's beautiful and it's peaceful and it's the place I finally realised my potential.

And, hopefully, it's the place where Audrey will agree to become my wife.

Emphasis on the hopefully.

I'm hyper aware of the chance she might say no, but I need to show her how serious I am about her. About us.

I'd considered telling my dad, but I was running on thin ice after the whole 'you're going to be a grandad' bombshell and I wasn't willing to risk falling through. Plus, he'd had enough shock for one day and he had one foot towards the car, ready to escape the wind and get back inside.

The barn style door to Noah's office is open slightly and when I approach, the distinct tapping at a keyboard gives away his presence. I poke my head through the gap instead of knocking.

"Sorry I'm late."

Noah looks up from the computer screen and whips his glasses off his face. I pretend I didn't notice, as per our informal agreement. He leans forward, clasping his hands together on the desk in front of him.

"I needed the time to get some dispatch orders in, anyway. You want to sit?"

I take the invitation and plant myself in one of the armchairs.

"I'm not actually here because of the build. Unless

you have any questions, then I can look into whatever. But I needed to ask you a favour."

Noah's face is stoic as he flips his palms over on the desk.

"Can you help me set something up? Here at the winery? Some nice spot on the grass or down the path where you can't see the building site? Something cutesy."

He clears his throat, and I swallow down the lump forming in mine. I wasn't expecting to feel itchy all over just trying to tell someone about my plan. I hate to think what I'll be like when I finally bring it to fruition.

"Go on …"

"I want to show Audrey that I'm not just here for the babies. That I want to be here for her. That I'm committed to her."

Noah's eyebrows dip, his mouth forming a tight, thin line.

"I want to propose."

He coughs. Clears his throat again. Opens his mouth to speak before closing it and leaning back in the chair. Crossing his arms he tips the chair back and forth.

"I love her," I add, in case it wasn't clear.

"I know you do. Does she know?"

"I told her."

"Did she tell you how she feels?"

I bounce in my chair a little, remembering how perfect the moment was. "She said she loves me too."

"And so … just like that you want to propose?"

I nod my head, a little too vigorously. Leaning forward to rest his arms back on the desk, Noah's face softens.

"Trust me when I say that it's best for you to wait. I … it's not fun if things don't go the way you planned."

I squeeze my fists against the armrests. "You don't think she'll say yes?"

"Do you?"

Every tense muscle in my body relaxes and I slouch down in the chair until my head tips against the low backrest.

"I think she'll say no," I admit to the ceiling. "But until she sees that I'm in this forever, I'm worried she'll always hold a piece of herself back. She says she loves me, but she is so hesitant to open up. I don't know if it's because of the babies or because of how I acted before I knew about the babies or if it's just because she doesn't know how she truly feels because her body is so full of lovey hormones. But I have to try something. And maybe she'll say no and I'm sure that will hurt, but at least then she will know, like really know, how I feel."

My knee bounces. My chest is tight and the room starts to spin. The edges of my vision blur.

Noah taps his knuckles on the desk. Without meaning to, I start to breathe to the sound of his tapping. The vice on my heart loosens and the room steadies. My vision returns to normal.

"I get it," he says when I have control of my senses again and look over at him. "But I still don't think proposing is the right idea. Especially at a winery when she can't drink. I mean, we make great food and the non-alcoholic wine is pretty good, but it's not the same when you can't taste the sampling."

"So, what do I do? How do I show her?"

He shakes his head. "I don't think you can. This isn't the kind of worry you can explain away. Her feelings are valid, and yours are too. You have to let her feel them."

I run my hands through my hair, scratching at the back of my head. "And I just, wait?"

He shakes his head again. "You keep showing up. Every day. Every chance you get. You show her with the little things. Bringing home her latest craving or remembering the show she wanted to watch. You go to her hospital appointments and those birthing class things and you remember everything they say. You take notes if you have to. You rub her feet when they are sore. You make her favourite warm drink before she even has to ask. You thank her and cherish her and honour her, and love her with everything that you do. And eventually the babies will be born and you'll keep doing all those things and she'll realise."

I can do that. I already do that, most of it, at least. I can show her.

"And then I ask her?"

Noah nods with a smirk. "Yeah mate, then you can ask her."

Chapter Twenty-Five

AUDREY

The map on my phone screen flickers, reloading as I drive past my destination for the fifth time. There are still no parking spaces along the street.

My chin tips up as I drop my head against the headrest, huffing. Gripping the steering wheel until my knuckles turn white, I turn up the nearest street to loop back around. Any other time, I would have driven a little further, parked up the street, or utilised the large parking lot behind the rows of shops. But I don't want to walk. I want the convenience of a fifteen-minute parking space so I can get in and get out without feeling bad when I inevitably shy away from the small talk. I want to take as few steps as possible to reduce the likelihood of my ankles swelling in the heat. But much to my dismay, the shopping strip is packed. It's to be expected, really, the week before Christmas.

It takes just as many laps of the parking lot to find an empty spot, and even then I have to chase down a woman carrying her loaded bags of shopping back to her car. The air in my oversized suburban SUV begins to heat as soon as I turn the ignition off. With no cool air flowing back into the space, it only takes a few seconds before the heat is unbearable. The summer sun glares through the windows, stealing away the breathable air only to replace it with a stifling dry heat that burns my throat. I step out, wanting to find relief but instead finding a muggy heat that sticks to my skin.

The babies flip in my stomach, and I wonder how much more of this I can take. My third trimester is only just beginning, but with two of them in there, my lungs are already as squished as I think possible, and the heat is only making it worse.

Cassidy's painting is propped in the rear of the car, but now that I'm parked a few hundred metres away I have no idea how to get it to the shop. It's too large for me to carry, especially now and certainly in this heat. In hindsight, I should have taken Callum up on his offer to pick it up, but I was determined to do this for myself. It was dumb really, not wanting to rely on my ex-husband. Considering the artwork is for his girlfriend and I can barely lift the thing up. Resigned, I pull my phone out to call Cassidy and ask for help.

When she doesn't answer, I have to search for the boutique's phone number. The phone rings and rings, and just when I'm about to give up and end the call, the receiver clicks.

"Thanks for calling Betty's, I'm Cassidy, how can I help today?"

"Oh, thank God," I sigh through the phone. "Cass, it's Audrey. I'm in the rear parking lot with the painting but I—"

"I'm coming, will I see you from the entrance?"

I look across the parking lot toward the boom gates. She might. "I'll walk down a bit so you can see where I am."

"Okay, see you in a sec!"

The line is cut short before I can respond.

I can't leave the painting to cook in the car, so I leave the boot open and waddle my way to the end of the aisle, thankful it's only a few cars down.

Cassidy's green summer dress floats behind her as she power walks into the carpark as I reach the end of the row. Her chocolate hair is scrunched on her head, and dark sunglasses shield her eyes. Her dark apron flaps against her legs, coming loose as she reaches a hand above her head to wave that she has seen me.

"Sorry." I puff the word out as she approaches but she shrugs off the apology.

Seeing my open boot, she heads over and pulls the painting out. It's not overly heavy, but the size is awkward, tilting off balance over her tiny frame. With the boot closed and car locked, I step toward Cassidy and help support the painting. Although she still carries most of the weight, it takes both of us awkwardly shuffling out of the parking lot and down the street to get the painting safely to her store.

A bouquet of scents hits me when we step through the open threshold and into her floristry cafe. Eucalyptus and florals mix with the deep aromatic smell of coffee and the sweet fruity flavours of all the baked goods on display next to the coffee machine.

Cassidy's friend from the housewarming steps out from behind the coffee bar cart to take my side of the painting.

"Thanks Amira," Cassidy says as they shuffle behind the long bench.

I say my own thanks and sit down on the edge of a low table scattered with buckets of flowers. My pulse races and my skin burns with the heat, but slowly under the cool flow of the giant overhead fan my heart returns to a steady rhythm and my panting breaths return to normal.

A young couple enters the shop as Cassidy and Amira prop the painting up against the wall.

Amira skitters over to the coffee cart and starts tinkering with glassware after taking the man's order. The coffee machine whirs to life. Cassidy excuses herself to help the couple, who are now admiring the wall of greenery along the back of the shop.

The space is exquisite. I'm not sure what I was picturing when Cassidy told me how she had grown her floristry business to also include the boutique, and how, with Amira's help and expertise, she added the coffee cart. I imagined a lot more pink, less native greenery, more cutesy decor and less exposed brick. But the rustic texture of the brick contrasts beautifully with the matte black fittings and the florals spread through the space. Most of the flowers are Australian natives, just like the Waratahs and Banksias I used in the painting. The low table I've made my chair, though, is full of more typical, brightly coloured flowers. Roses, Tulips, Dahlias and Gerberas in every colour of the rainbow.

It's overwhelming how beautiful the shop is. And it's inspiring to think that Cassidy created this all on her own. It refills that creative desire in my heart, threatening to spill over until I'm full from the inside out, ready to give up the career I've paved for my artwork. It wouldn't be the worst idea, and with every long day and painful interaction with my boss, I'm closer to deciding not to go back to real estate after my maternity leave than I've ever been.

The painting I created for Cassidy has been propped along the wall behind the counter, still wrapped as the women finish serving their customers. It was thrilling to finish the artwork and see Cassidy's payment hit my bank account. This piece will always be special to me.

"Can we open it now?" Cassidy asks as the couple leaves the store, iced drinks in hand, along with a posy of yellow flowers.

She yanks at the thick tissue paper and stands back with her hands on her hips. I can only see the side of her face, but her cheek puffs out as she beams down at the panting. I push off my makeshift chair, taking far too long to stand and shuffle my feet over to Cassidy.

"It's beautiful."

"Do you know how you're going to hang it?"

Amira chuckles from behind the cart. "Yeah, she is going to call her boyfriend to do it for us." Her hand slaps up to cover her mouth. A deep crimson tinge spreads to the tips of her ears as she looks over to me. "Oh my God, I'm sorry. Is that weird? Should I stop talking about her boyfriend? You know, because he is your ex and all?"

Cassidy grumbles. "Shut up."

Amira drops her hand to her front, wiping it on her apron. She steps out from the coffee cart and moves to throw an arm over Cassidy's shoulders. "Right, sorry. Probably weirder that *you* went on a date with her baby daddy."

I freeze. It's not news to me, Cassidy had mentioned it at the housewarming after all, but it's no easier hearing about it now than it was then. Come to think of it, it's probably harder now considering the new lines we've started marking out for our relationship. My stomach sinks and churns.

Cassidy turns to me. Her cheeks are brighter than Amira's ears.

"I promise it didn't mean anything. In fact, it was a pretty miserable date."

"Yeah, she *crawled* onto the couch afterwards. Moaning and whining about how bad it was." Amira nudges Cassidy, but her smile drops when she sees the agitation on my face.

I reach for the comforting edges of my cardigan, cursing myself when I come up short. It's too damn hot for anything more than my simple summer dress, but without a cardigan to wrap around me, I feel naked and exposed. I hug myself all the same.

"We just weren't right for each other." Cassidy's voice is soft as she tries to explain away awkward tension floating all through the room. "I was lofty and carefree and he was ... on a tighter time schedule."

"He had lunch plans. And dinner plans." Amira squeaks. Her mouth is tight as the words escape, and she throws a hand up to cover them again. "You know what, I've got some ... ah ... paperwork. Yeah, in the office." She scurries to the room behind the giant floral wall.

"He did," Cassidy says. "But from what I can tell, he has changed now. At the housewarming he might as well have been a different person. If it wasn't for the long blond hair and his gigantic muscles, I wouldn't have recognised him."

"The muscles, woah," Amira calls out from the back room. "Is he *ever* at home or does he live at the gym?"

I bite my lips together and nod, trying to ignore the pulling from deep in my chest.

"Amira!" Cassidy snaps.

I want to scream that it's not true. To tell her that he spends more time with me than he does at the gym. But I don't know if that's the truth. For all I know he probably does spend a lot of time there. He'd have to, for his muscles to still be as firm and delightful as they are. And the few times he's stayed he *did* rush off early in the morning. For work, he'd said, but maybe it was so he could go to the gym first?

"It's fine," I say instead, choking the words out through the pain and stepping towards the street. *It's not awkward unless I make it awkward.* Isn't that what I told myself when I first found out they had been on a date?

And it's still mostly true but finding out he also had plans with two other women on the same day has me questioning everything. I knew he had been with a lot of women before me. If that wasn't obvious by the expert way he knew a woman's body, he'd practically said as much when we first started to see each other more often. Long before the babies were involved and we spoke about our relationship the very first time. The exact words have erased from my memory but it was along the lines of him playing the field but finally feeling like he found the right person. I'd brushed it off as cheesy but now? Now it feels like a cop out.

Doubt starts to fester. I rush a goodbye to Cassidy and hobble my way back to my car. The seed rocks in my gut and nausea swirls. How can Michael be sure I'm the one if there have been so many others? There's nothing special about me. Nothing except the babies.

No. I force the spiteful feeling out before it has a chance to fertilise the tiny doubt seed that has been planted. He told me his feelings aren't because of them. I have to believe that. I *do* believe that. If I don't, everything crumbles right as it is beginning to bloom.

Forcibly, I swallow down the lump in my throat, burying the bitter seed down with it. I can't do anything to get rid of it now, but I can refuse to feed it. I won't let it grow. I won't let it sprout into something that could tear us apart for no good reason.

And if it grows on its own, without my negative thoughts feeding it? Well then maybe it was meant to be there all along.

Chapter Twenty-Six

MICHAEL

My feet twitch inside my boots. Not the work ones, for a change. A pair of nice leather ones Brendan assured me would make me 'look the part'. Sure, they look nice, but they squeeze at the sides of my feet and rub at the back of my heels. I'd much prefer my worn in steel caps, even if the seams are a little frayed and the years of mud has stained the black into a faded, murky grey.

I also wish I'd been to the gym this morning. Worked off some of the excess energy that swims through me. My calf cramps as I walk across the driveway, a painful reminder that I've skipped leg day most of all. But the truth is, going to the gym just hasn't had the same appeal lately. Not when I could be spending time with Audrey. I still care about my fitness and I do enough to maintain the physique I've grown accustomed to, but smashing endless weights day in and day out, fighting to lift that little bit more than the guy next to me, just doesn't have the same appeal anymore.

Even so, it's a good release when I need it, and I should have gone this morning. Should have anticipated the anxious way my limbs feel like they're on fire and my pulse pounds against my neck.

Too late to go back now though. I step up to Audrey's porch and freeze with my hand on the door handle. Should I knock? I stayed here the night before last, and the one before that. And plenty of other nights over the past few weeks. We agreed that I would make a gradual move into the house, eas-ing my way into Audrey's—and Maisie's—day-to-day lives.

This place is starting to feel like home, but I don't know if I should call it that yet. Or if I should act like it, or if I should knock on the door like a guest.

A shared laughter echoes from deep within the house, the low bass of Christmas music wafts through the windows. And then, Maisie's cheerful chatter, distinct as though she is right on the other side of the front door.

"I want … when … Michael …" I don't catch all the words as she chitters away at a breakneck speed, but that was definitely my name.

I wiggle my toes, hoping the itch disappears when they realise the boots are staying. It doesn't, at least not yet. Baxter steps in between my legs. His tail wags vigorously, slapping my legs with his playful force.

"Okay," I whisper down to him.

Straightening my shoulders, I turn the matte black knob and push into the house.

Maisie squeals from down the hall, barrelling towards me and cheering. Baxter pulls at his lead, bouncing to meet her. They've met before, but every time it's the same playful excitement. From both of them.

Once Baxter has found some chill, I unclip the lead and let him nuzzle against Maisie's stomach. She pets his back in long strokes.

"Oh Baxter, my sweet sweet boy."

I can't hold back the smile that spreads across my face as I watch the two of them. He'd never been around kids before, and I'd been so worried how he would react. To Maisie, sure, but also to the babies. But he has fully committed to the fur-brother role.

"Hi Michael," Maisie sings, keeping both hands on Baxter. He nuzzles against them when her movements slow to a stop.

"Hey Maisie."

"We're down here," Audrey's voice floats through the house, her gentle melody soaks into my skin, heating my soul from the inside out.

I make my way towards her, nudging Baxter out of the way as I move past. "Let me know if he gets annoying," I tell Maisie. She opens her mouth, eyes wide as she shakes her head.

The dining table has been turned into a spread, far too large for the four of us and Maisie. A small selection of deli meats is scattered between countless cheeses, fruit, dips, chocolate pretzels, veggie sticks, chips, mini cupcakes, candy canes and gingerbread. Nothing is missing. In the centre is the crystal vase my mum helped me pick out for Audrey's birthday. The lilies I got her started wilting a while ago, but they've been replaced with an abundance of greenery, deep burgundy flowers and bright red … berries? I think. They spill out onto the table in a way that can only be deliberate, the green gum leaves twisting around the plates of food. The flowers and berries are scattered throughout and the whole thing looks like it belongs in a Christmas catalogue. It begs me to start eating, and I'm desperate to fill the pit that's been forming in my stomach, but it's also incredibly *perfect*. I don't want to ruin it.

"I went a little overboard." Audrey gestures to the table from where she sits on one of the stools by the island bench.

Callum sits at the head of the table, holding Cassidy between his legs. He chuckles. "A little."

"Well, I did too." Cassidy steps away from him, arms folding. She glares down at her boyfriend before turning to me. "Hi Michael."

Bonus Family Christmas. That's what the women had called it when they came up with the idea. A new tradition because even though they are divorced, Maisie deserves a celebration with both her parents together. It makes sense, mostly because Audrey and Cassidy somehow get along so well. I wasn't going to question their decision either way though.

Maisie runs into the room demanding that it's time for presents.

"You said as soon as Michael gets her," she whines.

"No, I said we have to wait for Michael to get here. That's not the same thing." Callum's voice is calm but stern, a skill I'll have to master.

"Well, it's the same thing to me."

Audrey struggles off the stool and I race over to help her. "Christmas is not all about presents," she says once she is on her feet.

It's impossible for me not to hold her protectively while she stands so close to me. I wrap an arm around her, pulling her into my side. My free hand rests on her stomach, and our babies kick playfully under my touch. It's hard to believe she has two butternut pumpkin sized babies in there, according to the app I downloaded anyway. Although, the midwives did say they will probably be a little smaller. Regardless, I have no idea how they fit. Audrey's insides must be squished within an inch of their functionality, and the thought only makes me appreciate her more.

"Yes it *is*." Maisie stamps her foot in front of us.

I have to bite my lips together to hold back the laughter that threatens to spill out. "Um, yeah. It kind of is for a kid."

"And *I'm* a kid. See Mum."

Audrey whips her head towards me. "Michael."

"Sorry," I whisper before squeezing her closer. Time could stop, for all I know. She relaxes underneath my arms and I breathe in the fruity smell of her hair. Her breasts move against my chest as she breathes, slow and steady like she might fall asleep in my arms.

I forget where we are, forget who we are with. Nudging her neck up with my nose, I kiss the soft skin behind her ear.

She whimpers and I move to claim the sound with my mouth. Just a small kiss, a reminder. A promise.

A chirping voice screams, "Ew."

Audrey pulls away from me like we're teenagers caught making out behind the gym. Her cheeks are flushed.

"Sorry," I whisper to her again.

Her chin jerks in response, but she rolls her shoulders and spins to face the room with a wide grin. "Presents!" she cheers, shifting the attention back to Christmas.

Maisie cheers, racing over to the tree in the corner. When I left yesterday evening, the pine tree was still bare. I'd lugged it inside and figured out how to make it stand straight in the base, but it took longer than I anticipated. Once it was safely standing it was time for dinner, and then for Maisie to go to bed. Audrey had to *swear* she wouldn't do the decorations while Maisie was in bed.

They must have spent all morning decorating it. Baubles and handmade ornaments are scattered around the needles, heavily focused on the lower half. Fairy lights wrap around the tree, twinkling a gorgeous snowy white glow that leaves little reflections all through the room.

Maisie crawls under the branches to retrieve a gold wrapped bundle. Baxter follows her in, knocking a few dangling baubles on his way. When he emerges from under the tree, pine needles stick to his fur. Before I can call him over, Cassidy crouches beside the couch. He bounds over for a pet and she works to pick each one out.

Maisie takes a few steps away from the tree and looks between her mother and father. Audrey gives a little nod.

My mouth drops open when Maisie walks over to me, shuffling her feet along the mat and holding the present in front of her. Something tingles along my spine and settles in my stomach. Not like the anxious pit that was there moments ago, this is light and airy. I spent hours trying to come up with the perfect gift for Maisie. Audrey said she likes Bluey and Frozen and singing and dancing but nothing felt right. I scoured the shops, and every online retailer I could think of, and I doubt the silly little token gift is enough. I drop to my knees, hoping that it is because the last thing I expected was Maisie to get *me* something.

"This is for you." She forces the present into my hands. My fingers tremble as I take it from her.

"Wait here."

I stand, turning to see Audrey holding out the small wrapped box I left under the tree last night. Taking it from her, I drop back to the ground.

"And this is for you."

Maisie snatches the present from me and tears away the red paper. Her eyes light up and I've never seen her cheeks puff so much with her smile. She beams brighter than all the Christmas lights on the street. In the entire suburb.

"A microphone?!" She squeals, jumps, twirls, in excitement. She rips at the box to get to the bright pink, battery operated microphone. Turning it on, her squeals are amplified through the house. "Oh my golly Michael, this is the best thing ever!"

Audrey's hand rests on my shoulder as I start to open my present. "Maisie chose it herself."

Under the slightly wrinkled gold paper is a denim utility belt. The dark fabric is covered with pockets, loops, fasteners, and hangs from a wide black belt. It doesn't matter that I still have a perfectly fine belt in my ute. It doesn't matter that I don't use it as often now that I'm spending more time managing Noah's hotel build than I do on the tools. It's perfect. Because it's for me, from Maisie.

The little girl who once scared me shitless, who I once ran away from. Not only am I slowly getting used to being around her, not only am I not scared to see her anymore but sometimes I get kind of excited. And she *wanted* to get me a Christmas present. She cares about me.

Tears well in my eyes.

"Michael, are you okay?!" Maisie's voice still booms as she speaks directly into the microphone.

I reach my arms to hug her, and she squeezes her little body into mine. "Merry Christmas."

Hours later, when all the presents are unwrapped and most of the food on the table has been eaten, Maisie is still singing every line into the microphone.

"That stays here," Callum grumbles as he gathers their things.

There was tension, leading up to this weekend, it creeps back through the room. The air chills with it. It's nearing Maisie's bedtime, but when she leaves Audrey won't see her until after Christmas. Even though it was her choice, I can see the way she stands back, shoulders tense as they all say goodbye. I'm sure she'll be grateful for it next year, when she can spend the babies' first Christmas with Maisie as well, but that doesn't make this year any easier.

She squeezes Maisie a little harder than usual, pulling the thin fabric of her cardigan around over her bump.

"You'll leave the sign for Santa? Just in case he comes here by accident?" Maisie voice tremors, the microphone finally falling limp in her hands.

"Of course I will."

Once they are gone, I steer Audrey away from the kitchen and towards the couch.

"Put your feet up." I tell her as I walk back towards the kitchen.

She protests but leans against the cushions and props her feet on the coffee table. Her head falls right back until she is looking off the back of the couch and up at me. There's a twinkle in her eye. She watches me intently as she pulls her lower lip into her mouth and lets it out slowly. My cock twitches, thinking of all the things we could do with her in that position. Well, of one very particular thing. I step towards her, thinking with my dick.

The back of the couch is low, and my crotch is right in her face. Even with her upside-down there's no hiding the rapidly forming bulge in my pants. Her tongue darts out to lick her lips. With the tips of my fingers, I tickle her cheek, one thumb pressing on her mouth. She swallows, her throat bobbing.

"Audrey?"

Stretching her arms over her head, she grabs the back of my legs and pulls me closer. Her face is pressed against my erection. I let my hands explore down her body. One holds loosely around her throat, the other stretching lower to massage her breasts. She moans, and I crumble at the sound.

"Audrey?" I ask again.

In answer, she bites playfully through the fabric of my pants. A grumble forms in my chest as she fumbles with the button and zipper. I help her get them undone and she pulls my jeans down along with my briefs.

Her warm breath coasts along my shaft, sending a shiver that stretches right through me. With a long languid lick, Audrey teases me from base to tip.

"You'll need to do most of the work," she whispers. Adjusting herself, she lets her head tip back over the couch and drops her mouth open. My heart races with anticipation.

I nudge the tip of my cock past her lips and adjust one of her hands to rest on the back of my thigh.

"Pinch if it's too much."

Audrey tickles me, humming in response. The vibrations in her throat edge me forward until she takes every inch of my dick in her mouth. I pull out before she gags, but she hollows her cheeks and sucks me down.

Fucking her face, I dip my hand into her top and toy with her nipple. She moans again and I nearly come apart. My balls draw tight against her face as I pump in and out, her tongue flat against my shaft and the tip falling deep into her throat. Pleasure is a wave that washes over me until I can't hold it in anymore.

"Audrey I'm going to …"

With the hand still wrapped around my leg, she holds me inside her. My release comes hard and fast as I spill deep in her throat. She sucks every last drop out of me and only then does she release her hold so I can pull back.

My chest heaves as my vision blurs and returns. I hoist myself over the couch until I'm straddling Audrey, all my weight on my knees either side of her legs.

Mascara runs down her cheeks but … fuck. I can't get enough of her. I bunch my fingers in her hair and lean down to kiss her puffy and swollen lips. Her tongue carries my salty taste but I savour it.

"Fuck, I love you."

She giggles under me. "I love you, too."

Chapter Twenty-Seven

AUDREY

Christmas and New Year's came and went like a thirty-minute episode of a binge worthy reality TV rerun. Here one second, gone the next and then life moved on to the next instalment. My two weeks of forced leave while the real estate office shut down disappeared just as quickly.

Returning to work this morning, knowing I only have a handful more weeks before my maternity leave starts, was rough. Harder than all those mornings I crawled out of bed while Maisie was a baby, still waking multiple times a night. She spent the day with Callum while I pushed through the hardest days of my career. I lived for it, but now, it hardly feels worth it.

The computer strains my eyes, my raspberry leaf tea warms my insides, but does nothing to help me wake up. My inbox loads and loads and loads as I sip at my tea and eat the pineapple Michael cut up for me to 'celebrate' the babies reaching thirty-two weeks. All these fruit comparisons are starting to make zero sense, but I love how invested Michael has become, tracking the size of the babies and showing me, in his own crazy way, how much he cares.

Hundreds of emails continue pouring into my inbox. I should have checked it before returning. I knew that. I thought about it, but the idea was too painful. I wanted to enjoy my break, for once.

I scroll to the very bottom of my inbox. Wrapping my fingers around my mug, I take a long sip of the bitter, herbal tea. It burns at my throat, but I roll my neck and focus on my emails. The sooner I start to clear the seemingly endless list, the sooner I can move on to some other mindless task.

The morning drags, and I'm not even halfway through clearing my emails when my boss struts his way across the office. He stops behind me, a hand on the back of my chair preventing me from twisting to face him. His disgusting, snuffly breath is hot over my shoulder as he peers past me to read what's on the screen.

"Most of us logged on during the break to clear through our emails, you know." His stern voice grates against my ears and he leans in. "So we could start working on the more productive stuff straight away."

My ears are hot, and my pulse pounds against my temples. I bring my hands to my face to press my palms into my forehead.

"Well, I didn't," I snap. "I shouldn't have to. I was on leave."

He scoffs. "We all were Audrey. I sure hope this attitude won't continue when you take your little break in a month's time. When can we expect you back?"

I roll my shoulders to sit up as straight as I can. He drops his hand at the movement, and I turn the chair to face him. I'm startled by how close he is, but I keep my face neutral and he, thankfully, leans back out of my space. A piece of his greasy, slick backed hair falls out of place.

"I plan on taking my full twelve months off. I've already worked with payroll regarding both the employer and government maternity leave payments, and I've given them my expected return to work date." My chest is lighter as I say the words, but the thumping in my temples intensifies.

"A year? We can't have you gone for that long."

"Brett, with all due respect, that's not my problem. At your request, I've been working with the other agents to ensure a smooth transition. If you need to hire someone to temporarily fill the position, you can arrange to do so."

He takes a step back and shoves his hands into the pockets of his too short suit pants. His shirt buttons pull at his beer belly.

"Audrey this is …" He trails off, bobbing his head as he searches for whatever words he wants.

I reach for my phone, opening a voice memo. "Brett, I'm letting you know I'm now recording this conversation for my records," I let him know as I turn on the microphone.

The little lines appear across the screen as he splutters. "Very well." He turns on his heel, walking away. A small piece of me crumbles, thankful I didn't have to put up more of a fight, but a swirl of disappointment mingles with the otherwise settled feeling. It would have been good to get one of his misogynistic outbursts on record.

I close off the voice record app, but as the screen locks away I notice a missed message.

With Brett gone, I open up my phone again to read it.

> **Cassidy: I have two separate customers who asked about your painting and want one of their own. One owns the little clothing store down the street and the other is some boujee woman who wanted an almost exact replica for her 'sitting room'. I said I'd forward you their details. I think you should do it!**

I read the message over four times, letting the words sink in and making sure I'm not reading something that wasn't actually there. People want my artwork. Strangers!

Following the message are two shared contacts. My thumb twitches over the first one, willing me to call her *right now* to organise all the details. But when would I have time? I have five weeks left before my maternity leave is due to start, and then I'll be busy trying to relax while I get all the last bits and pieces ready for the babies' arrival. Resigning myself not to be hasty, I return my phone to my bag and turn back to the computer.

My baron desk dries my soul. I can still see the pin marks in the backboard where my photos used to be. They were of Maisie, mostly. The yearly calendar she made complete with her handprints took pride of place next to my monitor. Until Brett decided we needed a 'cleaner' workplace and made me, and the other parents, take them all down.

The yearning to just quit haunts me.

I still have hundreds of emails left to sort through, the number keeps growing as the day goes on, instead of shrinking as I work my way through the list. But I have no desire to hustle through getting them all done. I don't care. I have, as they say, zero fucks left to give.

Fuck it.

I lock the screen and wheel my chair back from the desk so I have room to stand. Walking past Brett's office on my way to the Human Resources department, I give him a little wave. My fingers dance in the air, as light as the smirk on my face. Brett's eyebrows squeeze together, thick lines forming in what was already a small gap. His eyes squint as he watches me.

On the other side of the mid-sized office, three women chat at their desks. Each of their desks has a small plant, and their backboards are filled with family photos, quotes, and children's drawings. The empty desk in their quad is covered with snacks. And there's a pleasant vibe in the air that stirs something green inside me. Maybe the next five weeks wouldn't have been so bad if I was over here. But I chose the wrong career path, apparently.

The women look up at me and the youngest calls me over with a friendly wave. Her blonde hair is pulled back in the sleekest ponytail. Perfect eyebrows and bright pink glasses frame her narrow face. I pull at the edges of the cardigan I wear to fight the chill from the air-conditioning but fight the urge to wrap my arms around my middle.

"Not much longer now?" She asks as she gestures for me to sit in the spare chair in their cluster of four work desks. The other two turn towards their computers, fake nails clicking against their keyboards.

"I wanted to talk about that actually." My fingers and legs twitch in discomfort. I twist in the spinning office chair to release some of the urge to *move*. "I made that plan before I knew I was having twins. With two of them in there, everything is getting harder. I'd like to pull my leave forward."

Her hand flies up to clutch her chest. "Of course. We can arrange that. When were you thinking?"

My breath hitches, I hadn't expected it to be so easy. No doubt Brett will kick up a massive stink, but if Human Resources supports me, there's nothing he will be able to do.

"As soon as possible. I'm finding it really hard to concentrate today, and I don't think I'll be productive if I have to keep working much longer."

"Start tomorrow!" She spins in her chair and begins to type an email addressed to Brett. "I'm sure it won't be an issue, considering Bitter Brett was having other agents ghost you anyway."

I hold in my laugh at the nickname, a weight lifting off my shoulders. "So, that's it?"

She holds up a finger, then returns to typing her email. I don't lean close enough to read what it says, but it's brief. Brett will hate it.

When she hits send, a weight lifts off my shoulders, and I slump in the chair with relief.

"Thank you." The word chokes its way out as I hold back the tears that want to form.

"Go pack up your desk, set an out of office, then head home. I'll handle Brett."

We walk together to my sorrowful corner of the office, parting ways when we reach Brett's office. She raps her knuckles on the door briefly as she waltzes in.

"Audrey." Brett's indignant tone floats past me. I ignore him, with a skip in my step as I approach my desk.

I don't even sit down, I just set up the out of office email and turn the computer off. The few belongings I kept in my drawer spill into my bag. Brett's grumbling is muted as my saviour from Human Resources closes the door. I admire her through the window. She stands tall against Brett's dismissive posture, holding her ground. For me. I'll have to thank her some day.

As though she senses me spying on her, she glances over to wave goodbye. I hold up my hand, dancing my fingers again. Brett's face goes red, but I let it wash over me as I sling my bag over my shoulder and leave.

I turn the car on but sit with it idling as I organise the details for *both* of the new commissioned artworks. I send a message to Michael, letting him know because I want to share my news with him *immediately*, and I can't wipe the smile off my face when he messages me back.

Michael: Proud of you. Love you.

I order a hamper to send to Cassidy as thanks, and my smile grows as I decide 'fuck it' and order one for myself. The wine will have to wait, but chocolates, bath bombs, a face mask, a cute pair of fluffy bed socks ... I deserve all that.

And I'm beaming, fully content with my decision to go on maternity leave early when I visit the art supply store to pick up the canvases and some extra paints.

But none of those grins compare to the one on Michael's face when I pull into the driveway. His arms are wrapped around a massive bunch of flowers, the non-alcoholic wine I've been enjoying, and paintbrushes. His deep amber eyes glow golden, just like his loose wavy hair, and I can see every one of his teeth.

"You made the right choice," he whispers in my ear, and the tiny speck of uncertainty that had started creeping into my vision floats away on the breeze.

Chapter Twenty-Eight

MICHAEL

"Hey Michael, since you'll be the babies' daddy, and you'll live here when they are born, will that make you my daddy too?"

I freeze, one hand poised over the UNO deck. I suppose, considering I've been practically living here since Christmas, this question was to be expected. Maisie accepted me into her house with arms wide open. She loves coming home to Baxter and has taken claim to the responsibility of giving him his breakfast. In turn, Baxter has found a new favourite spot— wherever Maisie happens to be.

Still though, her question catches me by surprise.

I need help and turn to Audrey for guidance on how to answer this question only to find she has conveniently disappeared after winning the round on her last turn.

The bridge of Maisie's nose scrunches, her mouth tilting almost completely into one cheek as she cocks her head. The dramatic movement makes her high pony of dark, thick waves flop over her shoulder. "But I already have a daddy, so would I have two daddies? Danny from school has two daddies, but he has no mummy and I definitely have a mummy. Almost two mummies because Cassidy lives with Daddy even though she said that does not make her my mummy. So, would I have two daddies *and* a mummy *and* an almost mummy? I'm confused."

She throws her head back with a huff.

"I'm confused too," I admit, choosing to lead with honesty over making up an answer that will probably only lead to Maisie asking more questions. "I'm not very good at this parent stuff."

"Mummy said you were pretty good at helping her when she needed to go to the doctor."

My lips turn up. I'd promised Audrey, when she first told me about the babies, that I was there for her no matter what, and I had meant it. Taking her to the hospital when she was worried she was in early labour was just a small part of that promise. Besides, truthfully, I had been panicking just as much as Audrey was. I just managed to hold it all on the inside. I hadn't realised that me being there for her in that moment had such a profound impact. Had meant so much that she told her five-year-old daughter. The feeling chips away at the few stony pieces left on my heart.

Maybe I'll be okay at this?

Still, I'm not sure if there is a 'right' way to answer Maisie's question. It's so loaded, even though I'm sure she never meant it that way. I adjust in my seat position on the floor, trying to alleviate some of the numbing in my butt. With my legs now crossed in front of me, I rest my elbows on my knees and lean in towards Maisie. She's laying on her stomach, head propped on a pillow and legs kicking in the air. Her hand of cards hangs haphazardly from her grip, giving me a full view of her streak of red cards and the sneaky Draw Four. I do my best to eliminate her cards from my short-term memory.

"I won't be your daddy, Maisie. Because like you said, you have a daddy. And I know he loves you a billion. But yeah, I'm going to be around, so maybe I can be something else. Something almost like a daddy but not really? Like an uncle but ... different. Honestly, I don't know."

A hand rests gently on my shoulder. "It's okay not to know. I don't really know either."

Audrey's voice rings through my ears, settling my

nervous heart. Her weight falls onto my shoulder as she struggles to sit down next to me.

"We should have moved to the table. How did you even get up before?"

Her bottom finally lands on the floor, and Audrey adjusts to find a comfortable way to sit. Her baby bump is more than just a bump now, it's a beautiful round home for our babies. It looks uncomfortable at the best of times, let alone trying to sit on the floor. "Sorry," I add, placing a hand on her knee.

Audrey sighs as she settles, back leaning against me with her legs straight out past where Maisie sits. "I crawled to the couch and pulled myself up." Her tone is light, but there's an undercurrent of despair that she can't shake off with her silent chuckle.

Dropping her cards, Maisie crawls across the deck sitting forgotten between us to rest her hand on her mother's stomach.

She looks up at me with her bright blue eyes. "So, if you won't be my daddy, but you're more than just Michael, what should I call you?"

I ponder her question. I hadn't thought about being called 'dad' by anyone just yet, let alone Maisie. 'Daddy' definitely doesn't feel right, and she is on the right track with me being more than just 'Michael'. I want to be something more to her than that. Words slip off my tongue as I contemplate. "Dad … Michael … Daddy"

"Michael Daddy," she giggles. "That sounds funny. Like Michaeldaddy. Mikedaddy."

Audrey runs her fingers through Maisie's long brown hair. "Mikaddy?" she muses.

"Maddy?" Maisie shortens the word even further into something that, oddly, feels kind of right. She gasps, throwing both hands over her face and kicking her legs.

"Maddy," I repeat. It's a playful nickname. One that only we would know the true meaning of.

Audrey twists her head until her eyes meet mine. "Maddy?"

I shrug a shoulder and reach an arm around her to hug both her and Maisie together. "Yeah, I like it."

Wriggling free from the embrace, Maisie jumps up and moves to stand in front of me. "Maddy," she squeals before running off to her bedroom.

Something warm settles itself deep in my chest, filling a hole I never noticed was there. I keep my arms wrapped around Audrey and rest my hands on her belly. Everything feels so easy, so perfect in a way I never imagined was possible. I'm constantly holding my breath, waiting for the penny to drop. But it hasn't, at least not yet. And the closer we get to Audrey's due date, the more everything seems to fall into place.

My dad's words echo in my thoughts. *'You're in love.'*

I've known for a long time that I love Audrey, but to be *in love* with someone? Doesn't that take years of getting to know each other and slowly falling, bit by bit? Maybe for some people. But Audrey and I were thrown down the hill together and now, we aren't just making our way back to the top, we're soaring above it.

I lean in, soaking in the fruity scent of her hair, stroking her belly as the twins wriggle about inside her, finding peace in the gentle rise and fall of her chest. She leans her head back onto my shoulder and sighs. We sit, in peaceful silence, caring about nothing and no one else. The box of packed up Christmas decorations calls to me from the corner, begging to be returned to its place in the garage, but I ignore it. We have time for all those little tasks. We have all the time in the world.

"Maddy."

My eyes jolt open at the sound of Maisie's shrill whisper. Audrey sleeps curled on her side next to me, the blankets loose around her waist. Her bare, round, stomach catches the moonlight that peaks in through a tiny gap in the shutters. Beautiful, always. But not the reason I was forced awake. I turn to Maisie, who's standing far too close and looks eerily like a ghost in the dim, blue-ish light. Her eyes are bloodshot, and her mane of wavy hair sticks up in every direction. There's none of her usual childish glow, the bright pink of her cheeks faded away along with most of the colour from her skin.

In all the scattered times I've stayed here, she has never come in overnight. Not in the beginning, not now that I spend more nights here than I do back at the apartment. Never. Until now.

"Maisie, what's wrong?"

She holds a hand over her mouth before she speaks. "I'm sorry Maddy. I was sick." Tears stream down her face, dripping over her cheeks.

I push up in the bed to hold her close. "Don't be sorry, shh." I'm way out of my depth here. Like, I've swam too far out at the beach and the tide is dragging me from shore. "Sick, how?"

She chokes, hiccupping as she answers. "I woke up and … I tried not to but … it went everywhere."

I pull her close, realising too late that everywhere included her nightie. The sticky remains of her illness cling to my arms and chest. I gulp.

Beside me, Audrey stirs, pushing up on an arm to see around me. "What's wrong?"

She must see Maisie and just *know*, because she goes into full survival mode.

"Fuck," she whispers as she pushes out of the bed. Her legs swing over the side and she takes a few deep inhales before standing. "Michael, can you go to the twenty-four-hour pharmacy around the corner? We need Hydralyte and ginger ale, get some of those glucose jelly beans too. Disinfectant spray, maybe even gloves and some facemasks. I really don't want to get sick. I can't get sick. Fuck, the babies. Michael?"

Aware of the vomit stuck to my arms and chest, I place my clean hand on Audrey's shoulder and rest my forehead on her back.

"You stay in bed I'll take care of Maisie and hopefully that way you won't get sick. We can worry about all the other stuff in the morning."

Maisie whimpers from the foot of the bed. "I don't want to make mummy or the babies sick."

"Then it's sorted." I kiss between Audrey's shoulders, then climb out of the bed to help Maisie.

Audrey whispers a faint "thank you" as we head for the bathroom.

After her quick rinse and a clean pair of pyjamas, Maisie is exhausted. Her bed is still out of action, so I put her back to bed on the couch. She hasn't vomited again, but I still lay towels underneath her and prop a bucket from the laundry beside her head.

"Maddy?" she whimpers, her eyes still closed as she snuggles against the pillows.

I sit on the floor beside her, tracing my fingers around her face. "Yeah Maisie?"

"Thank you."

Once she falls asleep, I strip her bed, setting everything in the washing machine ready to be washed tomorrow when the noise won't keep the house awake. I find clean sheets in the linen cupboard and go about making up her bed again. Shuffled footsteps make their way down the front hallway, and I stifle a yawn and tiptoe to stop Audrey.

Seeing me, Audrey's mouth drops open in a yawn of her own. Her eyes are puffy and her shoulders droop underneath her dressing gown. "Is she okay?"

I hug her close, kissing her forehead. "Maisie is asleep on the couch. I changed her bed and will wash the sheets in the morning. You head back to bed."

She hesitates, but I kiss her forehead and nudge her back towards her bedroom. She gives in easily, and I can only hope she falls back asleep without worrying.

Under the kitchen sink, I find disinfectant. My mind races as I go about spraying every surface Maisie might have touched.

Is this what my life is now?

It started with the very toned-down holiday season. Quiet family affairs that I thoroughly enjoyed but were so different to the wild celebrations of my past. We were even in bed before midnight on New Year's Eve, content with getting a full night's sleep over forcing ourselves to stay up until the clock ticked over.

Since then, mornings have been busier. I've had almost no time to do a workout session, and the few times I've been back to the apartment my home gym has screamed at me to be used. I could have, but I didn't *want* to. I wanted to get back to Audrey. And by default, Maisie too.

My life has changed, I have changed.

And I was okay with it, really. But cleaning up a child's vomit? It's another level that I wasn't expecting. And the thought of this becoming my new norm? A wave of nausea creeps through me, settling in my bones.

Not wanting to disturb Audrey, I curl up on the second couch. My knees are pulled right up to my feet to make room for my legs, and I wrap the thin throw blanket over my shoulders. Sleep never comes.

With every tiny movement or laboured sigh from the other couch, my eyes fly open, and I wait. For the second round of vomiting, and then the third. By the time the sky outside the back window is the muted orange of sunrise, I'm exhausted. Moving hurts, my stomach cramps, and my head pounds. I'm covered in a light layer of sticky sweat.

Maisie is still sleeping soundly, the towels under her scrunched up from her tossing and turning through the night. Footsteps echo up the hall.

"Stop," I stage whisper before Audrey can get too close. "You can't get sick."

All my unease aside, it's not worth the risk to Audrey and the babies.

"I'll call Callum," she responds, keeping her distance as she veers into the kitchen.

My insides twist, a fresh surge of nausea washing over me. "Thank you," I call out as I rush to the bathroom.

Chapter Twenty-Nine

AUDREY

Michael stands on the porch, shuffling his feet. He rubs at one arm, just below his bicep, shoulders hunched forward and face to the ground.

The morning sun leaves harsh shadows across his face, but as I open the door he looks up from his feet with half a smile. It grows the longer he looks at me, spreading until I can see the way his cheeks puff out in his silhouette.

Baxter runs through his legs, winding the leash around his ankles. Michael reaches down for the lead, unclasping it from Baxter's collar and stepping out of the loose knots. Baxter yelps in excitement, moving to lick the tops of my feet. Spying Maisie down the hall, he barrels through my legs to greet her. I knew when I asked Michael to stay that he was as much a package deal as I am. The dog goes everywhere with him, and I'd accepted that even when I wasn't thrilled about having fur all through the house. Two weeks without him running playfully around our feet though? I'll never admit it out loud, but I missed Baxter.

Even so, I wobble from the forceful movement as he pushes through my legs. Clutching at my stomach, I reach for the door frame to balance myself. Michael holds out a hand, supporting me while I find my balance. His hand is warm on the bare skin of my arm, sending a fire through me. One I thought was extinguished by the baby bump and the swollen feet and the daily, never ending, exhaustion.

Leaning into the touch, I rake my eyes over Michael. He's wearing a dark grey pair of sweats that sit loose over his thighs but cinch in at his ankles. The lighter, oversized tank gives me a full view of his muscular arms, and I fight to hold in the drool that forms when I remember how it feels when he holds me. Moves me. Uses me.

My breath catches when I go to speak and I feel every little bit of the distance between us. The small gap between our bodies as he holds me at arm's length. Plus the two weeks we spent barely talking while he and Maisie recovered from one of the worst stomach bugs I've ever seen, and I avoided both of them. I have Michael to thank for me not catching it, and I'm still in disbelief that I didn't. After he spent the night looking after Maisie, I called Callum, who rushed over in full supportive, protective dad mode and took Maisie back to his house. Michael emerged from the bathroom to watch over Maisie until Callum arrived. When they left, he sprayed the entire house with disinfectant before retreating to his apartment.

I don't blame him for escaping to his bachelor pad. I know that he was thinking of me just as much as he was thinking of himself. But still, it's nice to have him back. Except that he still hasn't closed the gap between us and the longer we stand here in silence, the harder it is for me to take the step towards him either. There's an icy chill to the air around us. I wrap my arms around me, wishing I had extra layers to hide behind.

"I missed you," I admit, forcing my gaze up to his face.

His smile has melted away into something softer. His lips are gently upturned and a glimmer that sparkles in his eye. Tracing his fingers up my arm, he rests his palm on my cheek.

"I'm glad you didn't get sick."

My heart drops, my head tilts down until I'm staring at the place my feet would be if my massive baby bump wasn't blocking my view. *That's all?*

"It would have been bad for the babies. Thank you."

He shakes his head and uses a thumb to tilt my face back up to his. "No Audrey, it would have been bad for you."

Finally, *finally*, he closes the gap, stepping forward as his other arm wraps around me. My stomach pushes against him but he leans in and kisses me like we were apart for two years, not just two weeks. Our lips and tongues tangle together and the warmth from his hands spreads *everywhere*. Down my spine, along my stomach, into my core. It's an all-consuming wave that threatens to topple me over and I have to break our kiss to catch my breath.

Michael leans down, planting a kiss on my stomach and picking up his duffle bag. Holding his other hand, I guide him into the house. He hesitates as he steps over the threshold, but takes the step when I turn back to grin at him.

In the kitchen, he pulls a cantaloupe from his bag.

"It's getting ridiculous now," he says as he chops the melon. "I highly doubt you have two of these in there."

I find a container for the fruit, popping a few of the bite size pieces into my mouth.

"Is that really what the app said for thirty-four weeks?"

Maisie announces her entrance into the kitchen with a ruffled, exaggerated sigh. "Can we *please* go through the box of my old stuff now?"

Baxter trails in behind her, and she reaches out to scratch behind his ears.

"What box?" Michael asks.

"All my old baby things!" Maisie squeals as she drags him to her room. "It's in my closet. Mummy said we could go through it to see what the babies might want, *buuut* it's too heavy for her to get down. So, we need you to."

"Thank you," I call down the hall as they disappear into her bedroom. As I make my way to the living room, a new wave of heat flows down my back, pulling tight at my stomach until it's hard to breathe. It's far from painful, but when it's not laced with the desire I felt when Michael and I were kissing, it's not pleasant. I head towards the couch, grabbing my water bottle from the coffee table to take a large sip. I reason with myself; it's too early, I'm probably just dehydrated again, it's not contractions. But even with my voice of reason my heart picks up pace.

I gulp down more water, trying to swallow down the unnecessary panic bubbling to the surface. Baxter nudges me closer to the couch. Taking his advice, I sit down on the soft linen, leaning over one of the arms as I try to catch my breath. He rests his head on my knees, one paw propped against my leg. His weight pushed against mine grounds me, and I find my chest feels lighter. I scratch his neck, grateful for his presence.

From Maisie's bedroom, a thud sounds, followed by her enthusiastic squeals. She runs down the hall, Michael trailing behind her with the big plastic tub. I admire the way the muscles in his arms pull tight and a different kind of rush flows through my body. My cheeks grow hot and he winks when he sees me staring.

With the box on the coffee table, Maisie wastes no time pulling out the contents. Her soft green baby blanket is discarded on the floor as she searches for memories from her younger years. It's brighter than how I painted it, a vibrant mint green that pops against the soft cream of the rug. Michael, seeing the way I look at it, crawls around the floor to get it. He drapes it over my knees. Baxter whines at the disruption, but promptly rests his head back on my lap. Michael settles down to rest his back on the couch beside me, an arm wrapped around my leg.

"It was her favourite. Well, my favourite for her." I curl my fingers in the blanket. Nostalgia is a breath of fresh air that pushes aside my panic and I remember sitting on this very couch with a teeny tiny Maisie wrapped in this very blanket on my lap. I remember how perfect the world felt, how I thought nothing could get better than that moment. How wrong I was. Because now, with Michael, about to introduce two tiny souls into our world, feels more right than any moment before. I'm still scared, terrified, of what life will look like with two screaming babies while we juggle the freshness of our relationship, but I know we will tackle it together. My heart swells and tears form in my eyes as I choke back the love and joy that threatens to spill.

Michael plays with a tasselled corner, admiring the delicate fabric. "I wonder if we could get one to match?"

"I doubt they sell them anymore. I don't even know if the shop still exists."

"Then we can see if someone will make one. There has to be some crafty person making custom baby blankets. So both babies can have one." He turns his attention away from where Maisie is now holding tiny onesies against her chest. "Or we could get them their own blankets? Similar but different?"

I nod, slipping my hand under his to lock our fingers together. "I'd like that. Most of this stuff we would need to buy a second anyway. And how would we decide what baby gets the well-loved hand me downs and which baby gets the brand-new stuff? Plus, I didn't keep all these things to use again, I kept them as memories for Maisie. I don't want her to lose that."

Michael closes his fist around my fingers. With his free hand he holds my stomach. Both babies go to town kicking, like they always do when he is close. A satisfied sigh escapes him.

"So, she won't," he says. "We'll get them new stuff."

The babies' kicking stops, replaced by an intense pressure through my belly, like they are pushing out in every direction. I suck in air through gritted teeth, waiting for the pressure to release. Pain shoots up my spine.

And then, almost as fast as it came, it goes. All of it, the pain, the pressure, the tightness. My hand loosens its death grip on Michael's fingers. Concern is laced all over his face as he climbs onto the couch to sit beside me.

"You okay?"

"I think so." I breathe slowly, still catching my breath. My heart still races because that was *definitely* a contraction.

With her head inside the box, completely oblivious to my current state, Maisie squeals. Her voice somehow more high pitched than it has ever been, she reappears holding a greying teddy pressed against her face.

"Oh, oh, oh." She jumps around with each sound. "*My teddy*! I can't believe he was in here! I was *looking* for him!"

She disappears into her room.

"She definitely has not been looking for that teddy."

Michael kicks off his sneakers and curls his body onto the couch. He stretches out until he is laying with his head against my stomach.

"Do we need to call the hospital?"

"I don't think so. Not yet. But I think I should call Callum to come get Maisie just in case."

"It's too early."

My palms are sweaty, my heart squeezes. "I know."

Chapter Thirty

AUDREY

The afternoon passes in a blur, time counting not with the hours but with each new contraction.

Trying to hide my panic while Maisie complained because she only just got to see Michael again and it was supposed to be her weekend with mummy, not daddy. Callum's large hand on my shoulder, his calm smile and a promise it'll be okay—even though he can't possibly know that—before he whisked her into the back seat.

Michael pacing the living room, calling the hospital as soon as they left, and again when the contractions started getting longer, instead of shorter. And again when I started to bleed. Only a little, but enough. Packing a rushed bag for the hospital and crouching over the bed as I tried to catch my breath. A particularly painful contraction in the car, and another in the carpark. Michael standing behind me to hold me up when I couldn't stand from the pain.

I find myself disassociating as I'm led to a consultation room. As though I'm watching the nightmare unfold on a TV screen. It's not happening to me. Only it is, and I'm terrified. My hand clutches Michael's and I refuse to let go as a polite midwife talks through preterm birth and how the babies will have to go to the Neonatal Intensive Care Unit. Michael, guiding me to the bed as I break down at the news, only to have another contraction tear me apart from the inside out. I make him stay as I'm strapped to the monitor, and he wipes my tears after each new wave of terror and pain.

Two panicked midwives huddle over the read out from

the machine, whispering. One races off, returning with an obstetrician. The ultrasound gel is cool on my stomach, but the pressure from the wand brings a new kind of pain, this one in my chest. My heart is breaking because I know things are going terribly wrong, they don't need to tell me.

I'm rushed into a delivery room despite my protests that it's too early, and I can't shake the feeling that no one is listening. Not the doctor, not the midwives, not Michael, not my body.

Not yet, I try to tell them all. *Not yet.*

And then, time starts to drag and rush by somehow all at once. And everything is a million times worse. Worse than it was before, worse than it should be—I'm certain. Contraction after contraction feeling like daggers in my stomach, my back. Until now, I have no idea how long it's been, what day it is, when it will end. There's a drip of antibiotics in my wrist. A dose of something that should have stopped the contractions and then a dose of steroids when it didn't work. A thick, painful needle in my butt that stings and aches but is nothing like the searing pain of the contractions. And all the while, the pain that rushes through my body every few minutes.

Michael stands, sits, paces. He lays his head on my shoulder, he stands behind me while I bounce on the ball, he carries me around the room when the pain is too much and I can't move for myself. He ties my hair back, lets his hair down, runs his hands through its lengths and pulls at the ends. I doze and wake in searing pain, over and over until I can't take it anymore.

Wires are spread across my stomach, pads are changed, hands are shoved inside me to check progress. My water breaks in a gush of liquid and Michael holds me on the armchair while the sheets are changed in a rush. A deep stain forms on Michael's pants and he pretends not to notice even though the dark red stands out against his pale jeans.

Every moment comes and goes but everything stays the same. The same pressure, the same pain, the same feeling like I could die, and nothing at all like my memories of Maisie's birth.

Was it easier because she was full term, or because it was only her? Had I just forgotten all of this because then she was here and it all seemed worth it?

No.

I would have remembered if it was this bad, I would have decided one was enough. But then, I had, hadn't I?

I should have done another birthing class. Everything I learnt six years ago is gone and I have no idea if I should stand or sit or rock or try to walk. Should I scream or breathe or clench my jaw or just give up. Maybe I should have accepted the epidural and I want to ask if I can have one but the room is suddenly spinning.

Two midwives check me again—is one a student?—and whisper to each other. "… bleeding … placenta … delivery … doctor …" I have no idea what any of it means, but I'm scared.

"I can't do this," I moan as another contraction ends. Everything hurts, and there's no such thing as relief as the wave crashes into an endless pain filled with pressure and exhaustion and worry.

"You are," Michael strokes my hair and whispers in my ear. His voice shakes. "You *are* doing this and I am so proud of you."

But I can't. *I can't.*

I can barely keep my eyes open.

A machine beeps erratically and Michael is no longer resting beside me on the bed. I squeeze his hand as a contraction threatens to tear me in two. I cling to him like it's my final chance.

The fire in my abdomen eases, but my world begins to blur, blackened around the edges like I'm staring up at my life from somewhere far below the floor. My grip on Michael's hand falls away.

"BP has dropped to one hundred over sixty." The voice floats through the room as one of the midwives pushes past Michael. His face drops, mouth hanging open as his gaze darts back and forth around the room.

Blinding lights take over the room, the silhouettes of too many people casting shadows across my face.

This is not the plan, I try to say.

The plan was dim lights and no extra people and as little intervention as possible.

But the plan was also a full-term birth, so maybe we threw the plan away hours ago. The words are stuck in my throat as I fight to stay awake. My eyes blink slowly, all on their own and each time I have to open them it gets a little harder.

The bed drops until I am lying almost flat on my back. I didn't want this. We wanted to let gravity help. We needed to let gravity help me get two babies out.

Michael. I want Michael. But in the sea of bodies still rushing around the room he is lost. Until there he is, halfway out the door. His eyes are wide and his face is whiter than the walls and he wrings his hands together while his whole body shakes. A face I don't recognise leans close to talk to him, but he doesn't take his eyes of me. Even as they guide him out the door, he walks backwards in tiny, hesitant steps.

And all the while I can't keep my own eyes open. I'm fading.

This was not the plan.

"Audrey." The voice is right in my ear. I can feel how close she is, but the words are so very far away.

I'm rolled to my side, my arm goes cool as something flows through the drip, a mask is slipped over my face and I can't breathe through the panic.

"We need to move you now, okay?"

They don't wait for me to answer, maybe they know that I can't. The door stretches closer somehow even though I'm still lying flat on this bed. People in scrubs surround me as the bed is wheeled out the door and down the hall.

Oh no. Oh no, no, no.

Despite the chaos, despite how distant everything feels, I know where they are taking me.

"No." I try to protest but the word simply falls out of my mouth with a laboured breath, too quiet for anyone to hear.

In the hallway, I search for Michael, desperate to fight the deepest sleep that's calling me until I know he is by my side. But a ding sounds, and metal walls surround us, and Michael is still missing.

And the world fades away into nothing.

And Michael is gone.

Chapter Thirty-One

MICHAEL

Thirty seconds. That's all it took for things to go from crazy to scary. My ears ring and my heart pounds against my chest. It hurts to breathe. It's too early, and we all know it, but still, Audrey is in labour, in pain, and there is nothing I can do to help. My voice shakes as I try to comfort her. Because I heard what they said. She's losing too much blood.

It's not an early birth anymore, it's a medical emergency. And I'm terrified.

One of the midwives pushes past me to slam her hand on the wall. Doctors and nurses flood the room, pushing me further and further back. I lose count of how many rush to Audrey's side, but with each new figure in the room my heart picks up speed until it hurts. My body aches to be next to Audrey. I want to hold her, to be by her side, to tell her it will be okay even though I don't know if it will be. I can see the panic in her face, as she searches for me. I need to reach her, but I can't.

Audrey's bed is dropped back with a force I fear might have hurt her, but no one seems to care. No one seems to notice I'm here. Until a young woman in pink scrubs is guiding me out of the door.

"We need to get her to surgery; her placenta has detached from her uterus and it's causing her to lose a lot of blood."

"She didn't want ..."

She places a gloved hand on my arm and I flinch away

from the kind gesture. "It's too late for wants and wishes. We need to save her and her babies."

Save her?

My heart stops its running race. I flatline right there in the hospital room because I can't breathe. Instead of beating, my heart jumps through my chest and lands on Audrey's bed. Because it's hers, and I need her to be okay. I need all three of them to be okay. I try to follow my heart to be by her side, but the midwife holds me back. Audrey, my heart, is whisked past me. I race after her, down the hall, squeezing into the lift right as the doors are closing.

Tears flood down Audrey's cheeks as she searches the room. I try to stretch toward her, to show her I'm here, but there are too many people in the way.

The elevator doors slide open, revealing another stark white corridor, and once again I'm politely shoved aside. Audrey is wheeled down the corridor and into a room. Chasing after her, a nurse stops me at the door, covering my hair with a net, and draping a gown over my front.

I'm handed gloves, then she uses her back to open the swinging door. I follow her into the room. My stomach sinks to the floor. Audrey lays on the bed with her arms spread wide. A curtain hangs across her chest and I can't see her face past the nurse by her side.

My hands drop to my knees as all the blood drains from my face. I give myself only the smallest of moments to compose my racing thoughts. Audrey needs me. And she needs me to be calm.

Crying breaks the tension in the room and the surgical team breathes a collective sigh of relief.

"Dad, over here." Someone nudges me towards the sound of crying. I pivot, wanting to go to Audrey but being called away. And then a tiny, *tiny*, baby is placed in my arms.

The room is a busy swarm of bees, each knowing exactly

where they need to be and what they need to do, but it all fades away as I stare down at my child. Hands guide my shoulders to the corner of the room and the tiny baby, my son, is taken from my arms. I watch, helpless, as a team of scrubs check over every inch of him.

Behind us, mayhem spreads.

"She's losing a lot of blood."

"I need to get this baby out."

"BP is not responding."

"I can't control the bleeding."

The room somehow becomes more frantic than before. Men and women in scrubs rush around me, while a handful remain by Audrey's side. There's a new squeal of cries and another small moment of joy. But this baby isn't placed in my arms. A nurse places him straight into a crib.

"Put her under."

"Get dad and babies out, now."

The lady with the pink scrubs is back by my side. "Come on dad, we're going to the NICU."

They told us this would happen, but I don't want to go. I want to stay with Audrey. Machines beep all around and I'm lost.

"They'll work better without you here, let's go."

She takes my arm, her fingers gently tugging me to follow her. Both babies are wheeled out the door and I'm torn in two because I want to stay with Audrey but I *need* to go with them. I turn to tell Audrey, but the midwife's grip firms around my arm as she drags me out.

My butt is numb. I shift in the seat, uncomfortable in the baggy scrub pants one of the nurses found me. Slouching down, I clutch the two tiny babies on my chest. *My sons.*

It's been hours, but it could have been minutes. Time has lost all meaning because Audrey still isn't awake. There's a hole in my chest where my heart belongs. I left it with her when I was forcibly removed from the room. When the surgeons had to save her life.

They said she'll be okay. That she lost a lot of blood but they were able to stop the bleeding and stitch her back together. They said she is in recovery. That I'll be able to see her soon. That I'm more useful here, with my sons. Our sons. Our tiny little boys, who were so dependent on Audrey until only a few hours ago and now they are dependent on wires and monitors and warm lights.

And me.

Their father.

When the world was falling to pieces around me, I became a father. I became responsible for so much more than just these two babies. I filled out admission forms and signed paperwork. I called my parents and Audrey's family and Callum and organised for Brendan to pick up Baxter. I told my mum exactly what kind of green blankets we needed.

But I'm scared, terrified, because with these two little babies in my arms, I have no idea what I'm doing. I just do what I'm told. Take my shirt off, hold baby one here, baby two there. Support their heads. Press this button if I need help. Keep them close together, close to you. Mum will be okay.

I want to scream that her name isn't 'Mum'. That her name is Audrey and she is the most important thing in my life. Only, I'm not sure that's true anymore. The realisation hurts but feels somehow wonderful. I would do anything for these babies. But I would still do anything for Audrey. And all I can think about is what she would want.

"She wanted to try to breastfeed." I announce as a

midwife arrives with two medicine syringes of milk. The same one who was there when Audrey crashed, in her pink scrubs with her kind eyes.

She closes them with a sigh, a gentle smile and a sharp nod. "We can try to hand express some colostrum once she wakes up, but it would just be to start her supply. With the pain relief she is on, they will need this for now."

"What is it?"

"It's formula, only a tiny amount because their stomachs are so small. But if they don't drink it, we might need to get them onto feeding tubes."

More tubes, more wires, but they are already so fragile. They weigh nothing, their tiny arms and legs so thin. "How do we get them to drink it?"

She shows me, tucking the end of the syringe into one baby's mouth and tickling under his chin until he starts to suck.

I sit up, awkwardly as I hold both babies close. For the first time in hours—maybe days, I've lost track—I smile. A wide toothy grin that hurts my cheeks and forces my eyes to swell. "He's doing it."

Once the syringe is empty the midwife steps away to write on his chart. "Does he have a name yet? Baby one?"

"Not yet." There was only one name we'd agreed on as a definite. "I've been calling him Uno for now."

She nods, her mouth still a firm, straight line. But when baby two sucks up his milk too, she cracks. A single tear drips down her cheek, her lips turn up.

"You've got two fighters on your hands."

"Three."

She looks at me, eyebrows scrunched together. The smile drops and she purses her lips, tilting her head to one side.

"Audrey. She's a fighter too."

The midwife doesn't answer. Instead her face softens. "Want me to ask how she is going in recovery?"

"Please."

I sink back into the chair, kissing each of my sons on the top of their tiny heads. As their little murmurs give way into steady breaths, a weight is lifted from my shoulders. They'll be okay.

But dread still settles in my stomach. Because I need Audrey to be okay too.

The steady beeping of machines begins to echo as my eyes droop. My head falls slack as exhaustion wins over the panic and adrenaline. It can't be safe to fall asleep with my babies on my chest, but it's so hard to reach the button. I force my eyes open, sitting up taller again and twisting in the seat. My elbow finds the button and I press down hard, just to be sure.

Nothing happens. No alarm sounds, no light turns on. But the kind midwife in the pink scrubs returns and I almost feel bad for not knowing her name. 'Sarah' the tag on her hip says. I commit the name to memory, hoping it sticks.

"I was just coming back," she smiles. "Audrey is starting to wake up. And it looks like these guys are starting to sleep."

I stand, still clinging to both babies but needing to move. There's an urge to jump, to whoop, to throw my hands in the air. Because Audrey is waking up. She's okay.

The midwife takes baby one from my arms and places him in his tiny, heated crib. I pass her baby two, hopping on my feet while she lays him down and turns on the lights over his tiny body.

She turns to stare at me, crossing her arms with an odd look on her face.

"You gonna put a shirt on, or are you giving all the women a show on the way there?"

My cheeks burn, but I grab my tank top from the back of the chair and stretch it over my head. She scoffs, smirking.

"Much better …"

I don't care. I pause at each babies' bed before I follow her. Resting my hand on each of their tiny bodies in turn. "I'll be back soon, I promise. I will never let you down."

Chapter Thirty-Two

AUDREY

A gentle hum fills the room, coaxing me awake, but I fight against the reflex to open my eyes. My head hurts. My body aches all over. My stomach feels light. No, numb. And there is a very odd sensation between my legs.

I try to turn over, but my body refuses to cooperate. A groan escapes my lips and I keep my eyes shut, trying to pretend I'm not awake.

Everything is wrong.

The sound of shuffled footsteps and whispers reverberate through my ears. So quiet, yet so loud. I squeeze my eyes shut tighter, inadvertently forcing a tear to escape down my cheek, and turn my head away from the noise. Away from the square of bright light in the otherwise dim room.

Then a sob, from right beside me. A sound I've never heard but would know anywhere. Michael. He came back. And he is sobbing, holding my hand, head bowed so low over my arm I can feel his hair tumble over my chest.

"I'm okay," I choke out. My throat burns and the words croak. And then through the foggy haze that is my brain, I remember. "The babies?"

"They're okay. I just … I had to feed them. They are tiny, but they are okay. Some oxygen, some lights, but they fed and Sarah said that's a really good sign. They're okay."

I don't know who Sarah is or why she has met my babies before me. I groan, part from the pain that is starting to swell through me and part because it's all *wrong*.

Because it was too early, because my babies aren't by my side, because I can't even remember them being born. And because when I needed him by my side, Michael was gone. I flinch my arm away from his touch. I can't deal with this right now. I need my babies.

I sense movement in front of me, and open my eyes to see a woman in pink scrubs reading the chart next to my bed. She examines the bag of fluid still—gulp—connected to my wrist.

"How are you feeling, Audrey?"

What a stupid question. I don't answer. Instead I moan, squeezing my eyes shut again, curling into myself and pulling the flimsy blanket up towards my neck.

"Fair. Can I check your blood pressure?"

I open my eyes to find her staring down at me with a gentle smile. The dark blue cuff in her hands. I dip my chin and remove one arm from the nest I've created.

She fastens the velcro strap and as it tightens on my arm I feel a firm squeeze in my chest. I'm still hyper aware of what's missing, of everything that has gone wrong.

"Where are they?"

"They're in the NICU. I can take you there as soon as we get a strong read on all your vitals. You gave us all a bit of a scare, Audrey."

"I don't care about me, I need to see them."

The blood pressure cuff loosens rapidly and my arm tingles at the changing sensation. Removing the machine, the midwife allows her hand to linger on my arm. To my other side, I register the feeling of firm fingers trying to loop themselves through mine. I jerk my arm back and slink my hand under the covers. He doesn't get to pick and choose when he wants to be with me.

"You should be with them." I hiss the words over my shoulder, not fully turning to face him. His gentle breathing by my side screeches in my ears. It's loud and obnoxious and it shouldn't be, but it is. The two sides of my brain battle it out, knowing that he was with the babies and I cannot fault him for that, but at the same time feeling unwanted, uncared for, betrayed. He wasn't there when I needed him, and okay he had two tiny, but incredibly valid reasons, but *he wasn't there.* Now it feels like he made his choice, he should stick with it. It might even be easier that way. He withdraws his hand from my side, taking a step back until the cold air whisks between us.

Typing away at her tablet, the midwife turns to me. Sorrow lines her eyes despite the gentle upturn of her lips. "I'll take you to them soon, but your blood pressure is still really low. We need to let your body recoup a little bit longer before we try to sit you up and move you about. I'm going to add another dose of pain medication to your bag and then we will see how you feel."

My chest cracks, another giant wound to match the one across my belly.

"They're sleeping right now." Michael's voice is tender and breathy. He fights to hold in a yawn but I hear the deep exhale that pushes out against his will.

"Why don't you get a little more rest, and when they wake, we can see about getting you down there in a wheelchair?"

As the midwife leaves, Michael settles into the chair in the corner of the small room. "Do you want some light?"

"No." It could be the middle of the night, for all I know. Hours passed like minutes in the delivery room, and then I slept for all that time.

"What do—"

"You weren't there." I cut him off, not needing his pointless small talk or distractions. "I was so scared, and you weren't there."

He leaps off the chair to my side, kneeling down until

his face can rest on the pillow beside mine. "I was, I'm sorry. They pushed me out of the way, I kept trying to get closer to you but I couldn't. I followed you into that room, but then our first tiny baby was crying and they just handed him to me, like I was supposed to know what I was doing. And then … I don't even know Audrey … it all happened so fast, his brother was born and you were bleeding and they made me leave." Tears stream down his face, but I want to slap him.

I want to tell him that I know it was scary because I was there. Because I thought I was dying and I couldn't tell him I loved him and I was never going to meet my babies.

"Audrey, I wanted to stay with you, but I couldn't. Because you had the best team of doctors working to save your life and I couldn't leave our boys to be by themselves."

"Boys?"

He sniffs. Stretching a hand up, he uses his thumb to wipe away the tear that had threatened to spill from my eyes. His fingers lace into my hair and he pushes forward to kiss my forehead.

"I'm sorry," he whispers. "There was probably a better way for me to tell you that."

I nuzzle into his hand. "What are their names?"

"I was waiting for you. It was … rough … for a little while. They couldn't tell me if you were going to be okay, I think because they just didn't know. Your placenta tore a hole through your uterus and the doctor struggled to control the bleeding. You lost a lot of blood. You were out for … I don't know, I lost count of the hours. But all I could do was wait. With our tiny boys on my chest, I just waited for you to be okay."

"I need to see them."

"I know, you will. I'll go and check on them soon. But you need to rest."

"What about Maisie?"

"She's with Callum, he said she can stay as long as we need. He'll bring her in when you are ready."

Realising that Michael has everything somehow under control my eyelids grow heavy and I have to force myself to keep them open. "Stay with me, a little longer. Before you go back."

Michael kisses my head again, then leans down until his forehead rests against mine. His eyes are the colour of chocolate in the dim lighting of the room, but they twinkle with deep joy. "I'll stay with you always. I love you."

He doesn't stay, because when I wake again, Michael is gone. Again. But the wound doesn't cut so deep this time because I know, deep in my gut where my babies once lived, that he is with them.

The room is blurry as I open my eyes. The pain in my stomach is intense, but also somehow dull and I'm able to sit myself up the tiniest bit so I can sip at the water beside my bed. The first mouthful glides down, cooling the sore, dry edges of my throat. I refill the tiny plastic cup and have a second gulp, then a third. I push to sit up further, but the odd feeling between my legs is back. I hadn't thought earlier, but I know now what it is and I want it gone.

As though she can somehow sense I'm awake, the same midwife from earlier slips into the room. "Audrey," she all but sings my name.

"Are you Sarah?" I ask, remembering the name Michael mentioned earlier.

She gives a little curtsey, "I wouldn't have blamed you for not remembering. How are you feeling?"

"Better, I want to go see them. I tried to sit up but …" I

gesture at the catheter between my legs. The word sits like a lump in my stomach and it's hard enough to think about it, let alone actually say it. If I do, I might vomit up the water I just drank.

Sarah tips on her heels and rushes to check my chart. She taps at the tablet, swiping through notes. Reaching under the cabinet, she pulls out the blood pressure machine.

"We'll check this again. If it's all good, the next step would be to remove that and see how you go sitting. If your blood pressure stays stable, I can take you across the hall. Sound good?"

In lieu of answering, I reach my hand across to her. She smiles as the cuff inflates, and hums a little when it deflates and she jots down the number.

"This is going to be a little uncomfortable, you ready?" Sarah moves to the end of the bed and when I give her the okay, she goes about removing the catheter. Uncomfortable is one way of describing it. Humiliating would be another good one. But once I've regained some composure a lightness begins to spread through the room. I'm ready.

She helps me spin my legs off the bed, moving slowly and pausing with each step. Once I'm seated, albeit awkwardly because of the numbing pain through my core, she checks my blood pressure again.

"Okay," she says with a satisfied smile. "You ready to meet your boys? You've got three bloody beautiful ones down there."

Three? My heart skips enough beats that if I was still connected to the heart monitor it would have sounded like a novelty horn.

Sarah giggles. "Well, two little boys and one stunner of a man." She gasps and slaps a hand across her face. Her cheeks turn red as she tries to hide her embarrassment. "That's incredibly unprofessional of me, I'm so sorry."

"It's okay, you should see him without the shirt on." The memory chips away at the walls that had built around my heart.

"I have, he was doing skin on skin with the boys and …" She runs her hands across her face, trembling. "Sorry, I'm going to stop talking now. You're very lucky."

She skitters away to get the wheelchair from beside the door and when she turns to bring it back to me, the deep red in her cheeks has dissipated.

"I am," I finally answer her as she rolls me towards the NICU. Even though I'm doing a pretty shit job of showing Michael that.

Chapter Thirty-Three

AUDREY

This moment is nothing like I imagined. I imagined dim lights and soft music. I imagined holding Michael's hand and him kissing my sweaty forehead as our baby was laid gently across my chest. I imagined soaking in all the love and bringing our second child into a room full of joy.

Instead, my babies were whisked away while I was dying. They were carried by someone who wasn't me, while the doctors fought to save my life. Then they were cared for by someone else while my body healed. Not fully, but enough.

Sarah pushes me down a hallway so bright it hurts my eyes.

My incision aches a dull, slow pain, but moths swirl in my stomach. I pull the blanket on my lap tighter around me, and hold my breath as I'm wheeled towards my babies. Fluorescent tubes buzz overhead, guiding us towards the NICU ward. She pauses before we enter.

"You ready?"

I'm not. I'm scared. But instead of telling her and letting the tidal wave of emotions out on some poor, unsuspecting midwife, I nod. She guides me through the automatic doors and points out the hand sanitiser I must use before we go any further.

The rhythmic beeping of many, *too many*, machines echoes through the room. It smells like bleach and citrus, it's far too clinical and not at all homely. But even so, it is my boys' home for the foreseeable future. Sarah wheels me in between two enclosed cribs that look far too large for the tiny babies inside them.

The sterile air hitches in my throat. Sitting on a cold green plastic chair between the beds, Michael rests his head against the plastic wall of one. His hand stretches out to rest on the other. His eyes are closed and for a moment it looks like he could be sleeping, but he stands at the sound of my soft cries.

"This," he says, taking my hand and directing my attention to the baby on my right, "is Uno. Name definitely not official. Baby one."

Tiny fingers cling in two little fists beside red cheeks. His eyes are squeezed shut, fighting against the dim lighting of the room. Four little round pads are spread across his delicate chest, with wires that link to the machine next to his crib, and an oxygen tube sits under his nose. And he is perfect.

My fingers coast along the side of the crib, itching to reach in and hold him.

Michael shifts my attention to my left. "And this is Henry. Name also not official, but I couldn't keep calling them baby one and baby two, and I know it was on your list."

"Henry." He also has a breathing tube, and wires attached to his chest. A monitor is fastened around his foot, but even in his sleep he wriggles against it. He has the same button nose as his brother and his dad, but his cheeks are chubbier. "It's perfect."

I turn to Sarah, who has stepped back to give us space. "Can I?"

"Of course."

Her and Michael help me into the chair, which isn't the comfiest but is miles better than the wheelchair. Once I've adjusted my position Michael shows me how to pull down my top.

"Skin on skin is good for them. Kangaroo care."

"This is Henry," Sarah whispers, handing me my tiny baby boy. She guides him to my chest, rearranging all his wires and tubes until he is comfortably snuggled against my skin.

My free hand wipes at the tears on my cheeks before they drop onto his little head.

"And this is Uno."

Sarah tucks him against me. Again she adjusts all the cords until he is nestled on my chest, next to his brother.

"We're not keeping that name." I laugh, but it's barely a sigh as the gravity of the moment falls onto my shoulders.

"I know." Michael stands behind me, with his arms around my shoulders and my heart in his hands. He kisses my neck, just below my ear. "I love you."

I turn to face him. Kissing him on his cheek. My mouth lingers until he turns into me and our lips collide. But it's not sexy or passionate or rushed or wild. It's calm and laden with sheer delight and it's all encompassing. It's love. For each other, for our boys.

"What about William?"

Michael leans back, only a little but enough to wipe my cheeks dry. "I like it," he says as he reaches down to place his hand on William's back.

I stayed there for hours, that first day. I helped feed Henry and William when it was time, crying that I wouldn't be able to breastfeed after all. I knew it was a stretch goal, to breastfeed *twins* when my body had struggled to make enough milk for Maisie, but even so the finality of the decision hurt. Like I wasn't even given a chance to try. I wriggled in the chair when my bum turned numb and I held in my pain as the medication started to wear off. Michael sat on the floor at my feet, leaning his head on my lap. His breaths turned heavy as he fell asleep.

I stayed long after Sarah went home until eventually, a different midwife came and told me I needed rest. Michael helped settle the boys into their cribs and held my weight as I moved back to the wheelchair. He pushed me back to my room and he stayed by my side as a new dose of medication helped me fall into a deep sleep

In the days that followed, I lost all track of time. My hours were spent sleeping or sitting on that cold green chair with my boys on my chest. Michael seemed to never leave the hospital but always managed to be clean, sneaking out while I slept to eat and rest and shower.

Maisie came to visit and somehow she understood to be calm, to talk quietly, to be gentle as she held her brothers' hands. My parents offered to come up, but I told them to wait until we were home. Overhearing the conversation, Michael told his parents to do the same.

And then one day, when my incision had started to heal and my body was functioning to a satisfactory level, I had to go home. Without my babies. The wound in my stomach may have been healing, but the one through my heart was sliced a little deeper.

"They just need a little more time," Sarah said as I walked out of the NICU that day. Tears that had barely stopped since the day I first met them streamed across my face and onto my shirt.

At home, a new nightmare began. Waking every few hours knowing it was time to feed my boys even though they were miles away, still at the hospital, still being watched around the clock.

Maisie started school. We saw her off in a sea of tiny new students and teary-eyed families. Callum and me and Cassidy and Michael, all four of her grown up people waving until she was so far into the room we couldn't see her. And she thrived. Making new friends and learning how to write letters and read sounds. But she spends more time there than she does with me, and it eats at my insides that I've been so distant. So torn in every direction that no one seems to get all of me because I'm always so distracted by who's missing out.

I spend every waking moment juggling my time between being home and being present for Maisie and being here, at the hospital.

And when I was here, I was charting progress like markers on a map. One where the road was bumpy and the destination was the only thing keeping us going. Home day. I dreaded that the boys might be separated. I cried a thousand tears when Henry fed from a bottle instead of a syringe, but William needed a feeding tube inserted when he wasn't putting on weight.

Days were tracked with milestones. William's feeding tube coming out after only two days. Both boys maintaining their oxygen levels without help from the tubes. They were putting on weight, feeding well, and holding their body temperature. By every definition they were overachieving premature babies.

It was wonderful, but still, we waited. For almost a month I held my breath at every visit, waiting for the news to drop. Waiting to be told they could come home.

"You ready?"

Sarah has become my comfort. My companion when I was here and Michael couldn't be. She saw me laugh, saw me cry. Helped me hold both boys, helped me feed them, change them.

She showed me how to love them, how to be what they needed when everything still felt not quite right.

Tears well in her eyes as she peels back the first round pad from William's chest, and one escapes down her cheek when she moves on to the other three. She turns to repeat the process for Henry, while I do up William's tiny onesie.

I pick him up, cradling him close. "Say goodbye," I whisper in his ear.

Michael steps forward, holding the first capsule in place on the green plastic chair that after four weeks oddly feels like home now. I smile at him, loosely. It means nothing. Our relationship is strained, at best. When I wasn't here, he was. When he wasn't, I have no idea where he was. Was he going home, to the house I opened up for him, even when I wasn't there? Was he returning to his bachelor pad? Was he at work or at the gym? Was he living his life when I had been forced to hit pause on my own? I don't resent him for it. *I don't.* I just can't pretend I'm *thrilled* about it either. The idea of us playing happy families when the boys were born is just another dream that was taken from me.

I buckle William in place. The padded seat belt envelops his minute frame. My hand lingers on his cheek and I trail my fingers down his arm to the tiny wristband that still says "Baby Baker One."

We repeat the process for Henry. Then wrap their sage green blankets over them.

Michael picks up both carriers, his muscles strained not against the weight, but against the awkward shape of the car seats. I turn to Sarah. Her cheeks are wet as she checks off the last few bits of paperwork.

"You're off," she says. Her lips turn up and she grins the biggest smile I've seen from her. "I'll miss you, but gosh I'm happy to see you all go."

Chapter Thirty-Four

MICHAEL

In the space of a few months, I've had more than my share of hardest moments. Audrey, too. So many that were so bad that no matter how shitty right now feels, it doesn't even come close.

Still, I hate that I am here. Hate that the day after our boys came home, to Audrey's house, I had to leave. Hate that I'm letting her down. Hate that my actions are doing nothing but reinforcing the idea of me she has in her head. That I leave when things get tough.

She has no idea what I've been doing the past few weeks—months, even—and it's eating her inside. I can see the sorrow behind her eyes when she smiles at me. I can feel the ice in her touch when we cross paths. There have been many, many times I was so close to throwing in the towel and telling her everything. But she deserves all of what I am doing and more. The last thing I want is for her to feel like she is stuck waiting.

So this morning I helped her feed Henry and William their morning bottles and settled her on the couch with a cup of tea and a book and the TV remote and everything else she might possibly need while I'm gone. I premeasured bottles and got the boys back to sleep in their cots. I hugged Audrey from behind the couch, kissing the soft skin below her ear and promising her I'd be back soon. She shrugged away from my touch, so I slid out the door before I ruined the surprise.

The sun glares through the windows of the car, heating

the interior until the air is thick. A thin layer of sweat beads on the tops of my arms as I shake away my thoughts.

Brendan slams a hand on the car door. "Get out."

I oblige, not because he asked, but because it was starting to hurt to breathe in there anyway.

"Can we make this quick?" I ask, taking a hint of my frustration out on my mate. It's not his fault we happened to plan this meeting to be the day after the boys could finally come home. It's not his fault I didn't have the foresight to re-schedule after the hospital told us the news. What's done is done, though, and I want to get this over with as soon as I can.

"How the fuck did I get stuck running your site?"

"Because you're the one who convinced me to run the big hotel site. Blame yourself."

Glaring at him, I turn towards the building site. My building site. Audrey's home. "Come on, I want to get through this walkthrough, so I can go see Noah about the hotel and then get back to Audrey." The other meeting I stupidly planned and ignorantly didn't think to reschedule.

"Is she at the hospital with the boys?"

"She's at home," I snap. "With the boys."

Brendan's mouth drops open. The folder in his hand threatens to fall to the ground as his grip loosens. "When did they come home?"

"Yesterday. So, I'd really like to get back there."

"We could have done this another day."

I shake my head, stalking past Brendan to let Baxter down from the tray. He bounds through the mud towards the exterior of the property. It's dirty, like any job site, with mud splattered on the windows and dust covering the panelling. But it's stunning. The facade is the perfect blend of modern and historical, giving a cute cottage vibe without feeling like it belongs to a grandma. The patio wraps around the perimeter of the house, but the railing is a cleaner, modern take on a picket fence with clean posts and long horizontal bars.

"I don't want to delay the build."

Brendan scoffs something that sounds oddly like "whipped", but I let it slide. I am, and I don't care who knows it. I grab Baxter's long lead and chase after him, tying him to one of the posts on the patio with plenty of slack to move around.

"The boys must be doing okay then?" Brendan asks as we enter the house.

"Yeah, better than. Even the doctors were surprised at their progress. They've put on plenty of weight and they don't need any of the extra support now. Just Audrey. And me."

"And how are you, and Audrey?"

Depends on what he's asking, really. I'm fine. Still scared shitless every day, still terrified every time I pick up one of the boys, still worried I'm doing everything wrong and nothing right. But beyond that, I'm okay. I've accepted the way they entered the world. Sure, it wasn't our plan, and it was far from ideal, but it is what it is. I'm just grateful for the team that surrounded us and supported us through their earliest, roughest, days. I can't shake how awful it felt when I thought I was losing Audrey, when my life started to crumble and I was forced to go with the boys instead of staying by her side. But I can accept that it was a moment in time, and that time has passed.

Audrey is doing well, too, from what I can tell. It's been even harder on her. She has Maisie to worry about too. And a major surgery to recover from. Everything takes more effort, standing, walking, sitting. She's only just now able to drive again and even then, she gets uncomfortable sitting in that position for too long. But she is the best mother I ever could have imagined for my children and I love her more and more every day. There has been a distance behind every smile, but her face lit up when we walked out of the hospital.

But, if he's asking about me *and* Audrey, together. I don't know. Everything feels hard and not because it is but because we are exhausted and nothing has gone to plan and it's difficult to accept the change in our relationship. Just as we were settling into something that felt an awful lot like love, just when we were making plans for a future where we were together—instead of just co-parenting—the universe threw us a massive curve ball.

Instead of supporting each other through the boys' earliest days and weeks, we've been forced to separate. To take turns. We barely see each other, choosing instead to make sure one of us was always at the hospital with the boys. The few times we managed to both be there together, it was a blur of bottle feeds and routine checks and kangaroo care. Our conversation was hushed, forced small talk to drown out the rhythmic beeping and the heaviness in the air.

When I wasn't there, I was here, building her house, or at the winery trying to prove to my dad—and Audrey—that I've changed. That I'm not some stupid kid anymore, I'm an adult and I'm ready. It felt wrong, staying at Audrey's house when she was at the hospital, so I spent what little free time I had at my old apartment.

"I didn't realise that was such a loaded question." Brendan breaks the lingering silence as I ponder his question. His expression is soft as he leans against an empty door frame, tucking the folder under an arm.

"It's been … tough. For her, for me. And for us."

He scratches his temple with the corner of his folder. "Does she know this is what you're doing when you're not around?"

I shake my head, staring down at my shuffling feet. Embarrassed because as soon as someone other than me said it, the idea of the surprise feels childish. She doesn't need, and probably doesn't even want, to move house in the near future. Sure, she complained that her house was too small. But the boys *just* came home, she's still recovering, everyone is still adjusting.

"You should probably tell her."

"I know. But now it's so close to being ready, maybe I should keep the surprise."

He pushes off the doorway and stands with his legs apart and arms crossed. A power stance if I ever saw one. The guy is me, twelve months ago. Never been in a serious relationship but out here thinking he knows everything about them anyway.

"I think she deserves to know what you're doing."

"I don't want her to worry about the idea of moving. Okay, so the end result is great because she gets the big house she wanted, but the stress of moving house when the boys have only just come home? I want to let her have some time to focus on that, first. Worry about moving when it's time and we are all ready."

Brendan rolls his eyes. "Your call mate."

We go through the rest of the walkthrough without dragging the conversation through the mud. It resonates as I sign away my satisfaction, and I dwell on it as I secure Baxter back in the tray of the ute. One more stop, then I'll be home.

Noah is a little more understanding when I tell him I need to make the meeting quick. He starts rushing me out of his office as soon as I tell him the boys are home. We fly through the progress report. Everything's on track, the site is in lock up and all the inside carpentry is complete. Nearly ready to start all the finishings. The hotel will be ready for bookings before the next Spring/Summer season.

Pride swells as Noah thanks me for my hard work, assuring me he never would have known it was my first big project if we hadn't told him. And he is right, everything went off without a hitch. I renegotiated contracts and timelines with tradies and suppliers. I've managed all the paperwork and invoices. We've had plenty of these progress meetings, and each one has been positive. It's still a big step to think my dad is gearing me towards running the whole business. But if I can do this, maybe I can do that after all.

"Why are you even still here?" Noah asks after I pack up my small stack of papers. I slide them into the folder I purchased after our first meeting. "Surely you can take some parental leave? It's your dad's business, right?"

"He offered." I mumble.

"Huh?" Noah moves around his desk and opens the door. He's pushing me out, knowing more than I do that I need to get home. To Audrey. To our boys.

I stand from the chair and pivot on my heel. "He said he would get someone else to cover the job while I took some time off. But I wanted to finish this. I need to finish this. To show myself, him, that I can."

Noah closes the door and takes a step towards me, ready to give me what I'm sure will be another one of his meaningful TED talks about life and relationships, and how terrible I am at them. He sucks in a breath and places a firm hand on my shoulder. I have to look up at him, and I hate how small I feel in this moment. I'm not short, but the man is tall. And even though I have a good few kilos of muscle on him, I feel like a child as he looks down on me.

"You can, Michael. Remember how you were the only one who doubted that?"

I clear my throat, trying to rid it of the lump that forms against my will.

"It's easier for me to keep up with the progress on Audrey's house while I'm still working anyway."

His brow furrows.

"She was complaining about how small the townhouse was. She lost all her painting space when Maisie's toys had to be moved into the sunroom, and the boys' cots are squished into their bedroom. I had land just sitting there. So, I'm building her a house. I just hate that it means I keep having to sneak away, and at least while I'm working I can say I have meetings."

I step away from Noah's reach as I tell him. His face doesn't soften, if anything, the line between his brows deepens. He purses his lips into a tight thin line.

"Does she know?"

"Not yet."

"*Not yet?* You mean you haven't told her? Fucking hell, Michael. You don't think she deserves to know that you're building her a house? That she might want to know that?"

Noah takes a few steps back until he is leaning against the wall. He props one knee up and crosses his arms over his chest. My shoulders sink and I drop, sideways, into the chair behind me. The armrest juts against my leg, but I ignore it, leaning forward until my head falls between my knees.

"I wanted it to be a surprise. But then the boys were born early and there's been no good time to tell her. When I left today she was so distant."

Noah sighs, long and hard. His eyes close and I get the sense he is carefully thinking through each word he is about to say. A skill I probably need to master.

"Her life is on hold, right?" he asks, but continues before I can answer. "She's on maternity leave, juggling between the boys and Maisie and trying to find maybe a sliver of time to herself to process everything she has been through. And the day after you can finally bring the boys home from hospital, you rush off to 'meetings'. No wonder she seemed distant."

"Fuck."

"Yeah. I get that you wanted to keep busy while the boys were in the hospital. And as sideways as building a house for Audrey might be, I get why you're doing it. But now that the boys are home, Audrey is going to need your help. A lot of it. You can't keep walking out on her and you especially can't keep doing it without telling her where you are."

"But the surprise …"

Noah shakes his head and opens the sliding door. Noise from the winery filters into his office, glasses clinking, cutlery shuffling, people laughing. But it's white noise against the steady pounding in my ear as I realise how royally I've fucked up.

Noah pulls me out of the chair and shoves me through the door. Pointing to the exit, he pats the back of my shoulder, nudging me forward. "Fuck the surprise."

Chapter Thirty-Five

AUDREY

Amidst the noise I suspect will become my new normal, I miss the rhythmic sounds of the hospital. The scurried footsteps in the hall would be worlds better than the steady thumping of Maisie bouncing her basketball in the backyard. And I'd take beeping monitors and the gentle buzz from the lights over the crying and shushing. Times two.

Because everything is times two.

Henry screams in my arms, and no amount of swaddling or rocking or bouncing or shushing or feeding seems to help. He spits out his dummy, over and over again, and I put it back in, holding it in place, hoping he sucks it.

Over the noise that pulls at my heart and hurts in my bones, I hear Cassidy fighting the same battle down the hall. William crying out, just like his brother. Cassidy's trim nail tapping against his dummy as she tries to keep it in his mouth. Her *sh, sh, shh*ing in time with her footsteps.

They weren't supposed to stay. They might have even had plans. But when they came to drop Maisie off, they found me trapped on the couch. Two crying babies wriggling against my chest, my own tears dripping onto their soft heads.

When they woke, I'd tried to feed William and Henry the bottles that Michael had got ready, but neither of them drank much. I managed to change both their nappies before the screaming really kicked up. Nothing worked. Nothing is working. And if only Michael was here maybe I wouldn't have fallen apart.

He's not though. I have no idea where he is because he said he had a 'meeting', but he has been gone for hours.

Disappointment began to brew the minute the door clicked shut behind him. Anger mixed in as his car drove off down the length of the driveway. The boys slept soundly in their cots but resentment swirled through me until my head hurt.

How dare he? Have the nerve to just leave as soon as we were settled. It better have been some damn important meeting to have left.

It's always the leaving, with Michael. There's always a reason, but he's always leaving. And I am never afforded the luxury. Imagine, if I just up and left him with the boys without any hint of when I'd return. I couldn't. And even if I could, I wouldn't.

"Do you think maybe they want to be close?" Cassidy walks back down the hall, bouncing with each step. She slides right next to me until the boys are close enough to hold hands.

As though they sense each other, an instant calm washes over both of them. Henry starts to suck on his dummy, and with my hand no longer holding it in his mouth, I can shift him in my arms. My stomach aches, the thick scar tissue that slices me in two stretching from all the standing and bouncing and holding.

In Cassidy's arms, William lets out a tiny whimper, but settles against her chest. One of his tiny arms stretched out to rest on Henry's head.

"Woah," Cassidy mutters, the awe in her voice apparent despite her hushed tone. "Should we try to sit?"

"Let's give them a second, then we'll try."

When the boys settle into sleep, we move in tandem to the couch, sitting in sync. My thigh rests against hers as we stay close so that the twins can still reach each other.

"Is this a twin thing?"

I look down at Henry's near bald head. "Maybe?"

I hope so, but I also hope not. I was blissfully ignorant about how much time I would spend on my own with both boys. I physically can't carry them both around all the time. The sad truth is that they will have to get used to being apart. Just like I'll have to get used to being on my own. Again.

I gnaw at the inside of my cheek, hoping to hide the self-loathing that spreads across my skin. It tingles like sunburn that's ready to peel and I wriggle against the sensation. I should have known. People don't change. Not the way I wanted Michael to. Not the way I hoped he had. I push him from my thoughts, not ready to face the cold truth anymore.

Cassidy shifts her weight next to me, swapping the hand that rests under William's bottom. Her new free hand traces tiny circles on his back. With her eyes closed, Cassidy lets out a breath, it hitches in the middle, but she sucks air back with a sniff.

"I'm sorry if this is hard for you." It would be hard for me, if I'd been dealt Cassidy's cards.

She shakes her head. "It's not, which surprises me. It just feels right. To have these boys in my life in this way. I know it must be hard for you, with everything right now. But for me this feels right."

I don't force out any unnecessary words, instead falling into a silence that's broken only by soft whimpers from the boys and heavy sighs from me.

"Did Michael say when he would be home?"

I purse my lips. "No."

Cassidy shifts to turn her body towards mine. William wriggles in her lap and we hold our breaths, waiting to see if the movement has broken the spell. It hasn't, because he settles back into place, sucking at his dummy.

"I still think he has changed. This was a massive error in judgement, but Noah says he is determined to make the hotel build a success. He's desperate to prove himself. To his dad, and to you."

Before I can answer, the sound of a car coming up the driveway echoes through the hall. Maisie runs into the house. She stops in her tracks when she sees us on the couch. Creeping over, she pats each of her brothers tenderly on the head before turning to the front of the house.

"Michael!" She stage whispers before running to open the front door for him.

Callum follows Maisie into the house, detouring into the kitchen.

Beside me, Cassidy stands awkwardly, inching the boys apart. Neither of them protest, so she stalks off through the house. I hear hushed words, the shuffling of fabric, and eventually three very different sets of footsteps coming through the house.

"Maisie, why don't you practise some of your new ballet positions in your room. Do you have the book we got you?" Cassidy directs Maisie into her bedroom.

Michael stands at the end of the hallway, William on his chest and a bunch of lilies hanging by his side. His chin is low as he shuffles his feet. He searches the room for me, but drops his gaze down to his feet when he sees me on the couch. If it wasn't for Henry, now fast asleep on my chest, it would look like I hadn't moved in the hours Michael has been gone. And from the look on his face, I'd say he knows it.

Pulling Callum around the kitchen bench, Cassidy opens the back door to let Baxter out and turns to look at me. She rolls her eyes towards Michael, dropping them low to the flowers that hang by his side. Her eyebrows jump and she tilts her head to the side.

"We'll get going. Thank you for letting us help Audrey." I go to brush off her thanks, but she holds a hand up to stop me. "I mean it. Thank you."

With Callum dragging behind her, she skitters out of the house.

Tension hangs thick in the air as the door clicks behind them. It turns to lead as the grumble of their car on the gravel dies down.

"I'm sorry," Michael finally says. He drops the flowers on the table and joins me on the couch, but the gap between us is blinding. Cassidy and I were leg to leg the whole time, but Michael sits right up against the arm rest. He turns his body to face mine, one knee propping up on the cushions. I *dare* him to make himself comfier. To lean back or close his eyes. Thankfully for him, he doesn't.

I don't respond to his apology. I can't say it's okay when it's not.

"I shouldn't have left today, and I knew that as soon as I had. I did everything I could to get back as soon as possible, but I know that means nothing to you."

He adjusts William in his arms to free a hand, and uses it to pull the band out of his hair. It falls down over his shoulders and he brushes it back from his face with his fingers. A stray piece falls across his cheeks and I want to reach out and tuck it away. I want to run my fingers over his cheek and okay maybe I want to kiss him. But I also want to slap him and *fuck,* hormones are annoying.

"Can I tell you where I was?" he asks.

I slump back into the cushions behind me and tipping my head to face the ceiling. A flicker of heat trickles down my neck, remembering the last time I was in the position. But the ice in my head and in my heart douses the flame before it has a chance to catch. We were different then. I was naive, drunk in lust and hope.

"I don't want to talk about it. Go do you, it's fine." It's not. In fact, it's far from it. But resentment swells until baseless, emotionless remarks are all I can manage. "The boys will wake up soon. I just want to enjoy the peace before it's over."

He shifts, one hand on William's back as he sits up. With his free hand, Michael wraps his large arm around Henry's tiny frame, rolling him off my chest. With the boys snuggled into his chest, Michael makes my ovaries explode. If I hadn't just *been* pregnant I—*No*. I cut the thought off and snap my eyes shut. Never again.

"Before the boys, you said you needed a grown up. Not another child. That's what I'm trying to be. I just know that I'm shit at it. I made a promise to myself that I would be the man you deserve, the man all three of you deserve—four if you count Maisie, which we should. I said I would step up and make something of myself. That's what I'm trying to do. I made a commitment to my dad to manage Noah's project and prove that I am capable. Not just of a job, but of eventually running his business. I should never have prioritised that over being here with you today. I fucked up, and I'm sorry."

My neck begins to ache from the stretch. I roll it to the side, facing Michael but keeping my eyes closed so I don't get distracted by all the soft masculinity he's displaying. "Thank you for acknowledging it."

"There's something else." He continues and there it is. Not for the first time, and probably not for the last, I hold my breath as I prepare for the blow.

He nudges me with his knee. "You don't just deserve a man who has his shit together. You also deserve to do what you love, every day. And you deserve the space to do it, properly, not crammed in next to Maisie's toys."

"Kids take up space."

"Right, so it's a good thing I have plenty of space to give you."

My heart sinks to my stomach and my throat closes. My

lip quivers and I want to tell him to stop, that I don't need to hear it.

"That came out wrong. I had land," he rushes out. "I'm building you a house."

A house? I open my eyes, my lip no longer quivering but instead hanging so low my chin hits my shoulder. He did not just say what I think he did. *Did he?*

Because I swear I thought I heard him say he was building me a whole damn house, after what, one—maybe two—comments about this one being too small. All so I can have room to paint again. Regardless of the fact I don't have *time* to paint again right now. The two half-finished commission canvases sit on easels in the now crowded sunroom, along with the promise to get them done as soon as possible and the reassurance that the women understand and I should take my time.

Time. I start to spiral, counting up the minutes and the hours and the sheer effort required to move into a new house. Never mind the two time thieves currently cuddled up on Michael's chest. I'll have to feed them soon, and the cycle will begin all over again.

"I don't have time."

Michael shushes Henry, who has started wriggling and whimpering, as if on cue. Although, it may be William. Without being able to see the little dab of blue nail polish on Henry's big toenail, and especially without being able to see the extra puffiness of his cheeks, I can't be certain.

"You don't need to do anything Audrey, I promise. It's nearly done. I'll handle the final walk through. I'll organise landscaping before you move in and I'll help with everything on moving day, and leading up to it."

"Fine."

There's a small, tiny—miniscule really—piece of me that's excited. Hell, I might even have swooned a little in an alternate universe. He's doing what he can, in the way that he can. This is his grand gesture, in a very Michael way, to show me he will do anything for me and the boys. I can hear the love and good intentions in his voice. I can appreciate the effort he is going to and how he just wants me to have everything he thinks I deserve. And that he is the man who can give it all to me. Plus, I do genuinely think this house is too small and we need a bigger backyard for Baxter. The poor dog is currently trapped in a tiny courtyard of an outdoor area.

But I'm still mad. Moving house is a big deal, and Michael has come in and made all the decisions for me.

"I should have told you."

"You should have asked me," I snap. I jump up, and am halfway to the kitchen before Michael tries to respond. I cut him off, "I don't want to talk about this right now. Build your house, go to your meetings, I have enough to worry about without adding more."

Bottles slam against the counter under my fingers. I spill a scoop of formula, cursing at the loss because that shit is expensive. I force myself to slow down, to breathe, as I carefully measure out the water and drop the bottles into the warmer.

"They'll need a feed soon," I say, turning on my heel and pushing my shoulders back. The rushed movement and forced posture pulls at my scar until I'm forced to hunch over a little. "I'm having a shower."

I don't let him answer, instead stalking to the bathroom and slamming the door shut.

I make quick work of turning the shower as hot as it will go, stripping down, and stepping into the steady stream. Scorching water rushes over me, burning away the worst of the rage. A tiny sliver of anger is left when I'm done, softened by the hint of appreciation that tries to push through.

I can be angry and thankful at the same time, right?

Chapter Thirty-Six

MICHAEL

Audrey races around the house, Henry wrapped to her front. His tiny toes poke through the stretchy fabric, one foot either side of her chest. Lately, on our chests has been the only place he will sleep. It's exhausting, but since Callum's sister stopped past with a basket of baby wearing accessories, it's been a little easier.

I haven't quite mastered how to tie the long stretch of fabric. When it's my turn—which would be more often if she would let me—Audrey still has to wrap me up while I hold Henry to my chest. Once it's done though, we're free to go about the rest of the day with our hands free. No more being trapped on the couch. It's a start.

William finishes his bottle and I sit him up in my lap. Just as Audrey taught me, one hand supports under his chin while the other pats against his back. After a few gentle taps he grunts, but the adult sized burp I'm hoping for doesn't come. I pull a cloth over my shoulder, hoisting him up so his arms dangle down my back. Standing, I continue patting and rubbing his back.

"Audrey, you don't need to do that."

She's got the vacuum out and is steering it towards the hallway that leads to Maisie and the boys' rooms. Huffing, she turns to glare at me.

"I don't want your mother to think I can't keep my house clean."

William wiggles against my shoulder and burps in my ear.

"Good job buddy," I whisper to him as I adjust my hold on him. Propping him in one arm so his head nestles into the crook of my elbow, I step around the couch.

"I promise you she will not notice if you don't vacuum the floor. And if by some odd fluke she trips and lands face to the floor in Maisie's room to find a tiny crumb hidden in the carpet, she will blame me, not you."

With my free hand, I take the vacuum from Audrey and step back. She protests, moving towards me but my long strides are too quick for her. I spin on my heel and take the vacuum back to the linen closet off the laundry. The sound of clattering dishes starts up in the kitchen, so I kick the cupboard closed and race out.

Audrey has one hand on the bench supporting her back as she unloads the dishwasher. Thank God she knows how to tie the wrap so tightly, because Henry hasn't moved an inch off her chest despite the way she leans forward.

Moving behind her, I place my hand around her middle and pull her upright. With William in one arm, I hold Audrey against my side until she drops her head back against my shoulder.

"You do not need to get the house ready for them. You've met my mother, she could not care less if the dishwasher is loaded."

Audrey shakes her head, her messy bun tickling under my chin. "She always finds things though. Dishes to wash or laundry to fold."

"She isn't judging you for not having them done, Audrey. She doesn't do it because she thinks you can't, she just wants to help." I squeeze my arm around her and kiss the top of her head. "If you want her to stop, I'll tell her to stop."

Audrey twists her head to me. Her mouth forms a thin, straight line, and I tip my head down to rest my forehead on hers.

"It's really helpful when she does it," Audrey admits. She frees her lip with a grin and slips out of my loose hold. "You know what else would be really helpful?"

I raise an eyebrow, humming for her to continue.

"If you could hold Henry while I shower?"

She's already untying the giant knot under Henry's bum. I stare in wonder as she unwraps the fabric, all while keeping Henry still and secure with her other hand.

"Want me to wrap you up?" she asks once she has successfully untwisted herself.

I reach for Henry, taking him from her arms and holding him on my chest, nestled close to William. The boys reach for each other, linking tiny hands above my heart. I let out a deep satisfied breath. I hope they never lose this connection.

"Nah, I'll be fine like this."

"Are you sure?"

"As I'll ever be, Audrey. Go have your shower, take your time."

She slinks off down the hall calling over her shoulder, "I can't take my time, your parents will be here soon."

"So, they arrive and you're in the shower, no big deal."

She ignores me, slipping into her bedroom and waving an arm behind her. "I'll be quick!"

Sitting down on the living room floor, I place both boys on the playmat and hold my breath. Henry wriggles and I think maybe I was too sure of myself to not need the wrap, but I roll him onto his stomach so he can see his brother and he calms down. Facing each other, the boys fight to see who can hold their head up the longest. William is the winner, but not by much.

I stretch out on the floor next to them, tickling their toes and singing words of encouragement as they work on their neck muscles. Laying on my arms, I close my eyes and appreciate this tiny, miniscule really, moment of peace. Of both boys happily chilling in a place other than in mine or Audrey's arms. These minutes are few, and very far between. So, I'll soak in the silence while it lasts.

It doesn't though, but it's neither of the boys' fault. The doorbell chimes, echoing through the house and causing both boys to whine from their spots beside me. I roll over to sit up, grabbing Henry and William and cradling them against my chest.

Halfway down the hall I call out, "It's open!"

The low murmur of the shower still floats out from the ensuite, so I use my foot to pull closed the bedroom door as I walk past. Audrey deserves this. Fuck, she deserves so much more than just a shower right now, but some days it's all I can convince her to do. But in the couple of weeks since the boys have been home, she never wants to leave their sides. I get it, but I want her to remember herself again.

Mum steps into the house with arms wide open. Her features soften when she sees me and she sighs a gentle, "ohh," as she pats my shoulder.

Stretching her fingers around William, she carefully twists him into her arms and against her chest. He wriggles, whimpering at being shuffled around, but settles into her as she holds him close.

"Come on, um …" she looks down at his tiny face then up at me, "William?"

I chuckle. "Yeah Mum, that's William."

She scrunches her mouth into a smirk and shimmies her shoulders as she walks off into the house.

Dad stands at the door, his arms full of food containers. "Your mum's been busy. I think you have enough ready cooked meals here for a year."

"We'll be lucky if it lasts a week with the way Maisie eats. Audrey says she'll shoot up soon."

He strolls past me, and I follow him to the kitchen. His

expression is stoic as he loads a few of the meals into the fridge and stacks the rest in the freezer. When his arms are free, he turns to me and rests the back of his hips against the bench.

"How are you?"

"Good," I say, but my shoulders drop and I look down at the top of Henry's little head. His light hair swirls at his hairline. "Tired," I admit when a yawn escapes me.

"That's to be expected. What about with Maisie. She's what, six?"

"Five. What about her?"

He shoves his hands into his pockets and looks up at me with raised eyebrows. "If I remember correctly, once upon a time you freaked out about the little girl and damn near ruined any chance you had with Audrey."

"How do you know about that?"

"I talk to your mother, believe it or not. She tells me things."

Right, well that's the last time I'll be confiding in her. My chest sinks at the reminder of how I treated Audrey.

"You've been given a second chance, Michael. I just want to make sure you're not going to blow it."

"I'm trying. And things are fine with Maisie. Better than fine. She's great. I just don't know how to show Audrey that we can be more than what we are. It doesn't matter how much I help with the boys or Maisie, it's like our whole life revolves around these kids. We're a team, but I want to be more than that."

I clear my throat, trying to cough away the scratching feeling, and turn away from my father. Tears well in my eyes.

"I don't know how else to show her, Dad."

"You need to find yourselves again. Having a newborn baby is hard on any relationship. Your mother and I fought like rabid squirrels when you first came about. So, imagine having *two* babies, after the strain of the NICU and off the back of a new relationship. It's a recipe for fucking disaster if you ask me. I'm surprised you're still sleeping in the same room."

"There are no other rooms," I mumble. "Maybe if there were—"

"No time for maybes, son. Look, you want to be something more with Audrey, you need to show her that. Outside of looking after the kids. What if your mother and I babysat the boys one day, Maisie too if you need. You and Audrey can go out, get dinner. Be human adults for a little bit."

After filling up the kettle, he flicks it on and pulls four mugs out of the cupboard above the bench. I grab milk from the fridge and set it next to him.

"Audrey likes hers sweet," I tell him as he scoops a teaspoon of sugar into each mug.

Adjusting Henry's weight onto the other arm I move back and sit down at the table. With empty hands, my mother walks into the room with bright eyes and a wide smile.

"We would love to look after the babies," she sings. "William is asleep in his cot. Let me take Henry."

I let her, and when I sit back in the chair without the weight of a baby resting on my chest, my breaths are a little lighter. Maybe a night out would be good.

Leaving two mugs of steaming tea by the kettle, Dad carries the other two over and joins me at the table. I wrap my fingers around the mug he sets in front of me, allowing the warmth to spread through my hands.

"Talk to Audrey, then let us know," Dad says as he sits down. He sips at his drink, sputtering as the hot liquid presumably burns his tongue.

"I don't mean to change the subject so abruptly but—"

"But you're going to anyway?"

"Shut up. I've never been good at this so just listen."

I roll my shoulders, tilting my head to the side. He leans forward in his chair, resting his elbows either side of his mug.

"You should know I still plan to retire at the end of the year."

"I figured."

Shaking his head, Dad continues, "But I don't want you to feel like you have to step up if you don't feel ready. I can find someone else, even if it's only temporary."

"No." The word shocks me as I say it, but now that he is offering to hand the business over to someone else, bile rises in my throat. I take a long sip of my tea. It burns at my throat, eating away the unease.

"I'll do it," I say, placing my mug on the coaster. I lean back in my chair in an attempt to remain nonchalant. Can't have him knowing how the thought of someone else being my boss has made my skin crawl. "I'll do it, I just need to know that I can still call on you when I inevitably need help."

"You can Michael, you always can."

Chapter Thirty-Seven

MICHAEL

"I've measured out three bottles each, but they should only need one before we get back. We won't be long. Please don't overfeed them. If either of them is really unsettled just give them an extra bottle though. Especially William, his little cheeks are so much thinner than Henry's still and I know the nurses *say* it's okay even though they are identical, but I think maybe it would be good for him if he caught up."

Audrey rushes around the kitchen, pointing out bottles and sterilised dummies and the sheet of instructions she stuck to the fridge. "I'll keep my phone out the whole time, so please call me if you need anything. You have my number but I put both mine and Michael's on the sheet in case your phone dies." She turns to me, terror filling the space around her eyes. "Michael, where are we going? I need to add the restaurant's phone number in case *our* phones die."

I move around the island bench and place a hand on Audrey's shoulder. Her muscles tense under my touch. I pretend not to notice the way her body leans, ever so slightly, away from mine. I push down the loneliness that has come with the distance forged between us over the past few months.

Weeks passed so slowly while the boys were in the hospital, each day tracked in milestones, waiting until we could tick everything off the list and bring them home. But now that they are here, it's as though the universe hit the fast forward button. Four weeks passed in the blink of an eye.

Four weeks of Audrey's quiet resentment every time I leave the house. She keeps saying "it's fine", but I know it's not. I see the way her eyes roll, I feel the chill in the air when I return. It doesn't matter if I've just gone to pick up more formula, take Baxter for a walk, or take Maisie to the local park. It doesn't matter that I asked if she wanted to come, or to go in my place while I looked after the boys. The iciness to her tone—hell, her whole demeanour—each time I return is palpable.

Tonight is my attempt to bring some warmth back into her life. And into our relationship. I miss her, I miss us. It took a lot of convincing, but Audrey finally accepted my dad's offer.

Maisie is spending her week at Callum's. My mother bounces a sleeping Henry in her arms. Next to her, leaning the back of his legs against the benchtop is my father. Gone is the eternal scowl, replaced with soft adoration as he gazes down at William. I wonder sometimes if he ever looked at me like that? Like he would burn the whole world down to make sure I had what I needed. Maybe, when I was younger, before I fucked everything up over and over again. Before I became a disappointment of an adult son.

But he has softened all over now that I'm getting a few things right. Everything is still running smoothly with Noah's hotel, even with me stepping back to be with Audrey and the boys more. And okay, my relationship with Audrey needs a decent dose of tender loving care, but we make a good parenting team.

Pride blossoms over my father's face every time he asks how the hotel build was going and I tell him we were on track to finish early. It filtered through his entire stance when I passed him one of his grandson's the first time they met, and it's there again now.

He looks up from William, following Audrey as she paces back and forth in the tiny kitchen. A softness I never knew he possessed comes out as he tries to calm her. "Audrey, honey, we'll be fine."

It doesn't work. Instead she scoffs and rifles through the basket of baby things on the bench. You would think she knew the contents by heart, the number of times she has checked over it this afternoon. Everything our parents could possibly need for the boys while we are gone. Panicked, she whips her head up to look at me. "Do you think this is enough nappies? I've got ten. And two packets of wipes."

I take a chance, stepping behind her and placing my hands on her hips. Electricity tingles from my fingertips and when she sucks in the tiniest of gasps, I step closer. Our bodies pressing together, I dip my head low to kiss her ear. Her exhale is shaky and she shudders underneath my fingers. They twitch at the feeling, dipping into the soft skin of her sides. *One step at a time,* I remind myself.

"It's plenty, Audrey. And there's more in the boys room just in case. Let's go to dinner. The sooner we go, the sooner we can get back, yeah? But you deserve this break, and Mum and Dad will be fine."

"We really will, sweetie," my mum pipes up. "We will call you if you need, but it will do you good to get out of the house."

Audrey sniffs. Her head falls back on my shoulder and I wrap my arms around her. She squeezes my arms around her middle before pushing back to step out of the embrace.

"Okay, let's go."

She kisses Henry, then William, on the forehead, and shares a long hug with my mother. She hesitates at the front door, and again before stepping into the car.

The restaurant is buzzing when we arrive. The sound crawls over my skin like ants, making my back itch and my nose scrunch.

"I should have picked somewhere quieter, I'm sorry."

Audrey nudges me inside. "It's perfect. Maisie is always going on about how good the pasta is."

"She's five, how does she know what a good pasta is?"

"Because I make a mean Spaghetti Bolognese. I need to size up my competition."

The restaurant is only a block away from Callum and Cassidy's old apartment. And Audrey is right, Maisie is always talking about how good the pasta is. Audrey always mocks shock, claiming she must try it out. It was easy enough to find out where they got it from when Cassidy came to take Maisie to dance class last week, and I took a gamble that beneath the playful tone there was a hint of truth. I can't wipe the smirk off my face when Audrey all but admits the bet paid off.

She slips her hand into mine as we follow a young waiter through the restaurant to a small booth near the back. The space is cosy, all warm lights and natural textures. Wood grain tables line the side wall of painted brick, flourished with centrepieces of green and white. The plush maroon seats either side of the table the waitress leads us to are small, clearly meant for one person each, but Audrey tugs me down beside her after she sits. Rather than squeeze next to her, I pull her onto my knee, holding her tight when she tries to protest.

"You wanted to share the seat made for one," I whisper.

She giggles. *God*, she giggles and I swear I haven't heard her laugh in months. The sound reverberates down my spine, warming me from the inside out.

"I missed your laugh."

Her giggle melts into a soft sigh and she finally relaxes against me.

I dip my hand onto her side, squeezing her thigh. My thumb presses against the crease, following the line of her panties underneath her leggings. Her sigh morphs again, into something more guttural. The sound feeds me, building a fire in my bones.

"I missed *you*." I kiss the soft spot behind her ear, nipping at the sensitive skin. As she wriggles in my lap, the friction rubs against my groin until my dick is strained under the zipper of my pants. "Fuck, Audrey."

She pulls her lower lip between her teeth, pushing herself further into me. "I missed you, too."

"Audrey," I warn her.

I've been so starved for touch over the past few months, and it's not her fault but if she isn't careful I'm about to let all my pent-up sexual frustration out on her. No more giving her time to be ready, to heal—physically and emotionally. No more waiting for her to make the first move, although the way she moves in my lap might be just that. She grinds herself into me until I'm ready to hoist her onto the table and feast on her. Screw the pasta.

"Michael." It's a whisper on her lips. A memory of how she moaned my name into my ear. A promise that she will again.

And then she is gone. She's off my lap and sliding into the chair opposite me before I have a chance to pull her back.

'Later' she mouths, and I don't *want* to get my hopes up because I know later means home and the boys and all the crazy that having twin newborns brings. But the hope swells anyway. My cock, too. I reach between my legs to adjust myself, earning a wide, all-knowing grin from Audrey. Her eyes twinkle and maybe it's just from the overhead chandeliers but maybe it's also because she feels it too. The electricity between us that was so close to fizzling into nothing but is still there, waiting to be sparked again.

The waiter bounds over while we are still taking each other in, catching me with my hand on my lap and my eyes, surely pitch black, raking over Audrey. Her tits are still swollen from the pregnancy, and they threaten to bust open the buttons that run down her satin top. I'm going to tear them apart. Later, though. Because beside the table the waiter is clearing his throat, shuffling his feet. His pen is poised on his tiny notepad.

I compose myself enough to order a bottle of wine and a serving of Maisie's go to spaghetti.

"I'll have the same," Audrey says, but her eyes linger on the lower half of the menu where the woodfire pizzas are listed.

"Order the pizza," I tell her. "You can have some of mine and see what Maisie is raving about."

"Are you sure?"

I nudge my leg against hers, but let the touch linger and brush my calf up and down hers. I can't stop. "I'm sure."

She smiles again, and it's like when the moon comes out during the day. Awe inspiring even though it's more common than you think. I will never not be captivated by her. Turning to the waiter, she orders one of the restaurant's specialty pizzas. The waiter jots down the order, promises to be back with our wine, and scurries off. No doubt happy to remove himself from the sexual energy buzzing around us.

A blush creeps up Audrey's neck, covering her cheeks with a crimson glow. She bites her lip again and pulls her cardigan around her, holding on to the corners as she folds her arms below her chest. It pushes her breasts higher and I can't tear my gaze away.

"You're making it worse, you know."

She jumps a little in the chair, rearranging her arms so the cardigan covers her tits. There must be a speck, or something, on the table, because she stares down at it intently.

"I'm sorry. I'll stop."

Her head bobs a short nod and she settles back into the plush cushion of the booth seat.

"It's okay, though," she says as she builds up the courage to look at me again. I strain every muscle in my face to keep it neutral, to hide the almost animalistic desire raging through me.

"It was nice, even," she adds, "to feel wanted again."

"Audrey, I never stopped wanting you." Reaching a hand across the table, I pull her arm out of her tight hold and lace my fingers through hers. "I was just trying to give you space, I thought you needed it."

She traces small circles on the back of my hand with her thumb. Her mouth opens to talk, but she presses it shut, inhaling deep through her nose. She lets her breath out through a tiny gap in her teeth and starts again. "I did, and sometimes maybe I still do. And I don't want you to feel bad because it's hard to show someone you want them when they aren't showing it back. I needed to feel like myself again, and until tonight, I haven't."

"I told you a night off would do you good."

Squeezing my hand, she leans forward, resting her elbow on the table and dropping her head into her free hand.

"I'm not saying it."

"Say it Audrey," I tease, knowing she probably won't.

But she does. "You were right."

I clasp my hand over my chest, dropping my mouth open with a gasp. "I was *what*, sorry? I didn't hear you."

"You heard me just fine, I'm not saying it again."

"I will remember this night for the rest of my life." Not just because she admitted I was right about something though. I'll remember the moment we reconnected after months of intense strain on our relationship. I might be naive, but I'm not stupid enough to think that one night away—and a few lust-filled touches—is going to fix all our problems. But we are back on the right path, and that's a bloody good start.

The waiter returns with our wine, pouring two glasses

after Audrey takes the first sip and nods her approval. His eyes dart between the two of us, but he places the bottle in the centre of the table and moves away.

Audrey takes a long sip of her wine. "I was so worried about coming out," she says after she gulps down the deep red pinot noir. "After all those nights while the boys were in hospital, you'd think I was used to being away from them. But now they are home I feel like I owe them all my time."

"I get it, but you also owe yourself the freedom to do the things you love. You can't pour from an empty cup, isn't that what they say?" I down the last sips of my drink.

Audrey picks up the bottle to fill our long-stemmed glasses. "My cup was definitely empty."

Chapter Thirty-Eight

AUDREY

I drank too much wine. It was only two glasses, but considering I finished them both before dinner, and I haven't had so much as a sip in almost a year, it hit my head hard. It wasn't until our food arrived and I demolished the chicken pizza and half of Michael's spaghetti that the throbbing began to ease.

We didn't last long at the restaurant after that. I was itching to get back to the boys, to make sure they were okay. And my blood was pumping with something else. Something I had feared was gone forever. *Desire.*

I hadn't intended to make Michael hard when I wriggled in his lap. I was, honestly, just trying to get comfortable. But when I felt his erection swelling underneath me, it flipped a switch inside me. One that I had lost. After the boys were born, only darkness could be found in my core. I scoffed and rolled my eyes and called my obstetrician ridiculous when she told me I could resume having sex at one of my follow up appointments. It was the furthest thing from my mind. But feeling what my body did to Michael's, the light turned back on. It heated me from the inside out.

It was surprising, to feel such an untamed want on the back of all the other, heavier, emotions I carry around. My re-found desire hasn't turned all those worries off. We still have issues to work through, and I have a lot of self-reflecting to do. But in the moment, feeling wanted, and *wanting,* felt good. Really good.

We barely spoke through dinner. I was too busy shoving

all the food in my face because yeah, I was a little drunk and hungry, but I was also desperate to get home. To be with the boys, but also to be with Michael. Both needs equally strong but wildly different.

The drive home was silent, electricity buzzing louder than the static from the radio. We said a rushed thank you to Michael's parents. Both boys were—are—asleep. They'd had a bottle just before we got home, both loved bath time with their grandma and grandpa, and had settled back to bed soundly. Typical.

I feel bad, genuinely, for all but pushing Michael's parents out the door, but I was ready to be alone with Michael. My core aches, and not the way it did while I was healing from the emergency caesarean. No, this is a deep throbbing that sends waves of heat directly to my pussy. It's fuelled by a raw need and an overwhelming desire.

There's every chance Michael's mum can tell. Even if my red cheeks haven't given it away, I'm sure the huskiness in my voice has. She pretends not to notice though, right up until she winks at me as I close the door in her face.

Michael steps behind me, enclosing me in his arms and nuzzling against my neck. He breathes deep and a grumble reverberates through him. The sound, so guttural and unfiltered, only adds to the pulsing in my core. I moan, leaning back into him, but he spins me around, stepping into me, forcing me back until my butt hits the wall.

He cages me in, arms either side of my body. My chest heaves, and he watches the movement with dark eyes that pierce through my skin. My eyes dart to his lips, parted and wet and wanting.

I stretch up onto my toes, lifting his shirt over his head and wrapping my arms around his neck. "Just fun," I mumble under my breath, reminding myself that our relationship might need work, but we can still enjoy the moment.

"Always with the fun," he growls and slams his mouth against mine.

The kiss knocks all the worry and messy thoughts out of my mind, and I sink into him. He fuses his mouth against mine, licking and biting and teasing at my lips until I coax them open.

I savour his taste, the richness of the red wine still lingering on his tongue. Michael brings a hand to my cheek, tilting my head to deepen the kiss.

The throbbing in my core intensifies until I can't stand it, I need more, I need everything. With my back pressed against the wall I tug Michael closer. He steps forward with a leg in between my own and I grind my hips against the friction it creates.

"Audrey," he moans into my mouth. "Fuck."

I bite his lip.

"Please."

Michael drops his arms and palms at my ass before hoisting me up. I wrap my legs around his waist as he thrusts into me against the wall and I curse all the fabric between us.

"Not here," he groans with a thrust.

He steps away from the wall, bringing me with him as he races to the bedroom. Somehow, amidst our carnal need and the frenzy of our reconnection, he manages to lay me gently on the bed. Hovering over me, his pupils are so dilated there's no colour left in his eyes. His gaze drops to my chest, where my still swollen breasts threaten to tear away the buttons of my shirt. His fingers are delicate on my skin as he traces down my neck and teases at the first button.

"I've wanted to do this all dinner." There's the slightest of twinkles in his dark eyes before he yanks at my top. In one clean movement he tears through all the buttons, revealing my boring, beige maternity bra.

I suck in a breath, aware of all the changes to my body

and unsure how Michael will see them. The stretch marks on my breasts and waist, the extra weight that still clings around my middle, and the deep scar running across my abdomen. I squirm under Michael's gaze. His eyes are still dark, his breaths heavy, and his cock is still strained against his pants.

"You're fucking stunning," he says, pinning my arms above my head. "Every fucking inch of you, okay? Don't even think anything different."

He kisses me again, slower this time. Tenderly exploring my mouth with his tongue. He runs his hand down my front, teasing the waistband of my leggings. I nod underneath him, pushing my hips into him.

Dipping his hand into my pants, he pauses with his fingers at the apex of my thighs. "Is this okay?"

I nod against him, but hesitation and fear must be written all over me because he doesn't move his hand. He pulls back from our kiss, resting his forehead on mine.

"Audrey, are you sure?"

"I'm sure. I'm just … scared."

"I've got you," he whispers. He kisses me again, dropping his hands lower until he is tracing circles around my clit. "If you want me to stop, I will."

I don't, I don't want him to stop, but it's torture. The slow movements building a fire inside me that needs more. I whimper under his touch. "More."

He presses his thumb hard against my clit, and dips his fingers between my folds. Teasing my entrance, he rubs the moisture around my pussy. My hips buck up to meet his fingers.

With my butt still off the bed, I reach between us and pull down my leggings, taking my very unattractive panties with them. Michael adjusts himself so I can kick them off, then leans back down to kiss me.

His thumb is still pressed against my clit, small

movements creating the biggest sensations inside my core, when he dips one finger into me. It's tight, which is the exact opposite to what I expected, and I suck in a breath as I adjust to the feeling. When I relax underneath him again, Michael slowly pulls his finger out before pushing back in. He curls up to reach inside me, to caress the spot that only he seems to know how to find.

The fire spreads through me until it's hard to breathe under his kiss. He moves to nip at my neck, licking at the soft spot behind my ear. Every muscle in my body clenches. Even my heart. The intensity squeezes away all the doubt I had about us, all the pent-up anger and frustration, until all that's left is raw need, untamed desire, and overwhelming love.

Pulling his finger out, Michael kisses me ferociously, as though he can feel it too. He teases me, toying at my clit and dragging out my orgasm until I'm writhing underneath him. My hips buck up and he responds by pulling my lower lip between his teeth. Using two fingers this time, he presses deep into me as I lose control. Of my body, of my senses, of my heart. My body tightens around his fingers and under his embrace as the fire he lights inside me burns brighter than the sun. Heat everywhere, sparks all around me, and all I can see is him.

He removes his fingers slowly, keeping his thumb pressed down on my clit until I can't take any more.

"Michael," I breathe out his name, my voice raspy with exertion, and he steals it away with a kiss.

With our foreheads pressed together, I creep my eyes open as the beating in my chest returns to normal. He kisses me again, this time little more than pecks that plant their love all over my face; my lower lip, each corner, my cupid's bow, then my nose, and each cheek, behind my ear.

I'm spent, but pressed against my inner thigh I can feel how hard Michael is. He rolls his hips into me, softly, slowly, testing the waters. I try to reciprocate, lifting my hips to meet him. My body protests, melting into the mattress instead.

"Michael, I …"

How do I let him down gently? How do I tell him we can't do anything more and it's not because I don't want to but it's because my body is literally done. My core aches, exhausted from my orgasm, and my scar is starting to throb, ever so softly but enough to pull me out of the mood and remind me of everything.

"I can't, I'm sorry," I choose, and my heart sinks through the mattress and onto the floor. I turn my head away from Michael's, holding back the tears that threaten to form.

With his dry hand he holds my chin, turning me back to him so he can kiss me. He holds his mouth against mine until I relax into him and purse my lips to kiss him back.

"What happened to not being allowed to say sorry?"

He rolls off me, taking me with him so we're on our sides. I tuck my knees up between us and he cradles his body around the ball I become.

"You've done so much Audrey, I don't expect anything from you. Ever. I never needed this—sex—I just need you. I know it's like, eighty or ninety percent my fault, but I need us to be *us* again."

"It's going to take time Michael. Every relationship is rocky at best after a baby is born. We've had two, and our relationship had really only just begun. I fought against it for so long because I was petrified that we would crumble. Michael, we were crumbling."

He tucks a stray piece of hair behind my ear, then pushes his own hair further off his face. "Then we just need to find the right way to rebuild the foundations."

My lip turns up, smirking. "Did you just make a builders pun?"

"The dad jokes just fall out of me now, I can't help it."

"You make a good dad, Michael." I snuggle down, resting my face against his chest. Goosebumps start to prickle on my skin as the heat from earlier subsides into a comfortable afterglow.

"You make a wonderful mum, Audrey."

Chapter Thirty-Nine

MICHAEL

Audrey squeals as she gets out of the car. She tries to hide it, sucking the sound back in and forcing a cough, but I heard her excitement. I don't blame her.

The facade of her new home is stunning, and I'm glad I left all creative licence to the designers and landscapers. Making things pretty has never been my strong suit when it comes to building houses.

A small, paved path cuts the front garden in two, surrounded by flowering shrubs of various sizes. The open paddock we drove past up the long driveway has been mowed, and Baxter bounds off the tray as soon as I unclip his lead to explore the space. I hope he doesn't get used to having all this space, but at the same time I hope he *can*. His nose dives in and out of low spots in the grass, sniffing out what I'm assuming are field rabbits. Brendan said the pest control guy protected the house, but I have no idea what that means. As with most other finishing touches, I just went along with it. Still, I make a mental note to look up what we have to do, maintenance wise, to keep them outside.

Audrey hops from paver to paver along the path, her now natural brown hair flowing behind her. With a little encouraging, she finally went to the hairdresser last week. I was expecting the highlights to be back, but instead she trimmed off most of the blonde ends, leaving behind a shoulder length, light brown hairstyle that softens the sometimes sharp features of her face. She pauses before stepping onto the raised patio, taking in the cottage feeling facade.

Two rectangular planter beds line the front patio, rustic wooden boxes that will one day be overflowing with flowers. Until they grow and spread though, three lily plants are spaced evenly in the soil. White, hopefully. At least that's what the woman at the gardening centre had said.

These plants were my one condition when I handed over the reins to the landscaper Brendan recommended. For new life and hope. That's what Cassidy had said when I bought them for Audrey's birthday, so it's fitting that we have some permanently on display at our home. Ones that will never wilt. Ones that will, hopefully—if I can figure out how to care for them—never die.

Just like the love that fills our new family.

Audrey follows me up the steps, her fingers entwined in mine. I unlock the door and push it open. There's awe in her breath as she takes in the wide, open hallway of the entry. Turning, I scoop her into my arms and carry her across the threshold. Full nineties rom-com style, and she loves it.

She giggles and squirms, twisting until she can kiss my cheek. Just as her touch always does, it sends a spark through me. One that tingles on my skin and fizzes in my bones.

"I thought that was a married couple thing," she says.

"I'm just getting a head start."

Audrey wriggles out of my hold and steps back. The awe filled smile is gone, and hesitation is plastered all over her face. She wrings her hands in front of her, pulling her cardigan tight. I reach a hand towards her, but she steps back until she hits the side wall.

"Michael I … I don't know if I ever want to get married again." My heart sinks to my stomach and bile rises in my throat. I thought we were good. And sure, I didn't think we would get married any time soon, but I had figured that's where we were heading.

Fun, that's what she kept saying and I should have

believed her. Should have listened when she told me so clearly that was all we were destined to be. I step back this time. I slide my back down the wall opposite her, dropping to my knees as my world begins to crumble.

"Fuck, that's not what I meant," Audrey drops to the floor and crawls over to me. She shakes her head and reaches out to tuck my hair back from my face. I flinch at her touch, turning my head and reaching up to tie my loose hair into a messy bun on the nape of my neck.

"I never imagined we would be more than something fun," Audrey continues, even though I've shied away, looking at the shiny wooden floorboards instead of anywhere near her. "When we first started dating, when we first got together after we found out I was pregnant. I never expected to fall in love. But I did. I can't imagine my life without you. And not because of the boys, but because I need you. I want to spend every morning waking up next to you, and fall asleep in your arms every night. I just don't know if I want to get married. And maybe we should have spoken about it before but it never came up and I'm sorry. I did it once, and it fell apart. It hurt. Marriage is not for me. Not anymore. But you are, Michael."

She creeps closer, nudging my legs further apart so she can sit between them. She wraps my arms around her and nestles her cheek against the crook of my shoulder. Her body is tiny in my arms, even all the bits she thinks are too big, or worries I don't like. She is made to fit perfectly in my embrace and I don't ever want her to leave.

"You're for me too, Audrey."

The silence that follows isn't uncomfortable, and for the first time I'm happy to just sit, to find peace, in the quiet. A cool breeze blows in through the still open door and I squeeze my arms a little tighter around Audrey.

"Are you going to show me your house or what?" she asks as she shuffles out of my arms and pushes herself to stand.

I push myself onto my knees and wrap my arms back around her waist. Her tits look fucking incredible from this view, and I'll never get tired of admiring her body, of worshipping her. "Your house," I remind her.

She ignores me, rolling her eyes and pulling me up from my underarms.

I take her hand in mine and walk her through the house. Her eyes light up at the giant master bedroom. Pendant lights hang where the bedside tables will sit once we move in, and soft sheer curtains hang over the window. They shift the bright sun into a gentle glow that lights up the room.

In the kitchen, she marvels at the space, and the so-called butler's pantry that is almost as big as the main kitchen. Marble bench tops are finished with a backsplash of tiles in an intricate zig zag pattern. The cabinetry is off white, with plenty of storage and large drawers in the place of most cupboards. I trusted the designer's judgement, and it paid off. The space is beautiful. If someone had asked me twelve months ago if a kitchen would ever be my favourite room of the house, I would have scoffed. But here we are.

Audrey clearly loves it too. Her eyes twinkle as she caresses the bench top.

I stand next to the only blank wall in the room, the tiny sliver between the main kitchen and the pantry. "This is where I thought we could measure how tall everyone is. Each year."

She skips towards me, happily turning to stand with her back against the wall and shoulders straight. With the pen in my pocket I mark her height on the wall. Handing her the pen, I swap our places. She has to stretch on her toes to reach above my head and once the mark is drawn I can't help but tickle her.

"The next room is the most special," I tell her, guiding her through the large main living space and into the sunroom.

Windows line the three exterior walls, with the same sheer curtains from the master bedroom. They look out into the garden, at the line of almost established fruit trees I had planted along the side fence and the gum tree we kept in the corner of the yard. The only pieces of furniture in the whole house sit in the centre of the room. A small stool, one that swivels and changes height and has a lower leg rest that can be used for crossed legs or pushed out of the way. And an easel. A light timber frame, large enough for the beautiful canvas pieces that have become Audrey's signature style. One day, I might even add an easel of my own to the room. If she'll let me. A small shelf lines the lower edge to hold all her paints and brushes.

Audrey freezes, just inside the room. Her eyes are wide and sheer joy is spread over her face as she takes in the space. Stepping in, she twirls to take it all in, before sitting in the chair. Her legs immediately curl underneath her, and I hold in the knowing smirk. The chair was the right call, even if Brendan said it looked weird.

"I wanted to put it closer to your bedroom, away from the busiest part of the house, but it wouldn't get enough light. With these windows, you'll get morning and afternoon sun, so it doesn't matter what time of day you manage to sneak away and have some time to yourself." I point my head above the windows to the large strip lighting that frames the perimeter of the room. "I added those lights, in case you ever want to paint at night. Or, you know, in Melbourne's dreary winter. They are—and this is a quote from the lighting salesperson—'the closest thing to natural light on the market.'"

She spins back and forth on the chair, her grin puffing up her cheeks until her eyes are squished almost shut. "Michael, you didn't need—"

"I did. You deserve it."

"Yes but it's your—"

"No Audrey, it's *yours*. Come on, I'll show you the rest."

She lingers on the chair, silhouetted by the warm sun that spills in through the sheer curtains.

"It's not as special as this room though," I tell her when she finally takes my outstretched hand.

"Michael, I don't think anything will ever beat this room."

It doesn't. Her grin remains, but nothing I have left to show her brings back the intense joy that was filtering through her body in her painting room. She squeezes my hand as I show her Maisie's room, with its feature wall of pale pink, as requested by our little ballerina. The boys' rooms, opposite each other down the hall, each painted a sage green to match the blankets we bought them. The crisp but functional bathroom, complete with heated towel racks and a large bath. And finally, at the end of the hall, my bedroom.

I freeze, pushing open the door to the bare, eggshell white room. It's not *small,* but it is technically the smallest of them all, designed as a toy room or spare room.

"And this is my bedroom," I mumble. I shuffle my feet, opting to change the subject before my chest explodes with anticipation. "So, that's your house, it's ready. Whenever you are."

"Michael, why do you need your own bedroom?"

So much for changing the subject.

My chin drops to my chest.

"Because it's your house. Not mine. We said I would stay while the boys were little. So I could help. And at the old house there's nowhere else for me to stay, so I share with you. But here, there's space. So ... my room. Because as much as I love you and want us to be together, I don't want us to keep being forced into taking steps we don't need to unless we both want to take them." I gesture into the room without looking up at her, too scared to see what's on her face.

Because I know what we said in the hallway no more

than ten minutes ago, and okay we've been sharing a room for over a month, and okay she says she loves me and wants to be with me, but there is no reason for our relationship to keep moving at the speed of a formula one car. I don't *want* us to slow down, but I can understand if she does.

I stare down at the floor, waiting for her response. I hear her take two steps, and her feet enter my line of sight, right in front of mine.

"Oh, you big dummy," she says.

She pushes my chin up and brings her mouth over mine.

Chapter Forty

AUDREY

"So … my room," Michael mumbles after his little speech about not sharing a bedroom. He gestures around the tiny white room and somehow everything clicks into place.

All the times he corrected me under his breath, every time I said this was his house or *our* house and he would murmur "yours" and I would pretend not to hear it. The flowers in the front yard, despite his claims to hate gardening and have whatever the opposite of a green thumb is. The way he added pot drawers to the kitchen after I said they would be helpful and he questioned their purpose over a standard cupboard. How he let Maisie choose the paint for her walls and took the boys' blankets to the paint shop to match the colour for their rooms. And the stunning sunroom, the painting room. So cleverly designed, just for me.

He was never building his house. He was building my house. And he told me so, but I never really listened. I never believed it. I always brushed it off.

But here he is, shuffling his feet and worried that I'm going to make him sleep in this tiny spare room.

"Oh, you big dummy," I say with a sigh. Stepping towards him, I grab his chin with my hand and drag his face away from the floor. His forehead wrinkles as he clears his throat. I watch his Adam's Apple bob as he swallows down his uncertainty.

Stretching up onto my toes, I press my mouth against his. He freezes, for only a fraction of a second, before wrapping his arms around my waist and pulling me closer.

I break the kiss, and he whimpers. "Michael, did you really think I would make you sleep in here?"

"I … I didn't know," he admits. "Everything between us has moved so fast, mostly because it was forced to. I didn't want to assume it would continue that way. I didn't want you to feel like I was forcing your hand. I realised, about halfway through building this house, that I've taken a lot of choice from you. The choice of who would be the father to your kids—if you ever wanted more kids and even though I didn't mean it. And then the choice of what your house would look like, what suburb it's in. I had to give you as much choice back. So, I am."

He reaches up between us to drag a hand over his face as he rolls his neck. "This house is yours, but you don't have to live here. If it's not what you want or where you want, you can sell it, and buy or build what *you* choose. If you do want it, you don't have to move in right away. You can rent it out until you're ready. And if and when you do move in, you don't have to let me stay. I'm willing to, I want to, for as long as you'll let me. But the choice is yours. I love you Audrey, and it will kill me to sleep in another room and it will kill me even more if you don't want me here. But I will respect that."

I wrap my arms around his shoulders, hanging some of my weight there and letting his arms support me. This burly young man with his heart of pure sunshine, and he's mine. He might get some things wrong, but he gets more things right than he gives himself credit for.

"It would kill me if you weren't here, Michael. It would kill me if you were here, but in this room. I want that wonderful master bedroom to be *ours,* not mine. I want this *house* to be ours."

He picks me up, and with my legs wrapped around his waist I plant another kiss on his mouth, then another on his neck. He groans, squeezing at my ass. The pressure builds through me, my heart starting to race. My back hits the wall as Michael pushes me against it, grinding his hips into me.

"Say it again," he moans, his mouth hot against my ear.

"This house is ours, Michael. It always was and it always will be."

He drops his head over my shoulder, resting his forehead on the wall. "I was so nervous. You are everything, you are perfect. I know when we met I wasn't even a fraction of the man you deserve. I've spent the past year learning and growing and just hoping to come close to that man, but always fearful you'll wake up one day and realise I'm not him."

His voice is a whisper in my ear, but his words echo through me until tears well in my eyes.

"Michael, the only man I want is you. Always. I love how carefree you are. I love your goofy smile and how your jokes bring light into even the darkest of rooms. I love how even when you had no idea what you were doing, you were nurturing and caring and you put everyone else first. You don't need to become the man I deserve, because you already are him. You just need to trust in yourself."

He carries me out of the room, giant footsteps racing down the hall. Reaching the open living space, he pauses, turning back and forth as he presumably realises there's no furniture. Nothing other than the easel in my art room and the stool—that yes lets me cross my legs underneath the seat but is far too small for what I'm thinking. For what Michael's thinking too, because he grunts as he carries me to the kitchen. The marble of the wide island bench is cool on my ass, but heat is pouring around us from every place my body is pressed against Michael's.

With my weight safely out of his arms, he lets his hands roam all over my body, palming at my breasts, grabbing at my hips. He touches me like he owns me, and he does. He owns my body, my heart, my soul. All of me. It's his.

"I love you so fucking much, Audrey."

His mouth meets mine with a deep kiss so passionate I might cry. His tongue explores my mouth and I savour in his taste, the way he always smells like home and the way I feel so small when I'm wrapped in his arms.

"When did you say we would need to pick up the boys?" he growls. His hand dips underneath my tank and his fingers tease the waistband of my leggings.

I lean back, pushing my breasts into his face and lifting my hips off the bench. "We've got time."

Three days after Michael showed me our home, we took Maisie and the boys to see their new house. That evening, we booked removalists. The two weeks that followed were a frenzy of packing and planning. Calling service providers and changing addresses with every business we could think of. Packing boxes while the kids slept.

Michael's parents came over just about every other day to help, and my parents came up on the weekends. And today, everyone is here. Including the three men we hired. Even with the professionals here to help, Michael, our dads, and Callum all stand around trying to look helpful.

Maisie chases Baxter through the now empty house, her squeals echoing off the bare walls. Nostalgia hits me like a wave as I remember the day Callum and I moved in. I wasn't pregnant yet, but we had always said we would start trying as soon as we had a house of our own. It wasn't long after that I was pregnant, and then Maisie was born. And we were happy for more than a while before we slowly drifted apart. It sucked, it hurt, and I hated that life hadn't gone to plan, but looking back I'm grateful for those moments. I know that this was the path we were always meant to take as a family. Because look at us now. Callum is happier than I've ever seen him, and he smiles at Cassidy with so much love I almost don't recognise him. Maisie has grown into the sweetest big sister imaginable, with parents who love her dearly and not-quite-but-almost stepparents who love her almost as much. And I've never felt more whole in my life. My boys were exactly what I never knew I needed. The twins, sure, but Michael too.

He steps up behind me, wrapping my arms around me and pulling my cardigan tight around my middle. I stare into the empty rooms and lean my head against his shoulder.

"The boys are in the car," he says.

I nod against him, a solitary tear escaping down my cheek.

Callum walks back in from outside, holding Cassidy's hand. "This is ... weird."

Cassidy puffs out a small laugh and I snort at Callum's choice of words.

"It's right," I say.

We walk out of the house one last time, and I'm not sad that my marriage with Callum ended. I'm thrilled to start the next chapter with Michael. With our boys and with Maisie. In the big, beautiful house that Michael built for us.

AUDREY

5 years later

Under the shade of the gum tree that grows in the corner of the yard, Henry and William bicker. Nothing serious, but enough that I turn my focus away from the half-constructed deck to face them. Hands on my hips, I'm about to call out when Michael whistles. Beside him, Noah shoves his hands over his ears.

"Boys, be friends or be apart," he calls out to them, his deep voice bellowing across the lawn.

The boys jump apart, no doubt with red ears and wide eyes after being caught.

"How do you do that?" Noah asks.

"Comes with the territory mate, you'll get used to it."

Noah looks to the boys. He holds one arm across his chest, rubbing his upper arm with the opposite hand, and sighs. Turning back to the deck, he rolls his head from side to side and picks up a stray hammer.

In their corner of the yard, William and Henry stand an arms width apart. I can't hear them, but from their stance there is no doubt they are whispering insults.

But that's them, best friends who love to fight. Always in each other's hair, calling names, wrestling, stealing toys. It's exhausting but, apparently, all part of the joys of raising boys.

Satisfied their argument won't turn physical—at least not yet—I step off the patio and head over to the deck Michael is building. His hair, still longer than mine, is tied in a low bun underneath his cap and the collar of his grey polo is popped up to protect his neck from the blasting summer sun. He leans down over the corner of the deck and I reach around his middle to pull him up.

"Are you sure this will be done before Maisie's birthday?"

Michael scratches at the back of his neck, hesitating before he answers. I don't have a lot of confidence in his answer when he nods shyly and looks away.

"You promised her."

"I know." He clips his measuring tape back onto his toolbelt. The denim fabric has faded over the years, and I've had to repair a few of the pockets more than once. But he still uses it every chance he gets. "I'll get it done. Brendan is taking over more of the residential builds, so I'll have more time."

"Good." He deserves it. More time. After his dad retired Michael stepped into the owner/manager position at full speed. In the past five years he has scaled the business to include more and more commercial builds, on top of the residential contracts that still flow through. I think, because he would never say as much, he was so proud of the way Noah's hotel turned out, he wanted to keep that momentum going. Once he was in, he was all in. A bit like being a father. Sure, the start was a little rocky, but he was all in from the very beginning and I can't fault him for that.

"Maisie's party is in a few weeks," I remind him. She's having her tenth birthday party one month early, because Callum and Cassidy are taking her to Disneyland for her birthday. She'll turn ten in front of Cinderella's castle, and she still has no idea. I'm only a little bit jealous.

Michael wraps his arms around me and pulls me close. "I'll finish the deck this week, then the boys can come landscape the garden beds, and then we can fill the pool," he tells me. "Plenty of time."

"Plenty of time, Audrey," Noah pipes up. "I'm getting us some drinks. And sunscreen." He disappears into the house.

Michael spins me around, reaching his arms around me to grab my ass. He squeezes playfully, nibbling at my ear. My heart flips, just like it always does when he holds me close.

Seeing us hugging, the boys run over and start to climb up Michael's legs. They're too big for this game now, but he plays along anyway, scooping them into his arms so they are squished between us.

The sweet embrace only lasts a second before Henry wriggles free and runs back to the tree. "I'm going to climb it!"

William jumps after him, "No, you said I could do it first!"

"You snooze, you lose Will!"

I relax back into Michael's arms, watching our boys climb the tree, its narrow branches bowing under their weight.

Michael kisses the top of my head and whispers, "Did you know that it was this day, five years ago, that the boys first came home?"

Tilting my head up, I kiss him. It's nothing like the hesitant kisses we once shared, or the frenzied clashing of our mouths we still enjoy. It's just peace. And love.

"I know, look at them now."

"Nah Audrey, look at *us* now."

READ ON FOR A SNEAK PEEK OF

Because of Me

NOAH

I've walked these stairs countless times. Hundreds, possibly, if you count the day I flew down from Sydney to help my cousin move in. But with all those steps, all the aching muscles and laboured breaths, it was still easier than today.

I pause, half way up the first flight, to swallow down the lump of concrete that keeps trying to settle in my throat. It lands in the pit in my stomach.

I can do this.

Lifting one foot above the other, I blow a steady breath out with each step I take, trying to remind myself that this is no big deal. Trying to ignore the way the collar of my shirt scratches against my neck and the blister I'm sure is forming underneath the fancy leather shoes I bought just for the occasion. I shake my foot, cursing at myself for thinking something as inconspicuous as my black dress shoes would matter.

I'm not supposed to be here to impress Amira, only that's exactly what I'm trying to do. She just doesn't know it. I've been fascinated by my cousin's roommate from that first day when I lugged boxes up three flights of stairs. She stood there, in the kitchen of their small apartment, in a grey sweater and a long sundress and I swear all the light in the room came from her.

But I lived in Sydney then, and the next day I was on a flight back home with barely more than a memory of her smile.

Now, I'm back in Melbourne for good, and I'll do anything to get to know Amira. Properly.

That's why I agreed to be her date for this wedding. To save her from whatever disastrous date her father was going to set her up with, sure, but also because I want her to start seeing me as more than just her roommate's cousin. So yeah, I'm not here to impress her in the way I would if we were on a real date, but I'm definitely trying to get her attention.

I just hate the anxious bubble of energy that's been floating around since I agreed to this. As though my body knows this could just as easily be the start of something great as it could be the beginning of nothing.

Because of Me

AMIRA

There's nothing fun about my family. They're full of old habits and overbearing views, and if I can't make my parents proud, I'll have to fake it instead.

Noah was the lifeline I needed to escape my father's scrutiny. My unexpected saviour in the form of my best friend's cousin.

But I've just spun our web of lies a little too thick, and now I need more of his help than either of us planned.

NOAH

Nothing in my life has come easily. So, when I inherited a winery from a grandmother I never met, I was determined to see it succeed. Now that it's thriving, I still thank luck, more than skill.

It was that same luck that found me at a wedding pretending to be Amira's boyfriend. Now more than ever, I can't get her out of my head.

I started by playing along, but now I'm playing for keeps.

Because of Me is a spicy fake dating romance about taking chances, and fighting for what, and who, you want. A standalone story, it is the third novel in Bookstagrammer Devon May's Because of Love series.

Because of Me will be released in May 2025

Acknowledgements

For a while there, I thought I was going to end up a 'one and done' kind of author. My first book was finished and this one sat, demanding attention that I just could not give it. I wanted to, but every time I tried, I froze.

It was a really scary thing, committing to writing a second novel before the first one had even been published. I was terrified that I was giving too much of my hopes and dreams away. But Michael and Audrey continued to scream at me, and now look at them. I love them, and I hope you do too.

As any author will tell you, there are countless unseen people that help bring a book to life. As such, I have so many people to thank, but I'll try to keep this short.

Chloe, Brooke, Deb, Hannah—your professional advice was immensely helpful. Thank you for reading the earliest of rough drafts and for guiding me to make a really tough situation believable and authentic.

Ash, Jess, Brittney, Bon, Elle, Jade, Bindi—my BETA readers. A few of these chapters are just for you. Michael and Audrey would not be who they are now if it wasn't for your advice, and I am immensely thankful that you gave me so much of your time.

Ashleigh, who does everything for me. Without you as my constant sounding board, I'd never be able to turn the stories in my head into real life, actual books. I appreciate your kindness, love, and support, more than I think you'll ever know. I'm sorry your name got cut (again), I'll make it up to you one day. I promise.

My real life book husband, Shannon, and my immediate and extended family. You guys support me through thick and thin. I'm sorry I'm always 'off writing'. Thank you for giving me the time and space to achieve my dreams.

Being an indie author has been a massive learning curve, and I wouldn't be where I am today without the support of other authors. Emma Mugglestone, Bindi Kennedy, Alexis Menard, Kylie Orr, Anne Freeman, everyone in the Romance Writers of Australia, and all the others. Your support is everything to me. Thank you.

And finally, as cliche as this last one is, *YOU*. Thank you, dearest reader, for taking a chance on a small indie author from Melbourne. You're making my dreams come true.

About the Author

When she was 10, Santa brought Devon a "how to write a book" journal. Publishing her debut novel more than 20 years later, she's glad it finally got put to good use.

Devon May resides in Melbourne, Australia with her husband and the two tiny humans who call her mum. When she isn't breaking up fights, she enjoys books that either break her heart, or turn her on. She carries her emotional support Kindle everywhere, drinks far too much coffee and will never be caught without a hair tie on her wrist.

You can find out more about her and her books at
www.devonmay.com

Instagram instagram.com/booksbydevonmay

TikTok tiktok.com/@booksbydevonmay

Facebook www.facebook.com/groups/devonmaysreaders